HECK'S ANGELS

SPECTERS ANONYMOUS: BOOK 5

PHIL BUDAHN

Cover designed by Bailey Hunter

www.SpectersAnonymous.Com

ISBN: 153757292X

ISBN 13: 978-1537572925

Phil Budahn's
Specters Anonymous
Novels

CHAPTER

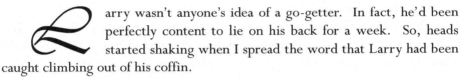arry wasn't anyone's idea of a go-getter. In fact, he'd been perfectly content to lie on his back for a week. So, heads started shaking when I spread the word that Larry had been caught climbing out of his coffin.

"A corpse will do what a corpse has gotta do," I said.

My friends around the casket in the funeral parlor smiled or grimaced or gagged, depending on whose face we're talking about. The shadows in the viewing room backed into the corners like frightened puppies.

"Is this going to be like last Halloween?" asked Gilda, our resident Goth. "My hair smelled of candy corn for a month."

I harrumphed discreetly into my hand, too polite to gloat and too respectful of my friends to say that I had no intention of repeating last October's childish prank. None whatsoever.

This year I was going to top it!

"You're looking at the real deal." I waved at Larry as he lay placidly on his satin pillow. "This stiff tried to join the cleaning crew a few nights ago. Newspapers, TV stations, bloggers—everyone's trying to find some dirt on him. As it were."

Veronica, the newest member of our 12-step support group, who arrived after last year's incident that has slipped into local lore as the Night of the Candy Corn, was the only one willing to lean over the casket for a better look.

"This gentleman isn't moving," she said. "Will someone tell me what we expect a dead man to do? The polka, perhaps?"

"To stay still. We expect dead men to stay still," said Gilda, always eager to seize a chance to disagree with Veronica.

"Okay, I'm beginning to understand," Veronica said. "We're wasting an evening in a mortuary to make sure a corpse isn't moving." Tall and lean, her brown hair hanging shawl-like to her shoulders, Veronica had the air of someone burdened by the ineptitude of lesser souls.

The chains on Gilda's black leather jacket clinked like a toilet handle jingling before it went *whoosh*. Tension had been building for nights between her and Veronica, and I didn't relish being in the same time zone when those two decided to quit playing nice.

My best friend Hank nudged me. "Admit it. You don't know which one to bet against."

I glanced beyond Hank at Fast Eddie, arched my eyebrows, crinkled my mouth and wished I'd had the foresight to have a message tattooed on my forehead, something along the lines of: *Okay, Fast Eddie, this would be a good moment for the animation to begin.*

Under the circumstances, no one could've guessed that Fast Eddie's nickname came from the speed he could careen around a scruple. He gave me a smile that was as shabby as his suit. His hands flopped in a what-are-you-gonna-do gesture, and my plans for the holiday crumpled like the downward arc of a geyser of candy corn.

Darleen inched closer to the coffin. Compared to Darleen, Pollyanna was a grump. Darleen couldn't work up the nerve to look Larry in the face, but she was the only one in the group who was thinking about our 12-step recovery program.

"Maybe he wants to find someone to talk to," she said. "Larry, if you're in there, I've got all night to listen."

Talking over our misdeeds and resentments is one of the cornerstones of our 12 steps, but no one seemed to know for a—pardon the rough language here—dead certainty how to get the unwilling to commence jabbering. The silence inside the funeral home was so thick it matched the drapes and carpet.

Eventually, Veronica straightened to her full height, which included eighteen inches of grandiosity and six inches of indignation. "I, for one, cannot imagine this corpse saying anything of interest."

Which, of course, set Gilda, Darleen and Hank on a fussing match that involved me only when someone needed a target, followed by a race to see who would be first to (A) remember a vital appointment, (B) register dissatisfaction with all concerned by stomping outside, or (C) grow bored and wander off.

Soon I was left in the darkness of the viewing parlor with Fast Eddie and Larry.

"One little thing," I said, spinning on Fast Eddie. "All I asked you to do is one little thing. But would you stoop to use your mojo to give my friends a little holiday squeal?" Wisely, Fast Eddie lifted his hands. Maybe he was surrendering, maybe trying to get me to stop before I lost control. Surrendering was the better choice.

"I've been trying to tell you, kid," he finally said, "but you won't listen. I can't walk into a mortuary and get the corpses to play poker with me. It can't be done."

"Can't? Or won't?"

"Both." Fast Eddie shot a glance at Larry as though he wanted to make sure Larry wouldn't contradict him. "You gotta know I had a long chat with Cal. And he says I should have better things to do than scare my friends."

"What's the point of having friends if you can't terrify them from time to time?"

"Explain it to Cal," he said, disappearing in a *poof*.

I jabbed a finger at the open air where Fast Eddie had just been. "Well, Cal ought to worry about explaining himself to me."

Larry lay there on the cushy pillow of his coffin, his eyes shut, the hint of a smile on his face. My mind raced through my repertoire of verbal persuaders, with emphasis upon remarks that were barbed, challenging or cringe-worthy. Surely, I could think of something that'd make the corpse come up with a significant twitch. After all, it hadn't been too many midnights ago that I'd been the one in the casket.

"We're dead," I muttered to Larry. "Let's get in the ol' Halloween spirit."

I EXPECTED A great many things after I had my own funeral. Feeling like a wallflower at the senior prom wasn't one of them.

In fairness to Fast Eddie, the 12-step program of Specters Anonymous discourages spooks from getting involved with the material world. We're in recovery—recovery from sunshine, working respiratory systems, long-term financial planning, love handles, haircuts, fashion accessories, bad breath and telemarketers.

Fast Eddie once had a reputation as a Tosser—the less formal, post-mortal nickname for poltergeists—then Cal talked him into trying the Specters Anonymous path to transcendence, and Fast Eddie went from being the sort of spook who took pride in sprinkling coffee beans around our meeting room for a little 12-step ambience, into becoming a spiritual entity who didn't see the humor in hoisting Larry from his coffin for a quick howdy-do.

I left the funeral home on Midlothian Pike with a hasty *Beam-Me-Up-Scotty* and pulled myself together on a sidewalk in the tree-lined south end of Broad Street. Houses with stately porches shared the blocks with new town houses that had lawns that'd fit in a flowerpot. Downtown Richmond glittered in the northwest.

Cal was waiting for me on the steps that led to the church basement where the St. Sears group met every night.

"I heard that Fast Eddie didn't put on a show for you," he said.

"Do I look entertained?"

"No," Cal crossed his arms and gave me an appraising look. "You look like a spook who ought to know better than to encourage a fellow specter to play games with the physical world, which includes ex-Breathers. That won't help Fast Eddie recover from his first life."

Never let a sponsor think he has the upper hand. "Everyone's up to their astral eyeballs in recovery. When do we get to recover our sense of humor?"

"When you're not hiding behind it." Cal didn't miss a beat.

Nor did I. "I'm here for you, Cal. What do you really want to talk about?"

Cal is unaffected by irony, sarcasm, attitudes or snarky remarks, which makes him either the most patient sponsor on this side of the daisies, or the only spook who bothered to bring a hearing impediment into the afterlife.

"You're real good with the snappy comeback, Ralph," he said. "It's time to see if you can find a snappy *go-forward*. You can't go forward and come back at the same time."

"You got a pencil? I want to write this down."

He did one of those funny things with his mouth that I've never been able to understand. Hank insists it's a smile, but I'm still sorting through the evidence.

"How about dropping the comedy routine?" Cal said. "Give it a try. Just for a while. I know you can do it."

I shook my head. "If it ain't snarky, it doesn't muss up my ectoplasm."

"Think about it." Cal gave me that look. I mean, *that* look before adding, "Let's go. The meeting's about to start."

INSIDE, THE REGULARS of our Specters Anonymous group floated above gray metal chairs arranged in a circle. Cal took his favorite place facing the door as newbies drifted to the chairs along the wall. I say *drifted* in a nonliteral sense, for the thing about newcomers is their inability to stay in one place. If they aren't floating through the walls, ceilings or floors, they're bumping into each other,

Our chairspook and senior grammarian patted her hair and smoothed her sensible skirt.

"Good evening, astral family," she said. "I am Rosetta, a recovering post-life spiritual force. Welcome to this meeting of the St. Sears group of Specters Anonymous. Is anyone new to our 12-step program?"

From the other side of the room, a hand rose that was attached to a guy who looked as though he'd entered the hereafter without a clue about anything. He was thin, nearly frail in appearance. His shirt was buttoned to his chin, his hair slicked against his head, and his feet twitched.

"I'm Fred-As," he said. "Would it be okay for me to listen?"

"*Fred as* in what?" Gwendolyn asked.

Gwendolyn was the spook you went to if you needed to remember what it was like to break things. He knows everyone in the hereafter named Vinny who started out in the adult entertainment rackets in New Jersey.

"Funny name, isn't it?" said Fred-As. "I wanted to change it. I even told a few spooks my name was Rocky. But that never felt right."

"Welcome, Fred-As, and please keep coming back." Rosetta straightened and inched closer to the edge of her chair. "The speaker who volunteered to lead our meeting tonight isn't here. She must have remembered she left a pot on the stove when she died."

The newbies snickered but the regulars knew that if Rosetta said something funny, it was a slip of the tongue and it would be bad manners to draw attention to it.

"Perhaps," she continued, "someone would like to get us started by sharing their *perplexities, tremors and uncertainties,* as our literature says."

Across the room, a slender arm snaked into the darkness. It was Fred-As, coming back for round two.

"I was wondering if someone could tell me where the Halloween party will be?" he asked.

The cigar stub that lived in Gwendolyn's mouth sagged. Hank suppressed a laugh. Gilda studied her purple fingernails. Cal recrossed his arms over his chest and looked steadily at me, daring me to open my mouth.

"When you say *party,*" I said, taking the dare, "might that include candy corn? Lots of it, a snowfall, a blizzard? Drifts of candy corn blocking city streets. Sugary orange-and-yellow hats on lampposts and parking meters? Candy corn spraying from windshield wipers, burying trash cans and storefronts and pet dogs?"

Fred-As's eyes glazed. "Sounds like you guys know how to have a swell time."

Two
CHAPTER

osetta is vigilant about stopping the overlapping conversations that are known in recovery meetings as *pretzel talk*. Tonight, she must have sensed that Fred-As might not show up at another 12-step gathering if we tried to dampen his enthusiasm, so she allowed the back-and-forth chatter to continue as we waited for the spook who was supposed to lead tonight's discussion.

I was about to take advantage of the situation by reminding everyone that the candy corn pieces last year existed for less than twenty seconds and were only visible to spectral residents of Richmond, but I saw an opportunity to bring some well-deserved confusion into the afterlife.

"Normally, I'd be happy to handle all the details for a proper Halloween party," I said, giving Fast Eddie a look that would make a more responsible spook check out his options for reincarnation. "But I need help with the technical stuff. That help doesn't seem to be available this year."

Fast Eddie eyed Cal, who didn't need to remind Eddie that he'd gotten out of the levitation business. No surprise there. Cal thought even newbies were closer to transcendence than Tossers.

If Fred-As noticed this undercurrent, he didn't let on. "Can I volunteer to help with the dance committee?"

With only half an ear, I listened to Fred-As describe his idea for a Halloween gala that, him now being on the dark side of the headstone, was too much like Christmas or someone's birthday party and not enough like an all-night Dean Koontz film fest.

"Okay, let's think outside the box," Fred-As said when I pointed this out.

"What's he saying?" Darleen whispered to Gilda. "If we weren't outside the box, we wouldn't be here."

Veronica snuffled. "Personally, I didn't go through the indignities of an autopsy to act like an idiot now."

"Come on," Fred-As said. "It'd be fun."

"I don't *do* fun," Veronica snapped. "And I don't do *creepy*, either."

"What do you do?" Fred-As asked.

There've been silences that let people hear a pin drop. The silence that followed Fred-As's question opened up the auditory channels for pins falling three counties down the road. Hank leaned forward. Gwendolyn's sleepy eyes locked on Veronica with more curiosity than I thought the old boy could muster. Darleen whispered to Gilda to explain why everyone was so quiet.

No moment ever existed on two dimensions that couldn't be improved by a smart-mouthed observation. I pursed my lips, puffed my astral cheeks and smiled at Cal, hoping he'd give me credit for restraint.

Rosetta, with the finesse befitting our arbiter of all questions involving deportment, knew exactly how to handle this awkward situation.

"Wouldn't this be a nice moment to take a break?" she said, cheerily.

HALFTIME IS OBSERVED at recovery meetings on all planes of existence. My spectral pals, not having money to toss into a basket, cigarettes to smoke or coffee mugs to refresh, gather on the steps outside the meeting room to discuss the previous discussion or plan the meeting after the meeting.

Hank and Gwendolyn usually beat me to the steps. When I slid through the door this time, only Cal was there.

"You're not thinking about repeating the episode with the candy corn?" he asked. "Or any other fiasco?"

"*Fiasco* can mean different things to different spooks," I countered.

"How many meanings can you find for *No?*" For a rare moment in our acquaintance, Cal looked me in the eye and didn't cross his arms. "Tell you what. Since you like games, I'll give you a game you'll never forget. Interested?"

"What's the deal?"

"Let's see how long you can go without any pranks, tricks, setups or put-downs."

A future in the hereafter opened up before me, and it was a wasteland. "Never? Forever and ever? Not at all? I gotta be dead *and* dull?"

"Just until Halloween."

"What's in it for me?"

"If you win, you choose my Halloween costume."

Can I describe, in the space of a mere afterlife, the images that flashed across my mind—Cal in a baby's diaper, Cal as a cringing newbie, Cal as a glow-in-the dark skeleton, Cal with the head of a pumpkin and the tail of a donkey.

"What's in it for you?" I asked.

"A couple nights when I can forget I'm sponsoring the biggest clown in the hereafter."

I thought about Cal dressed as Veronica. As fantasies go, this was too sweet to ignore. "You've got yourself a deal."

He crossed his arms over his chest in sync with the rumble of distant thunder. My sponsor crosses his arms the way writers use periods, hyphens, commas and question marks. This crossing was equivalent to triple exclamation points.

"Do I get credit for choking back snarky remarks in there?" I asked. "That situation with Fred-As was begging for sarcasm. Or, at a minimum, a small serving of irony."

"No wild tales, goofy pranks or smart-aleck language," he said, his voice softening. "Beginning now."

"What's Halloween without a booga-booga or two?"

"It's Halloween with someone else going booga-booga and you beginning to act as though you're serious about recovering from sunshine."

"Oh, that."

"Remember: *In recovery, you fall on your face* before *you have a stumblie*," Cal said, using a phrase from his Zen period.

The approaching storm growled in agreement. Windowpanes in the church rattled, a chorus of barking dogs filled the night, and panicked cats fled from the city. Instinctively I gritted my teeth for an ectoplasmicly searing bolt of lightning. Cal dropped his arms to his sides and, peering into the darkness, balled his fingers into fists.

No lightning bolt streaked across the darkness. Yet, the thunder grew louder until I was willing to believe the storm was stuck in my back pocket.

Down the middle of the street roared a column of ghostly motorcyclists, balancing twenty or thirty feet above the centerline. They wore black helmets studded with gleaming silver bolts, sunglasses that reflected the darkness, boots made less for walking than stomping on things, and black leather jackets emblazoned with runic figures and landscapes I'd never seen on my two planes of existence.

Chilly waves cascaded down whatever had replaced my spine, even though, in a strictly literal sense, there were no motorcycles, this being the hereafter and physical motorcycles being parked on the sunny side of the Great Divide, their major contribution to the afterlife being the hordes of folks for whom they created the need for a mortician.

As the first riders passed, I saw stitched in fiery letters on their backs the name of this ghastly cavalcade: *Heck's Angels*.

"Well," Cal said, barely moving his lips, "at least they won't run into trouble with Rosetta for inappropriate language."

Grim riders rumbled along with the confidence of spooks who don't worry about being the guest of honor at another funeral. The line was halfway past when, on cue, their engines joined in an irritated choral growl and all riders swung to the left. When they braked, every front wheel was aimed directly at Cal and me.

Just the two of us, facing down three dozen spooks in black, their faces hidden behind helmets and glasses and scowls, their massive shoulders rocking with the power of barely controlled engines that weren't, in an overly technical sense, there.

A lone rider rolled forward from the middle of the pack. "Tell our buddy inside that the boys are here," he snarled.

Before I could suggest the biker find his own messenger-spook, Cal whispered to me, "Remember our bet." He turned to the spook and said, "I don't think any friend of yours is inside."

The biker reared up on the motorcycle that hadn't joined him on this plane of existence, his fingers clenching the handles that weren't there, either, although the grumble of the spectral engine was surreal enough. Red whiskers bristled from the spook's chin and cheeks; each hair pulsed with a fiery glow.

"Are you calling me a liar?" the biker said.

"Who says your friend is inside?" Cal asked.

"Red Max," was the reply.

Things were going entirely too smoothly for my tastes. Bet or no bet, I stepped forward, shaking my head hard enough to set some vertebrae spinning.

"Red Max? Red Max? You couldn't possibly believe anything that moldy piece of roadkill says. His brain was smaller than a gnat's even before he hit the pavement for the last time."

The biker angled his head just so, twisting it in a way that made me think he was memorizing how I looked because I was seconds from being rearranged.

"I'm Red Max," he said.

I gave him a steely eyed glare, tugged up my astral belt, waited for the big fellow to blink, then said, "Your friend isn't inside, but you can look there if you want. You passed the test."

A biker in the line nudged his neighbor. "D'you hear that? Red Max passed the test."

The nudgee spat a glob of ectoplasm at the ground. "What'd you expect?"

"Ooowee. Weren't he smooth? *I'm Red Max*, he says. Like there weren't nothing to it."

"That spook was born to lead."

Red Max was twitchy around the corners of his eyes as murmurs of admiration swept to both ends of the row of ghostly bikers. He threw me a two-fingered salute, fired up his spectral Harley, slammed down the clutch that must exist in a dimension somewhere and went roaring into the church.

The armada of growling, whooping, helmet-waving, wheelie-making bikers zoomed through the walls behind him. There was a pause. Every car in the city must've hit a red light. The breeze took a breather. The crickets, sensing that things were about to go off at a 90-degree angle, made an urgent call for company for the night.

Then spookageddon hit.

From the roof and walls of the church, the cellar and the stained-glass windows, from the little dark places not even the votive candles can reach, specters erupted from our basement meeting room and the church upstairs. Spooks flew sideways from the building or feetfirst; a few newbies tried the *Beam-Me-Up-Scotty* route of escape but, owing to their inexperience with the astral plane, ended up winking in and out of existence as they skidded into the trees.

"That went nicely," Cal said.

"Yep, we've got them now where we want them."

Cal ducked to avoid decapitation by a grandmotherly spook in a jogging suit and red tennis shoes.

"Was that Mrs. Hannity?" he asked.

When the last spook caromed from the steeple in a direct flight to the Crab Nebula, a moment of silence that even the crickets respected settled again over the city. I was about to ask Cal if he saw any of the Heck's Angels leaving.

An eruption of spectral bikers blew out of the church through windows, bricks, roof tiles and gutters. Helmets askew, fists gripping non-material handle bars, black leather jackets ripped open to expose enough chest hair to carpet Belle Island, mouths wide with screams that didn't want to leave the safety of their necks.

Cal watched a spectral biker sail past, lying sideways on the air, pedaling furiously.

"Father Jenkins must be practicing his exorcisms," I said. "I never thought they were that bad."

"Some spooks still aren't prepared for everything," Cal answered, giving me a meaningful glance.

Last one out of the church was Red Max. He straddled his invisible machine like a nabob ambling through Calcutta on an elephant. I waved. Red Max swung toward me, surrounded by a bubble of rumbling, rattling, testosterone-saturated attitude, and I noticed someone on the rear seat—Fred-As.

"Gotta run," Fred-As said. "We'll get together later about that dance committee."

"Sure, happy to talk."

Red Max leaned toward me. I felt heat radiate from his blazing whiskers. "I thought you told me my buddy wasn't inside."

Fred-As caught my eye and shrugged.

"It was another test," I said. "You passed that one, too."

Three

CHAPTER

*T*urns out, I'd passed my own test. I'd spent entire seconds around a horde of no-neck spooks who strutted through the afterlife like conquering warriors when the only thing that could harm them is the stray photon, and not the slightest taunt had escaped my lips to suggest a real post-mortal risk taker would raid a tanning salon, not a dark church. Cal seemed to appreciate my restraint.

As he went into the church to check for stragglers, I headed to Shockoe Bottom at a Breather's pace. No sense hurrying to the diner for the meeting-after-the-meeting when most of the St. Sears group had probably stopped over the Dakotas to—using an insensitive phrase—catch their breaths.

Three spooks are a meeting, Cal likes to say. *Two are a problem and one is a disaster.*

After the run-in with Heck's Angels, I wasn't so sure about Cal's arithmetic. Those bikers were legends in the hereafter, which meant that most of what the afterworld knew about them was hokum and the rest was hooey.

Yes, they were restless spirits determined to roar through never-never land until something better occurred to them. Unconcerned with finding meaning or direction, uncommitted to any code or creed, individualists scornful of joining anything that doesn't come with a helmet, a poor muffler and the roar of a wounded mastodon.

I would cash in my Specters Anonymous chips and hop onto the back of the nearest Harley if I could shake the nagging thought that Heck's Angels had a fatal flaw, that I'd be setting myself on a short path to disaster if I hitched my future to that pack of ruffians, wastrels and derelicts.

So what was the problem?

They reminded me of me.

AS I GLIDED through the now-peaceful regions on the downslope of Church Hill, the leafless branches of trees lining the streets stretched their palsied fingers overhead. A quarter moon rocked on a chimney.

I felt good, I felt confident. I'd survived Heck's Angels without the smallest untoward syllable escaping from my lips. Why should I worry? My bona fides as the quickest quipster on the second dimension were well-established. A few nights of restraint would be worth seeing Cal dressed up as a Heck's Angel, or, better yet, riding an astral tricycle in a tutu with ballet slippers.

From the porch of a home overwhelmed by vines, a jack-o'-lantern watched me pass with a wary stare.

When I say it *watched me*, I don't mean that it sat there with a silly smile cut into its orange flesh. I mean that it locked its carved eyes on me as I floated past and rotated on the porch to keep me in sight. I veered toward the pulpy face. The silly smirk cut into the gourd disappeared, replaced by a glare of pure hate.

From the darkness and the shadows, a voice spoke: "The skies, they were ashen and sober; / The leaves, they were crispéd and sere—"

I didn't need to hear any more. "*Crisp-ED? Crisp-ED?* Couldn't you find a two-syllable word to fit your meter? Or show a little flexibility and just go with *crisp*? Isn't clarity a good reason to break your precious little rhythm?"

"A late contemporary of mine, with some limited promise, once wrote about *the viewless wings of poesy*. Those wings, being *viewless*, are easily trammeled by the unlettered."

"Poesy?" I asked.

From the shadows of a dogwood, a dark figure who was rather crispéd himself looked down on me. Wearing a thin black ribbon of a tie, a long black coat and a white shirt with enough ruffles to outfit the Rockettes was Richmond's most revered adopted dead son and the proud possessor of a signed, original edition of *American Rhyming Dictionary*.

Edgar Allan Poe gave a debonair tilt to his chin and echoed: "Yes, poesy."

My relations with Edgar A- had started badly, then plummeted. I suspect his bruised ego had something to do with a parody that appeared shortly after my arrival in town. A clever little ditty, if I may say so myself, that had a refrain that rang with the power of a bronze church bell: *Quoth the critic, This is crap.*

Still, Specters Anonymous teaches that whenever we find ourselves nervous about another spook, it's really the shadows in our own closet that are making us uncomfortable. A spirit of reconciliation and healing welled up in me, which, owing to my unfamiliarity with those notions, came out as: "What's up?"

Edgar A- floated down from his branch. Without thinking, I sidled backward, for his eyes shone with a dark light. I glanced from Poe to the jack-o'-lantern and back again, wondering if the poet was mimicking the pumpkin.

"At the urging of a few admirers who retain affection for my former labors with quill and inkwell," he said, "I've been persuaded to take up again the scrivener's escutcheon."

Edgar A- beamed in triumph.

"Could you possibly be more convoluted?" I asked.

"At the drop of a hat, old boy. But first, I wanted you to hear the grand news from my lips."

I felt a rant coming on. An unbecoming, childish harangue against puffery, flimflam and obfuscation. I gritted my teeth. Not a single word would roll off my tongue until I'd vetted it for trip wires and sharp edges. I'd act like a spook who wasn't racking up more train wrecks in the hereafter that I'd have to fix in my third plane of existence. Cal would be proud of me, and Rosetta wouldn't be too embarrassed. I'd amaze myself if I could get out of this situation without releasing an extremely barbed syllable.

"So, you're going to start writing again," I said cautiously. "How wonderful for you. And what will you be writing? A poem? Short story? Perhaps an essay?"

"I'm calling it *Poe's Potion for the Posthumously Lovelorn*."

The jack-o'-lantern on the porch gaped in amazement. From the distant river rose the chants of a spectral crew on a voyage to nowhere. Further inland came the muffled tread of deceased Confederate soldiers patrolling their fallen capital, weaving above the statues and trees on Monument Avenue and the sorority houses of Hamilton Street.

"And where would I read your . . . er . . . words?" I asked, not wanting to spoil the moment by drawing attention to the technical difficulties of a noncorporeal author pecking at a keyboard or hefting a Bic.

Edgar A- rocked on his heels, his fingers spazing at his sides. "'Tis a new and glorious age, my fine, semicoherent fellow. I shall avail myself of the marvelous communicative devices of this new twentieth century."

"Actually, it's the twenty-first century." I tried to anticipate the direction he was heading. "And your edifying words will appear in—"

Poe broke into a grin that was more terrifying than the dark, cold fire that simmered moments ago in his eyes.

"Son, I got me a blog!"

I HUNG AROUND for a while, not out of interest and certainly not from politeness, but because the tectonic plates of my afterlife had just shifted, and I struggled not to fall to the ground and curl into a tight ball of fetal ectoplasm.

By the time Poe started to explain a marvelous invention called Facebook which allows ordinary Breathers to transplant their cheeks, foreheads and jaws onto other skulls, I recovered the gumption to let the old boy know that I just remembered an important engagement at a funeral home.

"Don't jump into any hearses where I wouldn't go," he called with cheery bonhomie.

I gave him a thumbs-up, although passing the jack-o'-lantern I muttered, "Not a word from you."

Once again, I set my astral feet toward the diner in Shockoe Bottom favored by members of my 12-step group. I needed to smell a chocolate chip cookie, sense the chill rising from a cup of ice cream, be dazzled by the crispy shell of an apple pie. I needed the night to become paranormal again, not nutsy.

Passing another jack-o'-lantern on my way, I scrutinized it carefully on its perch in a second-floor window, relieved initially that I saw no evidence of sinister intentions, although crossing the next intersection, I realized it'd been studying me as carefully as I studied it.

Hank shared a booth in our favorite diner near the kitchen with a couple of students staring into the brightly lit world inside their smartphones.

"Do you realize that, at this very moment, you're practicing to be dead?" I whispered into the ear of one coed.

She shivered, her earrings jingled, and I slid into the bench opposite Hank. He nodded, and the tiny pigtail at the back of his *café au lait* neck bobbed in greeting.

"Where's the rest of our gang?" I asked.

"Recuperating from Heck's Angels. And figuring out a way to blame you."

"I was with Cal. There's no way they can pin it on me."

"Yeah, you also had an alibi for the Night of the Corn Candy."

Hank's eyes never left the slice of apple pie lying between the booth's two breathing occupants. I asked what happened when Red Max and the boys roared into our meeting.

Hank gave me the highlights: Rosetta lectured them for growling before they'd been formally recognized, Darleen looked for someone to explain why these new spooks weren't taking seats, Jingle Jim dashed into a corner to compose a poem memorializing the event and got stuck finding a rhyme for *assault*, Gwendolyn ripped one of the bikers off a motorcycle that was only there in a hypothetical sense, and Veronica got into a staring match with Red Max.

"How did Gilda take it?"

"With considerable annoyance." Hank looked up from the pie. "At first, the bikers thought she was one of them that we'd kidnapped and they wanted to kidnap her back. She straightened them out in no time. Then she started muttering, *Where's he at?* and looking behind the walls and underneath the floor tiles."

"I wonder who *he* is?" I said.

"Yeah, I've wondered myself who you were," Hank said.

My eyes went dreamy. "And to think of what I missed by being outside when those riders crashed our meeting—the confusion, the noise, the poor grammar, the breaches of etiquette."

"No, no." Hank's pigtail trembled. "If you're thinking of getting those goons involved in some Halloween prank—"

"You think they're freaky? Let me tell you what I've seen some pumpkins getting into."

"So that's what it's going to be this year—pumpkins and bikers instead of candy corn?"

"I'd never dream of such a thing," I protested. "I don't believe in repeating myself."

Hank pretended to stuff his fingers into his ears. "I've got my own recovery to worry about. And I've heard nothing that you've said. And I'm going to continue hearing nothing, regardless what you say."

And, *poof*, he was gone.

CHAPTER

'll always remember where I was when I heard the afterlife's saddest story. A few of us from the St. Sears group had decided to check out a meeting that John the Plain ran on campus. One of the sharers was an old-timer who gushed about the breakthrough he'd just had with his recovery: He actually remembered his last minutes as a Breather, when his entire first life flashed before him.

A great silence overcame the old-timer, which spread to John the Plain, then to his group, and began to get sticky until Darleen asked what happened next. "Dunno," he said. "I was so bored, I fell sleep."

I was thinking about that poor fellow after Hank left and I was stuck in the diner with a perfectly good apple pie on the table and two Sunshiners who couldn't take their noses out of their cell phones long enough to venerate their dessert. *(Note to self: How come those tiny phones are called* smartphones? *If those gadgets were so smart, they wouldn't distract Sunshiners from the precious things in life, like chocolate and caramel.)*

Did I have the same attitudes as those people when all my organs were working? When I finally got a grip on my own recovery, would I be like the old-timer who fell asleep during the story of his life? Was my reluctance to shut my mouth driven by fear that I'd discover I'm boring?

In a word: Nah.

I believe, with the sort of absolute confidence that only comes on my side of the Great Divide, that my own end-of-life Powerpoint presentation must've taken three or four days. Still, I've only been able to retrieve a few snippets to work with as I come to understand my first life.

I had a grandmother. My death may have had something to do with a car accident. I believe the 1950s sitcom *The Honeymooners* will provide me with vital background about my life in the sunshine. And the name *Ralph,* which I wrote in the big ledger by the entrance into the hereafter, was never my real name, but it's an important clue that will lead me from here *(wherever that is)* to the place I'm going *(ditto).*

Drifting in the diner beside two coeds who wouldn't know I was there even if they could see me, I had the strangest notion that I was being watched. Nonchalantly, I drifted up through the table for a few feet. Rosetta was coming through the door, glanced my way and went to a table on the other side of the restaurant. Not another other spook was in sight.

The only faces turned in my direction had been carved into the husks of a half dozen pumpkins scattered around the diner. I settled back on the bench to study the apple pie, which I'm sure hadn't harmed anyone in its brief post-oven existence, yet its thin brown crust was sinking tragically into the lumpish yellow interior.

Eyes were pressing on me hard enough to leave retinal imprints. I spun around and nearly bumped into a jack-o'-lantern balanced on the back of the booth. Where did it come from, and how did it get here? Those scooped-out eyes had a glimmer that had nothing to do with the candle stub inside.

I eased away. The pumpkin lifted its chin at the precise angle that a jack-o'-lantern would assume seconds before hurling his jagged, pulpy teeth at the neck of an innocent specter.

"I hope you're not planning to join me," Rosetta asked behind me.

Rosetta was seated at a table by the window with three Breathers—a mother and two young children. In her sturdy, all-season suit, Rosetta could be mistaken for the family's grandmother if you're willing to overlook the wee problem of interdimensional synchronicity.

I shot a glance at the pumpkin, which had turned back into a garden-variety vegetable.

"Did you see that?" I jabbed a finger over my shoulder for Rosetta's sake.

She was trying to tweezer fallen droplets from the Formica, while the youngsters at her table inhaled tall chocolate shakes. She gave me a look. "Not one smart remark from you. Call what I'm doing a test of faith. Optimism triumphing over experience."

"I don't remember seeing that line in our literature," I said.

"Which part?" she snapped. "Optimism or experience?"

"How about the part where physical objects sometimes interact with the spectral plane?"

Rosetta turned from the kids and their shakes. "You mean *repos* or Tossers?"

Every spook has been warned about repossessed houses. Same for Tossers like Fast Eddie who were able to flip the occasional stone onto a roof in their heyday. But malevolent pumpkins didn't fit into any tales I've heard about happily-ever-after.

Rosetta had the eagle-eyed alertness of a grammarian sensing that infinitives were about to be split. Time for me to pop my tongue into *race* and hope my brain catches up on the downhill slope.

"I overheard some spooks talking before the meeting," I said. "They said they noticed a certain restlessness among the jack-o'-lanterns this year. Something you could almost call hostility. They wondered if the farmers might have some new pesticide that really irritates the squash family."

"Killer pumpkins? Is that what this is about?"

"I wouldn't exactly call them *killer*."

A gleam came to Rosetta's eyes that I'd only seen during a discussion of the proper use of *who* and *whom*. "You've already disrupted our meeting tonight by sending a tribe of spectral bikers roaring through the church. Do you really need to stir up more mischief?"

"Mischief? Mischief? I ain't got no time for stinking mischief."

Rosetta leaned closer to the chocolate droplets on the table. "Right. As soon as you clear the major mayhem from your calendar, you'll be able to take on a little mischief."

WAS I THE only one who hadn't gotten out on the wrong side of the casket tonight? Leaving the diner seemed like a good idea until I reached the sidewalk. Outside was more of everything—more shadows, places to hide, directions to come from, open spaces, things to watch, and especially more room for my fears to set down roots and spring into full bloom.

Fortunately, it had less of one key ingredient: jack-o'-lanterns.

Or so I thought.

Like a lighthouse with a burnt-out bulb, I rotated slowly on the sidewalk in front of the diner. If I were stalking me, I'd think the old clock tower by the railroad station a few blocks away was the perfect observation post. Or the cars parked on the street would be an easy place to hide if I were planning to mug myself. But wouldn't it be more like me to creep up from behind my back, coming from the diner I'd just left?

I noticed the garbage can on the other side of the asphalt that was playing it real cool, its sides grimy and dented, its lid tipped at a rakish angle. All it needed was a sign that said: *Don't bother looking in here for a bushel or two of attack veggies.*

I was distracted by a limousine that glided to the curb, easing around a station wagon that had seen better years. The limo's chrome gleamed, its hood and roof sparkled like black ice, a powerful engine revved with the contented purr of a well-fed cougar.

Sliding through the rear door was Veronica, lean and stately, her long brown hair lying across her shoulders, not a single filament daring to get out of place. As stately as a cruise ship pulling from the pier, the limo flowed back into the street.

"I know I'm going to regret this," I said, "but has anyone pointed out that spooks don't need public transportation?"

Veronica bristled. "I would hardly call a limousine *public*."

"Okay, let's try this: Spooks don't need any kind of transportation."

Down the full length of her imperial nose rolled a glare that'd stop a charging rhino. "We're not supposed to move? Is that what you're trying to tell me?"

I liked this conversation less the deeper I slipped into it. "Let me try to be clear."

"Shouldn't you have made that effort before you opened your mouth?"

She turned and, in full hauteur, processed toward the door to the diner. Toward which, on the inside, the mother with the two kids who'd shared a table with Rosetta was walking.

Now, Veronica, like any spook, can pass through entities in the physical world. To include terriers, cockatiels, shellfish, whooping cranes and—What else? Oh, yeah—people.

Veronica, however, is not like other spooks, a subject on which she'll hold forth until daybreak. She has a tad more ectoplasm than the rest of us—just the barest amount of a negligibly measurable portion—enough to make her almost perceptible to Breathers. Mostly, they notice her out of the corners of their eyes as a shadow, a blurred movement, a flicker of the light that isn't there when they look directly at it. Or her.

Personally, I'll hop to the other side of the street before I'll pass through the sluggish interior of a pedestrian's intestines. Veronica, as I said, isn't like the rest of us. She kept gliding toward the door that the mother with the two kids was approaching from the other side.

At the last moment, the Breathers flinched. The woman did a quick side step, as did one of the kids, while mom jerked the youngest aside by the shoulder. And Veronica floated past.

"Well—I thought—but—" the woman said, flustered, not sure why she had felt something was coming at her.

I sidled out of the way for mom and the kids. The youngest, a little guy, was more puzzled than his mother. His squinty eyes darted wildly around the door where I stood. Infants and small kids are attuned to the goings-on on the spectral plane. A pudgy finger arose and I was sure he was going to jab my knees, but his arm deflected a bit and he said, "There's another one, Mommy."

I glanced where he was pointing. It wasn't a spook that he was calling to his mother's attention, but a pumpkin, a basketball-sized terror in orange that rested on the hood of the station wagon by the curb. Where no pumpkin had been seconds ago.

I looked at the jack-o'-lantern, its grin widened, its teeth took on the glint of razors. *You only die once*, is one of Hank's favorite sayings. I wonder if he got that in writing.

CHAPTER

ave you ever tried to stare down a jack-o'-lantern? It isn't easy. If your attention wavers, it'll glide closer, its mouth widening a smidgen, or tiny orange blurs will appear in the corners of your eye that aren't there if you look directly at them, and when you glance back at the station wagon by the curb, the pumpkin on the hood will have slid closer to the fender.

And you know it may all be in your mind, but a mind is a terrible thing to waste time in, so you struggle to think of somewhere you would be safe and hope that your mind doesn't follow you there. For me, no struggle is necessary to pick the one spot for those moments when the afterlife isn't large enough to contain both me and my imagination.

Home is a duplex on the eastern edge of the city on Libby Hill. On one side, the hill drops precipitously to the scraggly brush and packed dirt of the floodplain. On the other is a park with an obelisk to Confederate war dead.

I respecterized in the dining room where the mother of the house has a collection of coffeepots on the wall, each pot a potential sanctuary for a spook whose ectoplasm cannot survive more than a few seconds of direct sunlight.

Screeches and whoops and caws drifted from the living room. James William was stretched on his belly in front of the television, doodling in a coloring book and checking the screen only when a roar indicated that the program about the so-called natural world was going to discuss carnivores.

Mom and Dad were somewhere in the house doing motherly and fatherly things, which, since I'm rarely home at this hour, I don't know about. More importantly, I don't know Petey's routines at this time of night.

As I drifted through the ceiling to check James William's room, a distinctive *clickety-clickety-clickety* came from the kitchen, and suddenly the afterlife was alright again. Petey, my favorite beagle, the only dog on the first dimension of existence who can look a spook in the eye and waddle over for a good belly rub, must be inspecting the kitchen—no doubt for the eighteenth time since dinner ended—to make sure a T-bone steak hadn't escaped from a plate and managed to hide under the oven.

I drifted across the dining room and into the kitchen. "Hey, Petey. Did you find a good snack?"

Instead of a dog, a skeleton greeted me. Staring from eyes with bottomless sockets, glowing in the darkness on the counter, one leg crossed over the other, it raised a hand—*clickety, clickety*—and waved.

Wherever my heart was, it stopped again.

Faster than a bee's blink, I was out of there, down the street and accelerating. I didn't die to put up with this abuse. Not inquisitive pumpkins. And certainly not back-slapping skeletons.

Before I could hit orbital speed, I noticed a spectral army gathering around the Confederate memorial. Even for spooks, there's safety in numbers, especially numbers that've been itching for a fight for a hundred and fifty years. An officer gestured for me to join him at the base of the obelisk.

Unlike most of his unit, the Colonel had a beard that was trimmed and combed, a neat uniform, and the sword dangling from his side that was so highly polished that the lights of the city bouncing off the weapon had eroded the ectoplasm of his leg into semitransparency.

"It appears you have something to report," he said in an accent rubbed smooth by mint juleps and evening breezes on a veranda.

I pointed down the street. "Skeleton. I saw a skeleton back there."

"We do have a tendency to keep stepping over those things, don't we?" he said. "Anything else in the nature of suspicious activity? Troop movements? Strangers you don't recognize?"

I shook my head. "But the skeleton—"

"Did it show a hostile inclination?"

"Well, it waved at me." By then, I began to wonder if sticking my head in an open grave might be a wise move.

The Colonel was digesting my report when several soldiers rushed him, all jabbering at once. At issue was another trooper who was out of uniform because he was the only one in the enlisted ranks with boots. The Colonel held up a hand for patience. He was a stickler for thoroughness, even when questioning a slavering idiot like me who was startled to see bones in the hereafter.

"We're picking up reports of suspicious activity," he told me. "Was there anything peculiar about this skeleton—other than its friendliness?"

I saw in my mind's eye the bones loitering on the kitchen counter, coloring the room with an eerie greenish-yellow glow.

As I struggled to describe the exact shade, the Colonel pointed to a tree in a lawn across the street. A skeleton hung there, each plastic bone where it should be, bathed in the same fiendish glow that radiated from the skeleton in Petey's kitchen, although this one's movements were jerky and uncontrolled as it was shoved around by the wind sweeping through the trees.

"Could it have been plastic?" the Colonel asked. "I fail to see the allure of those effigies, although they seem quite popular at this time of year."

I shook my head. "I'm not sure. But even if it was, that wouldn't account for the one back home waving at me."

The Colonel bit his lower lip, and I was privy to a rare moment of uncertainty in the old soldier. He tugged the wrinkles out of his tunic and said, "I could send a patrol to check this animated plastic skeleton. But just last night, I heard one of the boys complain that he's still finding candy corn from last year in his musket."

"So, you think I'm lying."

"I have no question about your integrity, son." The colonel patted my arm. "It's the soundness of your mind that I have reservations about."

"I can certainly understand that," I rebutted.

I MUST HAVE spent half the night at the memorial. As the returning patrols reported to the Colonel, I maneuvered myself within listening range and if they didn't specifically mention the mood among the city's pumpkins and skeletons—a failure which, despite my admiration for the Colonel's outfit, all of his troops succumbed to—I was able to clarify the situation by shouting above the heads of the assembled officers and NCOs.

At least, that's what I did when the first few patrols came in, before I noticed the Colonel clutching the hilt of his sword and staring in my direction.

As the hours lengthened, I struggled against my predilection to turn up the hysteria. Say, to suggest the skeletons I saw were waving Union flags, but that would violate my pledge to Cal to curb the hyperbole during the run-up to Halloween. More patrols returned from the distant suburbs. Eventually, instead of sending those troops out on another reconnaissance, the Colonel told each squad to stand down for the night.

"You might as well get along home, too," he told me as another fatigued patrol drifted into the camp around the obelisk. "We're running out of shadows. If anyone's planning serious devilment tonight, they don't have time to do much."

I wound my way through knots of soldiers on the well-tended grass around the memorial. Somewhere a harmonica played a slow, mournful melody. No one noticed me leave.

Drifting down the tree-lined street to my duplex, the fears of the early evening seemed distant, almost something that belonged to another life, though I searched the trees, porches and home windows for signs of renegade holiday decorations. Everything was quiet.

Too quiet.

Gilda was waiting in the dining room beneath the shelves with the coffeepots. "I need to talk to you," she said.

My official IQ score these nights is a perfect zero, but I still registered the fact that she didn't suggest I'd have a speaking role in this conversation.

I lifted a finger. If a picture is worth a thousand words, then a visual display ought to be worth a thousand pictures. Warily, I went to the kitchen door and beckoned her to look inside. She leaned past me, examined the kitchen, then turned back, a quizzical crease to her forehead.

"Yes, it's a nice lunch box," she said.

I glanced inside. On the counter, where a bundle of luminescent bones had greeted me earlier, James William's lunch box lay.

"Is there something special about it?" she asked.

"Not anymore." I tried not to whine.

Gilda folded her hands and gazed at me with the full sincerity of her chalk-white face and heavily mascaraed eyes.

"I want you to know that I understand," she said.

"That's a relief." A somber glimmer came from the chains on her leather jacket, her purple fingernails glowed softly in the dark. "What are we talking about?"

"I understand what you're doing. You told us this story about a corpse who moved. Then you took us to the funeral home to watch him move. Even though you knew he wouldn't move."

"That wasn't quite what—"

"So we dropped our guard. We were supposed to be really surprised when you sent those bikers into our meeting to chase everyone out."

"Do you really think I had anything to do with those dim, unevolved, no-imagination specters?"

Gilda patted her black leather sleeve. "That's my Ralph. Always thinking three funerals ahead of everyone else. No one would expect spooks with that much testosterone in their systems to have anything to do with you."

"What are you going to say next? That I'm responsible for every irritating thing Veronica says?"

Gilda looked as though someone stepped on her grave, and she'd just discovered it was her own foot. "I don't know what you're talking about, Ralph. Veronica and I get along perfectly fine. *Be dead and let be dead*—that's my motto."

"If you and Veronica accidentally ended up in the same bucket some day, every Breather on the east coast would hear the uproar."

"Why would I dislike Veronica? What has she ever done to me?"

"She doesn't have to *do* anything. If there ever were two spooks who belonged in separate versions of the hereafter, it's you two."

"Next thing I know, you'll be suggesting I'm angry at Veronica because—"

I was barely tracking her words. The phrases tumbling through my mind were more interesting, a whirlwind of words that almost settled into place before they were knocked akimbo by more language anxious to get out of the shadows, with me struggling gamely to prove that I could control my own zingers if I wanted, especially now that I had a wager with Cal, when something strange entered the room.

It was called, I believe, silence.

"What was that about Veronica?" I asked.

"She's a very . . . sincere spirit. And I won't stand here while you insult her."

"Why would I insult her?"

"Why, indeed?"

Poof. Gilda retired for the day.

And I stared at the lunch box on the kitchen counter, almost missing the friendliness of a glowing plastic skeleton. At least, the bones weren't irritated at me for something I said.

Six
CHAPTER

*A*s a lighter shade of gray seeped across the eastern horizon, I huddled in the darkness of my hobo coffeepot on the dining room wall, waiting for the distinctive *clickety-click* of a plastic skeleton to sashay toward me or the long *ssshhh* of a jack-o'-lantern sliding across the floor in my direction. Was I obliged to stop spreading outrageous stories, as I'd promised Cal, when the tall tales happened to be true?

By the time Petey's family padded through the dining room and into the kitchen for breakfast, I knew I was safe for another eight or ten hours and collapsed into an exhausted ectoplasmic puddle at the bottom of my bucket.

I didn't stir enough during the daytime to send a ripple through my liquefied essence. Hours later, as night locked its grip on the city again, I started pulling myself together.

Pouring out of the spout, I emerged into a world with neat mats on the dining table, a tufted brown carpet in the living room, a toy helicopter on the edge of the coffee table, and a sofa by the front window where a bath towel marked the place Petey was allowed to sit.

Who'd ever guess that the afterlife would surround me with the things of the world? Things for entertainment, nourishment, play or learning, but only for those with a working respiratory system. As a recovering spook, those things only aggravate and confuse me.

But, of course, that was exactly the point.

A short time later—and I'm talking here about a fraction of a second that's so small it won't have a proper name for another forty years—I set down amid the red bricks and tired magnolias of Carytown, under the skeptical gaze of a cat on the ledge of a bay window where a neon sign once proclaimed *Psychic*

Advisor. Only, the neon was old and the wrapping was frayed and if anyone thought the sign said, *'syck Advisor*, that didn't affect the trade.

An odd collection of furniture waited on the other side of the door. Picture the contents of an 1880s bawdy house scattered throughout a dentist's office in a mall. If something didn't match the ornate paisley throw rugs and Tiffany lamps, then it was at home among the lava lamps, chrome chairs, and tables with smoked glass tops.

Two female Breathers glared at each other from different corners of the waiting room. The air between them crackled with electricity. Not the helpful, productive, friendly kind of electricity that waits patiently behind wall sockets to be of service. This was the kind of electricity that was in a hurry to shoot from a cattle prod.

A third corner was occupied by a spook I won't bother to call henpecked because that description was clear in every glance he took at the two women. He never drifted farther than a micron or two from being equidistant from both women at all times, and I knew he'd rather die again than be accused of favoritism.

The spook looked at me in desperation. "Do you know Bob? A specter named Bob?"

"I know a couple hundred Bobs," I said.

"Right." He sweated ectoplasm, squeegeed it from his forehead, then pressed it into the back of his neck. "Bob wouldn't set me wrong, would he? I mean, I can trust what he tells me."

"*Trust* is one of the biggest words in the—"

The spook collapsed into the wall. "I knew it. I knew Bob was up to no good. What kind of a friend would encourage me to take post-mortal couples' counseling?"

"Mrs. Wilson?"

At the sound of the name, the two women—both Mrs. Wilson, I presume—shot to their feet and headed toward the elderly woman in the hallway who called herself Sophia the Seer, known throughout the afterworld as Sophie the Fraud.

I met Sophie a long time ago, and I wouldn't hazard to guess whether the old girl thought she was dealing with one Mrs. Wilson, two Mrs. Wilsons or even more. Put that down to Sophie's long relationship with apricot brandy.

Sophie was a *twofer*. She lived in the physical world but was able to poke her nose into the astral plane far too frequently for anyone's good. Her best contact with the afterlife came on months with a *Q*, days of the week spelled with an *X*, and centuries marked with a decimal point. On all other occasions, Sophie's awareness of the paranormal is spotty. On this evening, Sophie's grip on the alleged real world was also iffy.

"Do go down to my psychic counseling parlor," Sophie said to the first Mrs. Wilson, while the second received a cordial, "Oops, so there you are again."

Last to join the cavalcade was the woeful spook who had to be Mr. Wilson, still stunned to discover the phrase *you can't take it with you* is void when talking about families. At least, he wouldn't waste decades trying to figure out what he did so wrong during his first life that rerouted him to this back alley in happily-ever-after.

Me, I was here on business. I'd finally made a vital connection: The jack-o'-lanterns and plastic skeletons that'd been stalking me were on the material plane. To fix a problem in the Breathers' world, get a Breather. And the only Breathers who'll listen to me are the twofers.

I joined the tail end of the parade down the hall. The aroma of apricot brandy rippled through a doorway, slinked into the corridor, hooked its fingers through my nostrils and pulled me through a curtain of glass beads to a small room where a crystal ball lay on a small table. Sophie worked her way into a chair.

"Please be seated," she said with a grand gesture to the other chair.

One Mrs. Wilson took the chair opposite Soph.

"Where am I supposed to sit?" the other Mrs. Wilson asked.

"I just told you," Sophie snapped, then muttered to herself, "Some people just don't pay attention."

Mr. Wilson was easing himself through the wall.

Sophie pinned him with a scowl. "You stay right there, Buster. You can have this woman's seat if she keeps popping up and down."

The second Mrs. Wilson seemed confused, the first Mrs. Wilson looked smug, and the sole Mr. Wilson had the skittery smile of someone who just learned that death isn't a hassle-free zone.

Boy, could I tell him stories.

MARGIE'S WORKROOM WAS a short glide down the hall, a domain of chrome furniture and brightly colored, molded plastic furnishings. A goldfish bowl sat on a table, with three or four residents of the silvery, algae-loving, finned variety. Margie had traded the stale cliché of a crystal ball for the ecofriendly cliché of a fishbowl.

A stack of papers and a pocket calculator took over most of the table. She fiddled with one, turned to the other, fiddled some more, then turned back to where she started. Like Sophie, Margie was a twofer. Unlike her partner, though, she was fully connected to the spiritual dimension.

"Do you think the IRS will let me claim dried flies as a business expense?" she asked, never looking up. "You don't know how lucky you are. No utility bills, no taxes, no food expenses, no upkeep."

"No sun in my eyes. No chocolate, cookies, cakes or pastries. Always wondering when I pass a cemetery if my bones are parked there."

"Tell me one of your problems that would send me screaming into the night."

"Jack-o'-lanterns and cheesy, glow-in-the-dark plastic skeletons. I think they're following me."

Margie glanced up. "Why would they do that?"

"Because someone in the first-life is moving them. Isn't that how things get around in your world?"

Margie took the news with the unflappability of a woman who grew up thinking that everyone can chat with spirits. Tightening her lips, she returned to her work. From paper, to calculator, and back again, her forehead knitted with worry.

"Do you know who's doing this?" she asked.

"Not yet. Do you have any ideas? Who'd play games with that stuff?"

"Dunno. They'd have to see you in order to do that. Sophie's the only other psychic I know who comes close to having real powers." Margie slapped down her pencil and three more zeroes appeared on her calculator's display. "But if she drives away another customer, I'll . . . I'll . . . shoot her."

"Don't bullets dissolve in alcohol?"

She looked at me, and a playful light began to glow in her eyes. She struggled with a snicker, lost the battle and let a guffaw rock the room. Sometimes I wonder what would have happened if I'd run into her during my sunshine period.

I let my feet sink through the floor until I was inches from her face. "If Sophie's so bad for business, why don't you let her go? She'll be out of work anyway if you go under."

Margie shook her head. "I can't do that. She doesn't have anyone to look after her."

"So the answer to your problem is—"

"Buy her a nice blouse. Something in Kevlar."

A gentle silence filled the space between us. She went back to balancing her books, and I decided that, since I seemed to be free of ominous Halloween ornaments at the moment, I might be able to do a good deed for a friend.

Something like—to pull an example out of the dusky air—using my connections in the spirit world to drive a pesky, bothersome, semicoherent twofer into the sobriety she should have considered three trainloads of apricot brandy ago.

I almost made it into the hall when my ectoplasm was curled by a yowl from a cat whose tail was sucked into a fan. In the corridor, I saw one Mrs. Wilson stomp out of Sophie's room, muttering, "I didn't come here to be insulted by a drunk."

"It's a miracle I don't drink more." Sophie swatted the glass beads that hung like baby pythons from her doorway. "First you're sitting over here. Then you jump up over there. Sit, jump, sit, jump. It's enough to give a girl the screeching apoplexies."

Meanwhile, the second Mrs. Wilson quietly eased the strands of glass aside in her bid to escape from Sophie's parlor.

Sophie spun on her. "I thought you just left. Will you make up your mind?"

"A full refund," this Mrs. Wilson insisted. "We paid for an hour. We barely got five minutes. I want my money back."

The spectral Mr. Wilson drifted to one side, trying not to look too relieved as he shooed this widow from Sophie.

"Just go, dear. This fraud isn't worth it." He flicked his hands toward the waiting room. "You've learned your lesson. Get out before you change your mind."

"I've changed my mind," the woman said, flinging a coil of glass beads into Sophie's face. "I'm going to the police. They ought to know that cheap con artists are masquerading as psychic advisors in this city. Then there's the newspaper and TV stations."

"Yes, yes, yes," Mr. Wilson said. "Great ideas. It's your civic duty. Why don't we do that right now?"

"No!" Margie flew out of her room and into the mêlée. "I think a full refund is more than reasonable. Maybe a little extra for your time. My colleague shouldn't see customers when she's still weak from the flu."

"If she's weak, it's from marinating her liver," the second Mrs. Wilson said.

Margie waggled her finger at Sophie. "Oh, you little scamp. Trying out another one of your herbal remedies."

By this time, the first Mrs. Wilson had clopped down the hallway, drawn by the scent of cash, while Margie was trying to persuade the second Mrs. Wilson that doubling her original payment for pain and suffering wasn't reasonable, and Sophie slumped against the door frame in a cocoon of glass beads.

Since they were well on the way to working out their problems, I still had that errand to run for Margie.

I LEFT THE hall and threaded my way through the ceilings and floors, weaving around sewage pipes and electrical lines and plowing through plasterboard, wooden supports, nails, crumpled caulking tubes and piles of acorns, with nary a pumpkin or skeleton in sight.

My destination was a room on the third floor of Margie's building where cardboard sheets were fastened to the windows to ward off the sun. Steel shelves jutted, library-style, from the walls, crammed with boxes of records from legal firms.

Drifting to a spot below a window where years of water seepage had created a Y-shaped patch of mold, I whispered, "Willbard, are you there? Willbard?"

A red light winked in the mold, like a tiny bolt of crimson lightning. It also flashed from the window sill. And the wall. And the ceiling. And, from behind me.

A voice pressed against the back of my neck and said: "Wwwwwwiiiiiilllllllbbbbbbbaaaaarrrrrddd!"

A lesser spook would have gone instantly to Katmandu. Being made of sturdier ectoplasm, I only made it as far as the Falklands before I turned around and, faster than an ant's twitch, returned to the third-floor storage room in Margie's brownstone.

"And good evening to you, too," I said, cool as an Eskimo's icebox.

Willbard was a spectral entity whose shape depended upon her mood. At the moment, she was a formless mass of swirling shadows, punctuated by reddish lightning bolts and eddies of blackness.

That meant she was in a good mood.

"Willbard, I was wondering if you'd like to play a game."

"Willbard likes games," said the creature. The maelstrom of darkness with flashing red thunderbolts disappeared and a Las Vegas-style roulette wheel sat in its place.

"Step right up, step right up. Place your bets, folks. Try your luck on the great wheel of destiny. She spins, she sparkles, she carries you off to a better world."

"Ah, I was thinking about something simpler."

"Oh."

The roulette wheel vanished. "Put 'er here, in your ear. Listen to the ivory. It's calling your name."

I needed a moment to trace the thin, reedy voice to the dice on the floor. One of the little cubes was talking to me. Without intercession from man or spook, the dice hopped into the air, jiggled a few times, hurled themselves at the wall, and when the ivory cubes stopped rolling, they showed a three and a four.

"Seven! We're hot tonight," the dice said. "Do you feel lucky, cowboy?"

"Perhaps I'm not being clear," I said.

"Then be clear."

Willbard's next transformation made her a snake-like entity with seven fiery eyes and a voice that came from rippling scales on her sinuous gray-green skin. Her voice sounded like thunder echoing in a desert canyon. Dozens of scales undulated to make each word, and underneath every scale was a mouth ringed with glistening, razor-sharp teeth.

I gritted my own teeth, leaned closer to Willbard and said, "Here's what I have in mind."

CHAPTER

left Willbard in her third-floor storage room and went for a victory lap through Margie's suite. Maybe I could casually let slip to ol' Marg the news of the wonderful favor that would shortly drop into her lap, courtesy of her bestest buddy Ralph. And let Cal know that I'd not only curbed my snarkiness, but I'd turned myself into a regular guardian ghost.

By the time I reached the second floor, the walls reverberated with Sophie snoring in her parlor while the two latest customers still whined in the hall, trying to get more money for the trauma of being in the same room with Soph for five minutes.

Why be hasty? I could wait until Margie digs her way out of the latest *snafu du jour* before mentioning that Willbard was going to give Sophie such a shock that the old girl would be sober for a month before she realized what hit her.

The clink of Willbard's ectoplasmic dice rattled through my mind. Hot dog, I felt lucky tonight.

Racing across the city, low enough to get comfortably edgy from the stream of photons from the streetlights below, I paused over Monument Avenue to observe a moment of silence out of respect for the Confederate veterans marching past memorials to their leaders.

Three quarters of the way to the meeting-before-the-meeting at the River City Diner, my euphoria began to erode. A nagging sensation returned. Something was out of place, unexpected, even a bit sinister. I turned to the railway station a half dozen blocks from the restaurant and drifted near the top of the clock tower.

Traffic still flowed through the eastern reach of Main Street. Around the railroad station, panhandlers shuffled and travelers scurried on their way. Several blocks beyond the diner, spooks at the Poe museum shot whooping into the air like spectral Roman candles. The master must be making an appearance tonight.

My reconnaissance tightened upon the diner. Whatever was happening— or wasn't happening when it should—involved the immediate area around the restaurant. Then I saw them: more than a dozen orange dots lining the restaurant's roof, plus three or four clumps of glowing green rods.

"What do you say to dropping into the diner?" a voice behind me asked. "I hear they've got a special tonight on German chocolate cake."

"I think I'll pass," I answered.

Fast Eddie lay near the sloping roof of the clock tower, his hands clasped behind his head, his shirt, trousers and coat as scruffy as ever, watching the scene below like a truant schoolboy loitering in a tree.

"Word around the cemetery is that we won't see that cake again," he said. "Too complicated to make, too pricey. And too much chocolate for the college kids."

"Really, I'm fine. I'm cutting down on the sweets I don't eat."

Fast Eddie swept a hand over his shirt to smooth it into place, managing to create more wrinkles. "You sure? It's the chance of an afterlifetime."

I glanced back at the diner. Jack-o'-lanterns and gleaming plastic skeletons continued to gather on the roof. Facing us. Staring at me. Pulpy voices and raspy, whispering clicks floated on the night, plotting, scheming, sharing tips about the unpleasant things they can do to ectoplasm.

"What about *them*?" I asked Fast Eddie.

His eyes followed the direction of my trembling finger. "What? Something special going on at the Poe museum?"

"No, at the diner."

Fast Eddie gave me a worried smile and squinted at the restaurant with more concentration than the old boy usually mustered. His expression was puzzled. "Is that a new sign in the window? Maybe it's about their German chocolate cake."

"I'm talking about the pumpkins on the roof."

His eyes flashed over the area, then from the street where the restaurant was located to the condos and offices along the river, looking everywhere for pumpkins.

"On the roof of the diner," I added.

He squinted into the distance. "Your eyes must be better than mine. Have you ever heard of a spook needing glasses?"

"Nope." I slipped some ice into my voice. "Another thing I haven't heard about is a spook needing a brain transplant."

"What do you mean?"

"I mean—Cut it out, Eddie. The hocus-pocus with the pumpkins and skeletons. I'm on to you."

FAST EDDIE DENIED on his word of honor as a Tosser with having anything to do with the vegetables and glowing plastic gadgets that've been ambling into my afterlife lately. Of course, what else could the spook say?

But I remember the Night of the Candy Corn and the slit-eyed appraisal Fast Eddie had given the astral landscape covered with white-capped yellow candy and the way he muttered, "Why didn't I think of that?" when it seemed no one was listening.

Fast Eddie thought he was going to top the ol' master this Halloween, but the ol' master knew how to tie his ectoplasm into so many knots Fast Eddie would spend the better part of his second life undoing the ropes. At least, that's how the *old* ol' master—as distinct from the *new* ol' master—would have handled the situation.

But Cal expected me to approach the hereafter more responsibly and with less *booga-booga*. What would be more responsible than having an earnest, caring, insightful consultation with my sponsor about Fast Eddie to let him know that that festering lump of roadkill had left the path to recovery and now had first-life toys?

Talking to Cal meant swallowing my pride, but that's okay. It'd just fall out of the bottom of my stomach, anyway.

If Cal wasn't at a meeting, or at a meeting before or after a meeting, he was usually around the cobblestone streets and brick walks of Shockoe Slip, a three- or four-block stretch of streets curving down to the floodplain that was old when Robert E. Lee did his fighting with tin soldiers.

The neighborhood bookstore and a few restaurants were still open, their windows fogged, their lights bright, their decors charming, but a restlessness was in the air. Sometimes, I wonder if sadness had stained the gray brick walls that had been brushed by the shoulders of people on the long retreat to the fields of Appomattox, and I puzzle over Cal's attraction to this place.

Cal says his first life was spent in the building trades, and old-time craftsmanship appealed to him. Or perhaps he just liked things that've been around longer than he has.

He was floating on the horizontal when I found him, inches from the knobby surface of the street. I imagined a horse-drawn buggy clomping down this road in an era when a large tush was considered the perfect shock absorber.

"Ever wonder why folks were so backwards then?" I said. "Maybe it's because they were knocking themselves senseless whenever they climbed into the old buckboard."

"Is this your way of easing into a talk about your recovery?" Cal's nose was inches from cobblestones that could have been smoothed during the last ice age.

"Can we take that up later? I've got a situation I need to discuss."

"*Every afterlife begins with two choices,*" he said, quoting from one of the many annoying sayings in the approved literature. "*Either clean house immediately. Or get used to living in a haunted house.*"

"It's not haunted houses I want to talk about. It's jack-o'-lanterns and plastic skeletons."

"There sure seem to be more of them than last year."

"No, you don't understand." I was beginning to feel the lift from my gyrating hands and arms. "They're stalking me."

"I thought we had a bet. You were going to give up fairy stories and tricks until Halloween."

"I'm telling you the truth. Pumpkins and glowing skeletons are following me. And I know Fast Eddie is behind it. He's just jealous because of what I did last year with the candy corn."

"These pumpkins and skeletons, are they carrying candy corn?"

"Forget the candy corn. This is about Fast Eddie manipulating pumpkins and skeletons. Making them come after me."

Cal rolled over to study me, carefully arranging his arms over his chest, one on top of the other, as though he were doing it for the first time. "In his prime—which was a long time ago—Fast Eddie might've been able to make a jack-o'-lantern twitch once or twice. Then he'd need a couple weeks to build up his strength."

"Then who's behind it?"

Cal turned back to his cobblestones and, with enough cynicism to fill a few fifty-five gallon barrels, said, "Can we rule out your own sense of guilt?"

"Yeah. I've always felt badly that I wasn't more guilty."

"So long as you don't stumble back to your wise-cracking, prank-playing ways, it doesn't matter," he said. "Just take it one night at a time."

"Why didn't I think of that?"

I FLOATED UP into the night sky, stung less by Cal's distrust than by the fact that his advice now came from skimming the top of our recovery program's platitudes.

On the interstate highway below, a caravan of vehicles with flashing red lights slowly made its way parallel to the river. Over-sized cargo poked from the sides of a truck in the center, probably something bound for the shipyard at the mouth of the James River. My mind was working as slowly as that convoy, my thoughts trying to manage a payload as bulky as the one below.

Cal was a recovering Tosser, and he knew what he was talking about when he assessed Fast Eddie's abilities. If he said Fast Eddie couldn't manipulate the things that were bothering me, then I had to strike Fast Eddie from my list of suspects. But if not Fast Eddie, then who? I needed solid evidence pointing to the spooks or Breathers behind this caper. At the word *evidence*, the foggy outline of a plan started to take shape.

I drifted towards the glow of Shockoe Bottom, where the roof of the diner was now bare of everything except shadows, as were the other roofs in the area. Carefully, warily, paranoically, I made my way to the streets, paying special attention to parked cars, garbage cans and anything else large enough to hide a gourd or two. Only after I was convinced the coast was clear did I dart through the door of the diner.

My pal Gwendolyn was in his usual spot near the stools in front. Gwendolyn had started the afterlife's first spectral detective agency and, until he found the right office—"Something that doesn't make me think of either NASA or Queen Victoria," he says—he was using the diner.

Before I could say a word, a Breather clambered onto one of the nearby stools.

"There's always one that didn't get the memo," Gwendolyn said, shaking his head.

Gwendolyn shifted to the same seat as the Breather which meant, for practical purposes, he was sitting *inside* the latest arrival, who shivered, looked over his shoulder and muttered about the draft before moving to a table further from the door.

"Nothing personal, buddy," Gwendolyn told the back of the retreating Sunshiner. "This is business. My customers got to know where to find me."

I slid onto an adjacent stool. "Speaking of customers, exactly how does one pay for your services?"

Gwendolyn pulled a hand from his trench coat pocket, held the index finger near my nose and in a few moments I saw a golden sparkle on his fingertip. A droplet of ectoplasm.

"What's the caper?" he asked.

"I want you to follow someone."

"Give me the details."

"It's a spook. About my height and shape. Spends his time in the places I'm usually at, carries himself like me, too. Face and general physical description identical to mine."

"Let me guess his name." When Gwendolyn blinked, he reminded me of a three-hundred-year-old tortoise trying to clear its vision. "Could it be . . . Ralph?"

"I'm impressed. You really know how to put things together."

"It's a gift." Gwendolyn pulled the cigar stub from his mouth, signaling that we were getting down to business. "Why do you want me to follow you? Are you just interested in learning where you hang out, or do you suspect you've been cheating on yourself?"

"I'm being stalked. And I want you to follow me, too, and tell me who else is in the parade."

"Very clever. Can you give me a physical description of the mugs I should be looking for?"

"The prime suspect is a vegetable. Orangish, round, with a green stub coming out the top. His buddies are greenish and bony. Think of a Breather and strip away anything that won't bounce off a tile floor."

"Sounds like pumpkins and plastic skeletons."

I shook my head and tried to whistle. "You're going to wrap up this case in no time."

Gwendolyn stared out the window. I was pleasantly surprised to see my story had touched him. He was a better friend than I'd imagined. Or had he also been tormented by Halloween bric-a-brac?

"Can I ask a question?" Gwendolyn drifted off his stool toward me. "Do I look like I died yesterday?"

"Pardon?"

"You and I have been pals for a while. Does that make me an idiot?"

"I don't—"

"You want to play a few Halloween pranks, go *booga-booga* at the spooks from out of town, you can count me in. Just don't try going *booga-booga* at me. *Capisce?*"

"I'm serious about the pumpkins and skeletons," I said.

"And I'm serious right back at you. I'm a *booga-booger*, not a *booga-boogee*."

Eight

CHAPTER

The literature of Specters Anonymous is filled with stories about spooks who went to their friends in the afterlife to confess some personal failing that injured the party on the listening end of the conversation. This is part of the process we call *graphing a spreadsheet*.

As these stories go, the listeners/victims, who often didn't know some wrong had been done to them or didn't suspect the speaker/reprobate was the source of the harm, always welcomed an honest revelation with open arms.

I, too, was greeted by open arms—in this case, Gilda's—when I met her outside the church basement where we held our nightly meetings and admitted that I might have had some involvement in last year's misunderstanding about the candy corn, but that had nothing to do with this year's problem with the jack-o'-lanterns and fright-night skeletons.

Gilda's arms lifted wide to the heavens in the interdimensionally recognized signal for *when-will-this-burden-be-lifted*.

"Did I say something wrong?" I asked.

Inside the meeting room, Cal rested above a gray metal chair facing the door, his arms crossed, listening to Veronica, who lapsed into silence when she caught my eye. Regulars filled the rest of the seats in the circle and newbies collected near the wall where, with a little luck, no one would notice them.

I found a seat beside Darleen, grateful that at least one spook wasn't treating me like a sputtering fuse.

"Ain't it nice to be with friends?" I whispered.

Darleen patted my hand. "I'm sure your friends will be happy to see you, too. But since you're here already, why don't you stay for the meeting?"

My jaw dropped, my head spun, my lips and tongue quivered for a retort that my brain couldn't deliver. Darleen? Mary Poppins of the afterlife? I had been cut to the core by Darleen? Ms. Spectral Hospitality? The spook voted least likely to find a thorn if she rolled all night in a cactus patch?

I gave her a meek smile.

Someone probably led the discussion, although I couldn't tell you who it was. And I'm a little vague about the topic. For that matter, I couldn't swear whether we had the usual halftime break or if I went outside to the steps.

Blank looks were locked on every face that swung in my direction; even then, spooks couldn't seem to focus on anything above my chest. Newbies made me the one spook in the room they managed never to bump into.

Then Fred-As caught my attention. His gaze didn't flick away. He smiled, and I felt a moist line of ectoplasm welling in my eyes. He had a dorky name and hung out with a bizarre bunch of spooks, but he liked me. That counted for something. In fact, the way my night was going, that counted for everything.

Before I knew what was happening, Rosetta said, "Thanks to all for a wonderfully transcendent meeting. We'll close in the usual way."

I pulled myself to a vertical position while spooks rose around me and began lining the sides of the room.

"Über-spirit," Rosetta began.

"Über-spirit," echoed the spooks in the room in a ragged volley as they adjusted to Rosetta's rhythm.

I closed my eyes and extended my arms from my sides.

". . . help me to do the things I can do," we said together.

I opened my hands. We held hands when we talked to the Über-Spirit.

". . . to stop trying to do the things I cannot do . . ."

I wiggled my fingers.

". . . and to give me a slap upside the head to quit analyzing the previous requests."

I opened my eyes.

The spooks of the St. Sears group had formed a circle, as they do every night to recite the Transcendence Prayer, one astral hand linked with another, with even the newbies getting the hang of it.

After all, how difficult is it to hold someone's hand?

I brought both of my hands—my empty, unclenched, shunned hands—under my chin.

Apparently, it was more difficult than I realized.

I SLUMPED ABOVE a gray metal chair as the regulars of the St. Sears meeting exited through the door and newbies left through the walls, floor and ceiling. I never felt the hereafter could be so lonely. What was left now? Should I pretend that I'd found my gravesite in some cemetery and, like Jedediah, become a tomb-squatter? How bleak eternity would be without an occasional whoopee cushion.

"You look like a spook who wasn't invited to his own funeral," a calm voice said.

I glanced into a small, confident smile. Fred-As was the only spook left in the room, and he gazed at me with the relaxed acceptance that I would expect from the Über-Spirit.

"You wouldn't happen to know of a good 12-step program?" I asked. "Something that specializes in personality disorders?"

"I got something better."

"A 13-step program?"

"An analyst," Fred-As said. "What do you say to hitting that long, astral highway?"

"Let's do that before it hits me."

FRED-AS GRIPPED my arm, gave me a yank, and before I knew it, we were respecterizing outside a ramshackle building on the banks of the river. *Squid's Beak Inn*, said the sign. Even without swirling clouds of fog or windows glazed by decades of dust, you knew it was the sort of place the riffraff favored when they wanted to test their luck.

Fred-As led me through the door and past the bar. Slumping figures were spaced along the stools; some were spooks looking especially glum, seeing as how they didn't even have empty shot glasses to stare into. Fred-As slapped one on the shoulder.

"How's that *spreadsheet* coming, Ernie?" he said.

Ernie shook his head and glared at the pitted counter.

Fred-As adjusted his buttoned collar. "Sad case," he whispered to me. "Under-active imagination."

"He can't remember his first life, either?" I said.

"He remembers a lot just fine. Problem is, he can't remember being close enough to anyone in his first life to do any damage."

"Tough," I said, surprised by the chill that swept through me.

Was that the legacy from my first life that I had to face if I want to transcend to a higher-quality afterlife? As they say on my side of the Great Divide, *If the casket fits, wear it.*

But did it really? My record in the hereafter shows a real knack for making friends. I've been the life of the post-mortal party. Take Gilda: I was one of the first spooks she reached out to in the afterlife. Then it was downhill and accelerating rapidly. Okay, let's look at Hank. My best friend, the spook who shared my major escapades. At least, the ones that happened while we were still speaking.

Ah, Cal? Nope.

Rosetta? Definitely not.

Veronica? Even more definitely not.

Fred-As glided lightly around the darkened tables and their glowering customers, then slid the last couple yards on one knee as he pointed at a closed door with the aplomb of a maître d' seating a big tipper.

I eased my head through the door and confronted a strange scene. Imagine a room filled with pagans in grass skirts, spears clutched in their hands, swaying around an open fire with a cast-iron pot containing a single puzzled missionary. Then take away the spears, the grass skirts, the fire, the pot and the missionary. For good measure, remove the cannibals and replace them with an equal number of lumbering figures in black leather jackets emblazoned with *Heck's Angels*. That'll give you a feel for what it was like to peek into the back room at the Squid's Beak Inn.

"This is the spook I was telling you about," Fred-As said.

The honcho who'd be stirring the pot if this were a cannibals' luncheon turned. He was a mountainous accumulation of ectoplasm, capped by red hair, a fiery beard and beady eyes that glowed with a dark fire. He was also the driver of Fred-As's motorcycle.

Red Max, that was his name. I flashed a grin and started to say hello, but my voice wasn't working. Did he remember our first meeting, and did he blame me for the fact that Father Jenkins was practicing exorcisms that night? I couldn't shake the notion that a big kettle was just out of sight in the shadows.

With a twitch of his head toward the door, Red Max emptied the room of bikers, including Fred-As.

"You're looking for me," the big fellow said, and I wasn't sure if it was a question, a statement, a challenge or a test.

"Actually, I'm here to meet this analyst," I said. "Silly, but I don't know his name."

Red Max loomed over me like a cliff that decided it wanted to be my buddy. "And you can't find the analyst in this room."

I took a quick count of noses, then a recount, then I triple-checked. I couldn't get beyond two noses—Red Max's and mine. I looked up, imagined what innocence felt like, then tried it on for size.

"My friend says you're the best analyst in two planes of existence." I said, shifting seamlessly into foot-out-of-the-mouth mode. "A real wizard when it comes to all sorts of adjustment problems. I imagine your schedule must be pretty full. Perhaps I can make an appointment for some time in the far future."

"Lie down."

"Pardon?"

"Lie down."

I was looking for a bed or a table when Red Max clamped a pickup-sized paw on my forehead, lifted me from the floor and gave a quarter twist that left me horizontal and three feet from the ground. He settled over a chair.

"Your biggest worry?" Red Max said. His beard and hair started to crackle and glow. "Don't think about it. Just say it. Your biggest worry. Out with it. Now!"

"Things," I stuttered. "That's what's on my mind now. Things that don't like me. That are out to get me."

"What sort of things?"

"Pumpkins are the worst. But lately they've been joined by skeletons. They've been popping up in the strangest places. They're even at my home."

Red Max held up a hand. "And your littlest worry. What is it?"

"I don't understand."

Red Max leaned closer, tiny flames jumped from the ends of his whiskers and flashed along the hairs on his head. "Tell me what word you don't understand— YOUR . . . LITTLEST . . . WORRY."

By this time, Red Max's eyes had joined the firestorm whipping through his hair, and I guessed his idea of counseling didn't include stuff like compassion, understanding or rapport.

"There's this dog where I live. She's called Petey," I said. "Most definitely, she's my littlest worry."

"Why do you worry about her?"

"I don't worry about her."

If Red Max could sigh, his sigh would have shaken the Squid's Beak Inn to its foundations. "Let's try again to find that word you don't understand."

"I get it, I get it. You want to know something that worries me. But it's at the bottom of my list of worries."

He gave me a smile that I didn't like any more than his scowl.

"My littlest worry. My worry that's the littlest. That would be, without any question—and I want to be honest here. We're talking about nailing down a situation that's still in flux."

Red Max tightened his mouth, and the floor trembled below me. Did I really want to irritate a spook whose mortal remains probably needed a bus for a casket?

Bus. But, of course, that was it.

"My littlest worry is this old TV show, *The Honeymooners.* It's about this bus driver, his wife and their neighbors."

"Now, we're getting somewhere." Red Max put a hand on my shoulder and rolled me in the air until I was facing him. "Tell me about the things in this TV show. The vegetables there. The bones. That kind of thing."

The question hit me like a searchlight in the face.

"But there aren't many things in the TV show. Vegetables, bones or anything else. Mostly, it happens in a bare apartment. The bus driver and his wife don't have much. They just have each other. And a few friends."

"And if things started talking to this bus driver, what would they say?"

"To the moon, Alice. To the moon."

CHAPTER

o the moon. Three simple words—repeated by the character Ralph in the *The Honeymooners* series whenever he was angry at his wife—had layers of meaning. They had a history and a smell. Now I understood how some Sunshiners could spend their first lives staring into their navels and repeating a handful of syllables.

"Sam, looks like we're the first," a voice said behind me.

The door to the back room of the Squid's Beak Inn opened, river fog flooded in from the main room, and silhouetted in the door frame were a pair of Breathers, each with a single rhinoceros horn stuck to the top of his forehead and carrying several boxes. Once inside, they opened collapsible tables stacked in a corner.

"Our time for using this room is up," Red Max said. "Why don't you see my assistant about scheduling an appointment for next week?"

Part of me knew the prudent thing was to leave while the big guy was distracted. But if my friends got word of me doing anything prudently, it'd never die down.

"But what does it mean?" I asked as Red Max ushered me to the door. "Is there supposed to be some connection between my littlest worry and my biggest one?"

He patted my shoulder and what in the afterlife replaced my collar bone threatened to collapse into places where Breathers keep ribs and intestines. "You're getting close. You can see the outline of the answer from here."

"And the question is—"

Everything in Red Max's face tightened. "Haven't you been paying attention? Didn't you learn anything?"

"Just a little spectral humor," I said. "Trying to see if I could catch you off guard."

"Do you think that would be funny?"

I looked at the flaming red eyes and the blazing red hair and was sure I smelled the contents of a very large kettle coming to a boil.

"I don't want to get a new biggest worry," I replied.

"You're catching on."

WITH MY BUDDIES in the hereafter convinced I was pulling a prank about the pumpkins and skeletons, and the twofers I know too involved in their own problems to be useful, only one spook came to mind who might help me untangle the knot of emotions I carried from the Squid's Beak Inn.

His name was Jack of Diamonds. He had settled on a chimney in Richmond after realizing he didn't have a good reason for going anyplace else, and ever since he could be found on the city's roofs, watching the worlds go by. He never met much in the afterlife that was worth losing sleep over, which was precisely the attitude I needed to get a grip on Red Max's cryptic insight.

Lately, Jack had taken up residence on the tops of the tallest buildings downtown. As I circled the business district looking for him, I asked myself why I kept digging my own grave deeper.

To the moon, Alice. It was a cliché from the 1950s TV sitcom that popped from my mouth when I tried to connect the old TV show to my current problems with jack-o'-lanterns and such. And Red Max reacted as though my ego, superego and id had crawled out from under my fears to strut down Broad Street in a Fourth of July parade doing the macarena.

"To the moon," I whispered to myself and, glancing into the starless sky, where the earth's lunar sidekick glowed like a gigantic bug light, saw exactly where my next step should take me. Actually, it was closer to a leap, although, operating in *Beam-Me-Up-Scotty* mode, it was even more like slipping into a shower and being able to dodge those little jets of water.

In mini-nanoseconds, the earth was a blue marble behind me, and dust and gray rocks stretched in every direction to a bleak, lunar horizon.

Take it from me, once you've been to the moon, you'll understand why no visitor ever bothered with a second trip. What with sunlight blasting much of its surface, the moon is especially unwelcome to members of the astral community. Nice dust, but being spectral, I can't kick it into little clouds. The odd rock might be fun to toss into low-earth orbit, but I'm not much at levitation and, besides, if Cal caught me skipping stones through the atmosphere, he'd call it a stumblie and send me back to the first step of Specters Anonymous.

Rosetta once said life used to exist there. Unique life, not like cats or jellyfish or people. Saying they were *thinking creatures* was using our labels for a completely different sort of being. The moon's inhabitants came and went long ago, Rosetta said, and what remains of them—calling them *spirits* is too terrestrial-centric to be even roughly accurate—were probably in their own post-sentient recovery period.

To which I say, there's hope for Rosetta if the most strait-laced resident of the afterlife can enjoy spreading such flimflam.

In this part of the lunar landscape, sunlight was close to the dark side of the moon, creating a wide band of perpetual twilight. Here the photons weren't intense enough to blast my spectral being to the outer rim of the galaxy, but at the same time, the shadows weren't so thick that I might as well be sitting in a basement in Richmond. I drifted across a plain of dust where mini-meteors had punched holes in the powdery surface no wider than the tip of a paper clip, reminding me of the breathing holes that clams leave on the beach.

Where on this Roth-forsaken country was a pumpkin when I needed a few questions answered?

I slipped behind a rock wall that shielded me from reflected sunlight, my thoughts darkening, too, as I sensed with a certainty that comes when life has thrown its last surprise that someone was watching me. Subtly, I scoured the barren vista, the small cliff that plunged me into darkness, the waveless ocean of gray dust.

"Come out, come out, wherever you are," I said.

Of course, this being the airless regions of the moon and me being an entity without a working respiratory system, my words didn't have any effect; I can't even claim they made me feel better.

Rounding a boulder that resembled the stern of a boat that had plowed bow-first into the dust, I almost stepped on an oddly shaped rock. Funny thing, instincts. Even if I stepped on it, it's not as though anything would happen. My foot would simply pass through it. But years of pre-posthumous training taught me to be wary of uneven surfaces, so my foot jerked away from the rock at the same instant the rock flinched away from my foot.

Faster than I could say, *S'cuse me, little fellow*, the rock shot up the side of a boulder and settled on a narrow ledge, level with my eyes.

Maybe the physics of the moon allow a rock to fly off the surface under certain conditions. But when I tried to analyze those conditions, I couldn't concentrate because the rock in question was making me nervous. I hitched up my astral pants, crossed some fingers behind my back, and drifted over for a better look.

On closer inspection, I can't explain why I mistook it for a rock, for it wasn't a member of the physical world, yet if it were a resident of the spectral plane, it came from no hereafter that I've visited.

What it looked like, I can't say with certainty because its appearance kept changing. Try mixing fog with a few handfuls of mud, then throw in a Siamese cat, the plaster gnome from the neighbor's garden and a newly hatched nest of tarantula spiders, and top it off with some photos taken in a fun house mirror of your ugliest cousin, and give the visual mash a spin every two seconds in a blender.

That'll give you a rough idea of what was squatting on the lunar ledge, looking at me.

As I ransacked my memory for anything else Rosetta had said about the moon's spectral inhabitants, my companion got comfortable on the ledge. In fact, for a moment I saw a gnome cross his tiny legs and settle against the rock, although that might have been a wisp of fog waving in the airless climate or a dozen spiders lunging at each other.

"Glips," I said. That was Rosetta's name for the clan of lunar spooks.

At the word, the changeable form of my new friend solidified for the briefest instant into a wizened, bearded, bemused face. I smiled back. And despite the difficulties of communicating across species and dimensions and celestial residences, despite the replacement of that gnome's face seconds later by features that were part pig and part fungus, a bond had been forged.

I can't say how long I hovered near that ledge. The Glip started talking, and though I couldn't hear a word and only had glimpses of its shape that made any sense, I was certain the little spook was pouring out its heart.

I was happy—honored even—to listen. Call it an obligation to stay in the narrow lunar valley for as long as the Glip wanted me there, if only on the chance something would happen that allowed me to understand what he was saying.

To the moon, Alice, I had told Red Max. That was the key that supposedly connected my big problems to my little ones.

Well, I was on the moon. Listening to a critter I couldn't hear. Studying an entity that changed every few seconds like a frantic kaleidoscope. And if that wasn't enough symbolistic mush to make a spook seriously consider the costs of getting repotted, I was here on the advice of a specter who thought that death wasn't a good reason to leave his Harley at home.

The Glip's unheard voice lowered—I could tell this by the slowing twitch of its many tarantula legs—and when the legs began to quiver and jerk, I suspected the Glip had gotten to a more outrageous part of his story, so I slapped my knee and laughed loud enough to be heard on Mars.

When the Glip's rotating features stopped, a prickly feeling warmed my ectoplasmic neck, and I knew I was being watched. I spun around. A pair of eyes lined with fiery veins glowered inches away, the sort of eyes that send homicidal maniacs scurrying for places to hide.

When I looked at the Glip for advice on handling the situation, the Glip wasn't there anymore.

"Perhaps I should have knocked," said a familiar voice.

A rolled wad of tobacco leaves quivered quizzically in the lunar twilight. Behind the stogie was a fedora, a trench coat and a pile of ectoplasm that went by the name of Gwendolyn.

"What are you doing here?" I said.

"Someone asked me to follow you."

"Was it anyone I know?"

"Only superficially," Gwendolyn replied.

CHAPTER *Ten*

Scooting into the long shadow the earth casts through space, Gwendolyn and I left the moon, then, protected by that tube of darkness, took a leisurely cruise back to *terra infirma*.

"Why were you really following me?" I asked Gwendolyn.

The first twitch of his lips, the one that sent his stogie from one side of his mouth to the other, told me everything I needed to know.

"Let me rephrase that," I added. "Who—besides me—told you to follow me?"

"You think someone else is interested in you?" he said with mock perplexity.

I've learned that deception wasn't a player in Gwendolyn's first life, and he hadn't gotten better at it in his second one. He still put his trust in skulking and breaking things.

I squinted at him. Really hard. He weakened.

"Just f'instance," he said, "say that I heard someone and his sponsor talking. And the sponsor was chewing out this spook for making things move around. Stuff on the physical plane."

Easing up on my squint, I said, "Just so I can follow you, let's say the stuff was Halloweeny things. Jack-o'-lanterns and skeletons and stuff."

"Yeah, whatever. And so Fast . . . er . . . Teddy . . . Fast Teddy gets an A-one reminder from his sponsor that the sponsor was about to levitate Fast . . . er . . . Teddy's sorry astrals back to the first step unless he'd cease and desist from having material playthings."

The need for a deep sigh filled my chest, but the feeling didn't know what to do with itself and went away. "So, I'm not hallucinating."

Gwendolyn had a cool, steady gaze. "Don't look at me. I see dead people. Around the clock, around the calendar and around every corner I come to. I wouldn't know a hallucination if I tripped over one."

"Thanks, pal."

THE DARK SIDE of the earth spread before us like a gigantic medical X-ray, getting larger and larger, as Gwendolyn and I rushed home. In the smallest dot of light on the earth, how many pumpkins, skeletons, fright masks and plastic tombstones could there be? Thousands? Tens of thousands? Millions? And not a single one of them was going to jump out of the shadows at me.

Unfortunately, not a single spook would pat me on the back and welcome me home, either.

Reversing direction, I shot back to the moon with a quick wave to Gwendolyn, who continued in an earthward course. I'll probably never know exactly what the Glip said, but we had made a connection. Glip let me feel that I was needed. That and more. Glip had worked a strange effect on me. Dare I call it magic?

Back to the narrow valley in the moon's twilight realm I went. There, between its searing sunlit half and terrain draped in unending blackness, I positioned myself in front of the small ledge in the rock where I'd met Glip. If the long-departed lunar resident had come here once, perhaps he would come again.

Time passed. The starless sky probably kept slowly spinning. When I grew bored with drifting with my nose inches from a dusty rock wall, I slipped onto the ledge myself.

I couldn't tear my eyes from the spot where the Glip had been. A specialness permeated that gnarled rocky surface. Something momentous, historical, beyond even my own list of adjectives had taken place here. An entity who may have spent hundreds of millions of years alone had walked out a door. As it were. And who would know if the eyes of man or spook would ever alight on its kind again?

And, more miraculously, it trusted me. Me. Even though I'm not privy to my own secrets.

I tried to imagine how Glip must have felt to find another astral creature and finally to unburden itself after thousands of millennia without a companion, and how I must have looked to it, floating above moon dust and rocks excavated by imploding meteors.

I hope Glip found some peace. Just being in this bleak gray region, where the landscape was either a tumult of rocks and hills or flat dusty plains stretching to the horizon, brought me a sense of comfort. I felt my spectral body begin to turn into liquid ectoplasm. Fortunately, there was a small cupped area on the ledge and the moon generated enough gravity to hold a liquefied spook in place.

Secure in the knowledge that the nearest jack-o'-lantern was a quarter million miles away, I let myself go.

ON THE PLUS side of eternity is the fact that spooks rarely dream and having memories of those dreams is about as frequent as having molars pulled in our first lives. And every bit as unpleasant.

So, you'll understand my consternation when I was yanked from my ectoplasmic rest by a premonition I couldn't name. Something that was powerful enough to send the spirits of any molars still stowed away in my mouth vibrating out of their sockets.

Respecterizing, I looked for the telltale marks of a pumpkin dragged through the lunar dust. Nothing. But that didn't fool me. I searched for claw marks from a bony plastic hand on a worn rock.

"Where are you?" I muttered.

The gray terrain responded with a landscape's version of a cold stare. It didn't move. But it was a more hostile version of motionlessness than the absence of movement that you'd normally expect from a clump of rocks.

Something was going on here. I could feel it.

Enough dust to cover the bottom of a teaspoon drifted from the side of my protective rock. I reminded myself that a lot of science has been done on the moon, and no one has detected the presence of a pumpkin patch. I was safe on a place that was so lifeless it didn't have a respectable cemetery.

A darker shadow passed through the shadows lying on my narrow valley. I looked up. And I remembered, too late, that things had been coming here for decades to die.

In this case, a squat metal spider, the size of a two-car garage, shuffled toward me on spindly legs. Its head was a gleaming sphere punctured in more than a dozen places by slender rods, reminding me—oddly—of a metallic soccer ball that'd been kicked onto an archery range. Or something that man had, as it were, kicked to the moon.

Once I realized the head was a Sputnik satellite, it wasn't difficult to identify the stocky body and awkward legs as parts of a U.S. lunar lander.

"Cool," I said.

The lander answered with a beep and a glimmer of lights and a sweep of a claw-like arm toward my head.

NASA has had many remarkable achievements, most having to do with putting people on top of large silos stuffed with high explosives, lighting a fuse and making sure everyone on the top of those silos was in the mood for milk and cookies afterwards. But I don't think the space agency is in the business of developing materials that can punch across the Great Divide.

However, I have underestimated my fellow spooks' technical prowess before.

I did a *Beam-Me-Up-Scotty*, and before the fastest motherboard could get a byte-sized handle on the situation, I was back in the dining room of the house on Libby Hill that I called home.

THE LIGHTS WERE dim, the family had gathered around the television set in the living room. James William, the nine-year-old who was second-in-charge of the house, squatted next to the coffee table and maneuvered rubber soldiers around the wooden legs. His mother slouched on the sofa to watch television for a few seconds, then spent a longer stretch watching her son. Father sat in his recliner.

When James William's father laughed, I dashed into the corner of the dining room with the best view of the TV set. Father was the Breather most attuned to the vintage humor of *The Honeymooners*: if he finds something on the tube funny, I pay attention.

No luck tonight. Another waste of time with some program about people who wore surgical scrubs and military uniforms. At least, I was safe from any assault by a lunar lander.

Clickety, clickety, clickety. I prepared to hurl myself into the nearest coffeepot on the wall. Cal may have told Fast Eddie to get out of the levitation business, but had Fast Eddie really accepted the plan? And did Cal have the foresight to include lunar landers on the list of prohibited toys.

I crouched in full Beam-Me-Up-Scotty mode. The *clickety-clickety* clicked louder, and around the corner from the kitchen came the master of the house, a bundle of brown, white and black fur, punctuated with a wet nose, lashing tongue and eyes the color of hot chocolate.

"Petey!" I said.

The beagle braked to keep from skidding across the hardwood floor into me. Not a pleasant experience for either of us. Soon Petey was rolling on her back as I rotated my hands inches from her fur in an astral massage that, to judge from the dog's reaction, was better than the real thing.

Next to Petey's thumping tail was the toe of a black boot, tapping with the impatience of a mortician on Saturday night.

"What?" I asked the boot.

"We're going to be late for the meeting," Gilda answered.

As a Gothic member of the afterlife, Gilda was usually too detached to take notice of me or anyone else. The rhythmic speed of that toe suggested that she had set aside her detachment for the moment, and I could guess why.

"Sorry I wasn't here yesterday, but I gotta tell you how I spent my day," I gushed. "I was on the moon. A Glip talked to me for hours. I have no idea what he said. But I don't have to worry about pumpkins and jack-o'-lanterns any more. That's because Gwendolyn—he was on the moon, too, and dropped by for a chat—Gwendolyn said it's all Fast Eddie's fault and Cal has brought Eddie into line. Although I'd appreciate a heads-up if you see any lunar landers hanging around."

The black leather toe hesitated as Gilda worked out the least pleasant direction to take the conversation.

"A Glip, huh? I can see why you didn't come home yesterday. You were having too much fun with your imaginary friends."

"But it was real, at least in a spectral sense. It wasn't imaginary."

Gilda looked puzzled. "I thought you said it was a friend."

"'Natch."

"Like I said, imaginary."

CHAPTER

inding a spectral entity on the moon and being pursued by a four-legged spacecraft didn't turn out to be my biggest adventures of the week. The chart topper sat inside the room in the church basement where the St. Sears group of Specters Anonymous held its nightly meetings. First, though, I had to get through the door.

The usual collection of regulars and newbies had gathered on the lawn and outside stairs. Gilda drifted off to talk to Rosetta, her sponsor. Fast Eddie glanced in my direction and started to sink through the lawn.

"If you leave now," I said, "I'm going to send the Great Pumpkin to bring you back."

"The Great Pumpkin? That doesn't exist." Fast Eddie's confidence crumbled around the edges. "Does it?"

Slowly, Fast Eddie rose high enough from the ground to bring his mouth out of the grass. He may have wanted to say something, but the way his lips were flapping, he couldn't settle on a topic.

Cal drifted over. Great, just what we needed: a referee.

"What do you want to say to Ralph?" Cal asked Fast Eddie.

Fast Eddie mumbled.

"What?" Cal said.

If Fast Eddie hadn't had me stalked, I might have felt sorry for him.

"I apologize for the pumpkins," he said. "And the skeletons."

"What about the lunar lander?" I asked.

He cast a wary glance at Cal. "Whatever."

Cal, who didn't do smiles, gave him a supportive flicker of his lips. "Don't you feel better now?"

"I probably feel better than the pumpkins," Fast Eddie said. "I'm going to go stick my head in a tectonic plate."

"Enjoy yourself," I said.

He sank from view, but that wriggly motion spread across Cal's mouth.

"I wasn't being snarky," I hastened to add. "I most sincerely hope he finds a home in some magma pool."

"Just keep a positive attitude."

DRIFTING INTO THE meeting room, I wanted to embrace my fellow specters and give them the joyous news. Not just about Fast Eddie apologizing for his pathetic pranks. But because the afterlife had grown. Vertically. I had been to the moon and met one of its resident spooks and he/she/it had a wonderful talk with me.

Granted, the Glip didn't shut up long enough for me to get a word in. Further granted that I hadn't the slightest idea what it said. But Specters Anonymous is, as Cal is quick to point out, an *us* program, and where's the *us* in comprehension or dialogue?

As I said, my adventures on the lunar landscape were not the most amazing part of the night. The entity with that distinction floated above a gray metal chair with one black trouser leg elegantly draped over the other, the cuffs of his ruffled shirt poking from the sleeves of his black coat and a silver-headed cane lying across his lap like a dead cat. Yes, gracing our meeting tonight was every Richmonder's ideal of post-mortal Southern gentility, Edgar Allan Poe.

Like a reigning monarch, Edgar A- nodded to the spooks as they glided into the room. Veronica passed her usual place in the inner circle of chairs to take a seat near the late great poet.

Jingle Jim, our group's official rhymester, who considers the author of *The Raven* to be a mere dabbler in verse, took the chair furthest from Edgar A-. In fact, he tried sitting inside the wall, but for reasons I'm not interested in investigating, decided to float back into the room.

I caught Poe's eye and acknowledged him with a dip of my chin, the sort of salute traded by international powers at the start of negotiations. Edgar A- leaned over to ask Veronica if she'd come to this meeting for her entire afterlife and she said, "Not yet."

Fred-As and a few stragglers scurried through the door while Rosetta called the meeting to order.

"Is anyone within their first thirty years of transcendence? Anyone who's never been to this meeting before?" She looked pointedly at Poe, and *pointedly* is the precise word for anything as razor-edged as Rosetta's glance.

Edgar A- leaned toward Veronica and stage-whispered, "I remember when this used to be a four-step program and your *Teeny Book* was called *The Long Paragraph*."

If that zinger had come from anyone else, Rosetta would have found something to quibble with, but she was too much of a librarian to take on a spook who had his own digits in the Dewey decimal system.

"I have asked a spiritual being whom——" she began.

Poe lifted an eyebrow.

Rosetta swallowed. "——who——"

Poe lifted the other eyebrow.

Rosetta patted her no-nonsense tweed skirt and said, "——a spiritual being I met at another meeting to join us tonight. I am pleased to introduce Bethany."

"Hello, my best of all possible friends." Bethany flashed a thousand-candlepower smile. "I can't thank you enough for coming out on this dark and dreary night to support me."

Everyone in the meeting had the same confused smile that I sensed was frozen on my own face. I'd never laid eyes on this spook before, and I'm sure I would have remembered. Not many specters arrive in the afterlife with their own hairstylist and fashion consultant.

With one hand clenching Rosetta's wrist and the other combing through her ectoplasmic locks, Bethany launched into a recital of the *dreadful* accommodations in the hereafter, the *appalling* shortage of written instructions for being dead, the *shocking* level of *unsophistication* among the spooks who dared to rub elbows with her and the *unconscionable* waste of time in meetings that failed to provide anything of importance to her, which I took to mean any meeting that wasn't about her.

Most spooks of a formerly testosterone-carrying variety watched Bethany with confused grins. Edgar Allan Poe tilted again toward Veronica and whispered, "Poor creature."

"And not a single cast member is here to support her drama," Veronica replied.

"One does what one can," the poet said.

Normally, I'd expect Veronica to be checking out Poe for his casket size or sparring with Bethany, but the afterlife's mistress of indignation was giving a master class in *restraint of fist and spit* this evening.

Sometime during Bethany's recital of helpful suggestions for spiffing up the decor of our meeting room, I noticed a radio on a table next to the wall. A faint light flickered from its dial, and by squinting and holding my head at a certain angle, I saw the light move and split, flaring up and joining together, rippling in a way that looked suspiciously like Cal's lips when he was planning to say something.

"What's wrong?" Hank asked.

"I think the radio is trying to talk to me."

"Yeah, they'll do that if you drop your guard."

Bethany was on the verge of gushing through the customary halftime break when Edgar A- started *tsking* and shaking his head, his face draped in mournful shadows.

Bethany must've been thrown off balance by Poe's deathly pallor and his disapproving *tsk* or maybe she needed a moment to find another word that conveyed how far we had dropped below her standards. Regardless, a wisp of silence snaked across the room, and Edgar A- pounced on it so quickly you'd think he'd found another rhyme for *Nevermore*.

"Nature, in her infinite wisdom, has placed the tender roses and the harsh gales of winter in different seasons," he said. "For true beauty does not deign to spend her preciousness in the company of the bitter, the dissolute, the unappreciative."

Bethany swatted the air. "Oh, go on. I couldn't have said that any better myself."

Poe gave the hem of his vest a confident tug that differed from a working man rolling up his sleeves only in the direction the cloth went.

Veronica's jaw was rigid, her back stiff, and I nearly heard her ectoplasm bubble under the pressure to contain itself.

The radio on the table winked at me.

"A true gentleman." Bethany gazed adoringly at Poe.

Newbies in the back of the room who operated bobby pins in their first lives leaned toward the poet, all wearing the same dazzled smile. If this hadn't been the afterlife, I might have warned Mrs. Poe about poachers.

"I have committed myself," Edgar A- continued, taking a grip of his lapel, "to spend the remainder of my time beyond the vale of mortal tears caring for the fairest flowers among us. I am availing my hard-won wisdom, my battered but unbowed experience, my struggling yet sincere encounters with language, to help the fairer sex in their toils against the vicissitudes of unfeeling post-mortality."

"Isn't that sweet?" Darleen said. "What does it mean?"

Mrs. Hannity and the newbies of a female persuasion in the back of the room tried to sigh.

If my smart-alecky ways weren't behind me, I'd've whipped the assembled spooks into a righteous ectoplasmic froth. Fortunately for the entertainment value of the meeting, we still had Veronica.

"*Vicissitudes?*" Veronica growled, to encouraging nods from Gilda and Rosetta.

"Yes, one *c* and three *s*'s in the plural form. You'll find it in all the better dictionaries," the poet answered.

"*Fairer sex?*" Veronica added.

Poe gave her a frank appraisal. "I'm sure someone can explain that to you after the meeting."

Veronica's eyes spun in their sockets.

Bethany, looking neglected, said, "*Très galant,*" with a French twirl.

"At your service." Poe bowed. "Bringing the utmost discretion and delicacy to the punctual resolution of any quandary."

"Have no care, Poe is there," Jingle Jim chimed. "Or should it be: Please beware, Poe is there?"

Edgar A- shot him a look that'd freeze the nose off a polar bear. Meanwhile, a torrent of invective—that's two *e*'s, one *c* and a sting measured in megatons—rushed quickly up Veronica's throat and spewed from her lips as:

"Ggggrrrraaaaawwwwwiiiii!"

"Right," agreed our unflappable chairspook. "Let's have halftime."

BETHANY RUSHED TO Poe, since that was where the attention was, trailed by Gwendolyn, who'd obviously never seen a prima donna before, his cigar stub lolling around his mouth.

Rosetta, Gilda and Veronica hurried to the exit, arms linked, heads nearly touching, jaws slack from the exertion of preventing them from dropping open during the last half hour.

"I'm sorry, I do apologize," Rosetta was telling them. "I had no idea egos got that big in the afterlife."

"You talking about Poe or Bethany?" Gilda whispered.

Rosetta and Veronica shared a look. Then they shared it with Gilda. Then, in chorus, all said, "Both," and broke into giggles.

The lights on the radio's face swung to the right. If those lights had been eyes, they would have been following the three gossiping spooks out the door before swinging back to the left, where they'd be watching me.

I told myself to snap out of it. This was silly. It's a radio, after all, not a pumpkin.

After a decent interval, I followed the parade out of the room, with Fred-As in hot pursuit. He did a subtle maneuver—part waltz step, part tap-dance routine—that took him to the top of the outside stairs to cut me off, then glided elegantly back down again.

"Pardon me for bringing up business at a time like this," he said, "but Red Max wants to schedule another appointment for you."

I looked at him and hesitated as a skittery wind sent dried leaves scuttling across the sidewalk. In the next block, three or four jack-o'-lanterns burned from porches and walkways, and a luminescent, glowing green skeleton swung from the limbs of a magnolia. Many houses had seasonal wreaths of pine branches, orange ribbons and pinecones on their doors.

Fred-As was motionless above the lawn. "Wasn't your first session with Red Max helpful?"

"It was the biggest and best thing that's happened since they played *Rock of Ages* just for me."

"So—"

Cal and Hank slipped between us on their way back into the room for the second half of the meeting. Cal gave me a certain look—sure of himself, confident of my loyalty, unsuspecting as a spook newly arrived on the path toward transcendence that I might get more helpful recovery advice from someone else.

"Let me check my calendar," I told Fred-As.

CHAPTER

drifted back into the basement room with everyone else as the break ended, and although I stayed for the rest of the meeting, Bethany was not as offensive, nor Veronica as indignant, nor Gwendolyn as infatuated, nor Poe as smug, nor Gilda as Gothic, nor Cal as oblivious as they all had been before.

I'd been to the moon—*To the moon, Alice*—and the problems that filled my afterlife seemed so . . . so . . . earthbound.

If it hadn't been for the radio, I might even say things were going smoothly. But the radio kept the room's anxiety level in the red zone. It didn't miss a thing: it sat on the table by the wall, pretending to be just a bunch of switches and wires carrying an electrical current.

At least, that's what it would have been pretending to do if it weren't actually doing that. And, with Fast Eddie hanging up his levitation skills, why would it need to pretend it was merely a household appliance? It could actually be one.

The second half of the meeting passed in a gray blur and the group had barely finished the last syllables of our communication with the Über-Spirit— "and a smack upside the head to quit analyzing the previous requests"—when I was heading out the door again.

"How about a meeting-after-the-meeting?" Hank called across the room.

I glanced over my shoulder at the radio. Had it moved a couple inches to the left where the view was better?

Hank tried to figure out what I was looking at. "You still worried about things coming after you?"

"Yeah, I picked up a bad case of PPSD."

"?"

"Post-Pumpkin Stress Disorder."

"Then I've got just the cure, most noble spook," said Hank. "A little fresh air. A change of scenery. And a double helping of manly companionship."

He gripped my shoulder, and before the small hand on an atomic clock could start its next twitch, we were on the edge of downtown where a line of austere buildings that once served as tobacco warehouses shielded the city from the James River. With Hank in the lead, we worked our way to the water at a Breather's pace, weaving around condominiums, renovated offices, night spots and exercise spas.

Taking the greatest care not to offend Hank with an ill-timed reminder that a good friend might have warned me that Fast Eddie had unleashed every jack-o'-lantern and cheap glow-in-the-dark skeleton in central Virginia in my direction, I inquired:

"How long did you know about Fast Eddie's prank with the pumpkins?" And to put Hank at ease, added: "That little scamp. Ha, ha, ha."

"I found out a few minutes before you did. Right before the meeting."

"Ha, ha, ha," I added, defusingly.

"Ha," he summarized.

I stared at his retreating back, not certain whether to be hurt, relieved or puzzled. One of the problems of getting in touch with what Specters Anonymous calls *our inner adult* is that it really puts a crimp on our tantrums.

Soon we had worked our way to the banks of the James. Silver glints of moonlight ricocheted from the waves; the river was a lively, narrow stretch of rough water near the city. The longer I stared at it, the more I struggled to keep from thinking this churning, foamy, rock-strewn patch of river was a metaphor for my afterlife.

"Manly companionship, huh?" I said.

"Arriving momentarily," Hank replied.

I spread my hands, tilted back my head and shouted, "If someone's got a more direct way of communicating with me, I'm ready to listen."

A quarter ton of forged metal plummeted through the darkness and plowed into the ground between Hank and me. The earth trembled, even though I wasn't, literally, standing on it. A thick rope tied to the buried metal hunk—a ship's anchor, as I could see—looped around my neck and tried to pop off my head like a pinched zit.

"Apologies, lad," said a voice overhead.

I traced the thick, tarry rope a few hundred feet through the mist to a two-masted sailing vessel that rocked gently in the sky.

Above me, the captain blustered and bellowed as he directed the crew to unloop the rope from my neck, a task accomplished by a crewman who switched his eye patch from one socket to the other to get a better angle on the job before freeing me with a single flick of his arm and a long undulating wave that coursed through the rope.

Hank and I drifted up to the ship.

(Technical note: Neither the anchor, the rope, nor the ship were physical presences, nor were they quite on the spectral plane. Like the motorcycles of Heck's Angels, their existence was closer to the virtual than the material. Closer, but not quite crossing the finish line. Even for a specter, though, a 500-pound, nearly non-physical anchor dropping a couple hundred feet can put a dent in more than our love of sailing.)

Twenty feet from the ship's railing it looked as though the crew were busy swabbing decks that weren't there with invisible mops. I slipped onboard, and the full details of the spectral vessel snapped into view. I saw the weathered hull and the sails flapping listlessly overhead and mops worn to the size of Q-tips by centuries of scrubbing.

Perhaps a spook more advanced in his recovery would have sensed an omen in the eroded mop heads, but I haven't advanced much in any direction since I was lowered into the ground.

I leaned on the rail as the moon glowed overhead like a benevolent deity and let myself believe I felt the wind tousling my hair. Richmond lay below like a field sown with lights: yellow, white, with the occasional blinking red and the rarer blue, all rendered harmless to an ectoplasmic entity by distance. Who could say what adventures lay ahead in the shrinking glaciers of Greenland, the lava flowing into the ocean from Hawaiian volcanoes or the rush-hour traffic of New York City?

Maybe this was what Hank had in mind. For a new perspective, how about going someplace new? I have my entire afterlife ahead of me. Why spend it in Richmond? How much more rewarding to wander through ancient ruins and modern capitals, empty deserts and howling jungles, the gray-green expanse of oceans that take weeks to cross and the lonely towns nestled in corn fields that can trap souls for a lifetime.

"You think you've signed on to a tourist boat, have you?" The captain was inches from my shoulder. "Shake a leg, laddies, and get up to the cockatiel's nest."

Hank stiffened. The captain pointed to the top of the tallest mast, where a small platform wove from side to side with the jerky rhythms of a broken metronome.

"You mean the crow's nest," I said.

"The cockatiel's nest is what I said. And the cockatiel's nest is what I meant."

I peered through the sails, booms and cordage. Sure enough, peering from the tippy-top of the tallest mast was a figure sporting the latest in beaks and the classic look in crested feathers. Mike the Cockatiel gave a courtly nod. He leaned to the left to offset a sudden lurch in the ship, then, as the vessel righted itself, glided down on his wide, gray wings to the captain's shoulder.

"Avast there, matey," the captain said to the bird.

"SWWWWWWAAAAAAKKKK!" replied Mike.

The captain and the cockatiel studied me with their heads held at matching 45-degree angles, both incredulous that my feet were still in the vicinity of the deck after the captain had ordered me into the rigging.

Mike the Cockatiel was the only former member of the animal kingdom I've met in the spirit world. He never gives up. He stops at every pet cemetery, veterinary hospital and splotch of roadkill to see if an animal-sized spook was nearby that he could set on the path to transcendence.

"Are you with us or not, laddies?" the captain asked.

Hank gave me a shrug. "Do what you want. I'm going to check the cockatiel's nest." He grabbed a rope and began hauling himself upward.

I studied Mike. Cal always told me that the helping hand of the Über-Spirit can be attached to any arm. He didn't mention whether the arm might have feathers.

"Can we do this later?" I asked the captain. "I just remembered a sick friend I promised to visit."

The captain nodded. "Aye, a shipmate in foul weather is worth some time ashore." But Mike the Cockatiel looked away, clearly disappointed with me.

I flipped a salute and dropped through the deck. Somehow, it didn't seem like much of an improvement to go from a place where a hulking, snarling, glowering motorcyclist was a source of wisdom to an afterlife alongside a spectral cockatiel searching for the avian version of Specters Anonymous.

I cleared the keel by the time the captain regained his voice. The force of his salty "AAAARRRRRR" propelled me into the tree-lined streets of Carytown.

FIRST STOP WAS the local psychic parlor. Slipping through the beads that hung over the door to Sophie's room, I was immediately assaulted by brandy vapors. Sophie lay with her head on the table; little puddles of drool stained the lace cloth. Two dead flies lay feet-up by her crystal ball, testimony to the intensity of the alcohol fumes.

Faster than a drunkard's snore, I left Soph's inert body and reappeared two floors up, next to the spot under a window where years of water seepage had turned a section of wallpaper back into wood pulp.

"Willbard, you come out here and explain yourself. Willbard! You were going to frighten Sophie until she stopped drinking."

I almost glided through a box on the floor, a squarish container that came to my knees, with a red ribbon on the top, tied neatly into a bow, and a tag attached to one end of the ribbon. I looked at the tag:

Do not pull this ribbon, it said.

I bent over to read the other side. *I really mean it*, it continued. *You'll be sorry if you do.*

"They certainly don't know how to scare me," I muttered.

I pulled the ribbon, which, being ectoplasmic, actually came undone, only dimly recognizing that anyone who knew me or any other member of Specters Anonymous would know precisely how to make me pull the ribbon.

The tag fluttered down, the ribbon slipped loose, the top of the box fell to the floor. And a head popped up from the box.

Smooth and white as a cue ball, with lips the color of a punctured artery, it bobbed, it weaved, it thrummed and shuddered on a neck no bigger than a gnawed-on pencil. And the eyes. If the head was a cue ball, then the eyes were a pair of black marbles. And they didn't look thrilled about leaving their box.

"WWWWWIIIIIIILLLLLLLBBBBAAAAAAAAARRRRRRRDDDDDDD!"   the clown screamed.

Tension flew from my shoulders and neck like the last exhalation of a spook in the making. An idiot's got to do what an idiot's got to do, and a ride in a hearse doesn't help anyone to keep his feet on the ground.

"Hello, Willbard," I said.

The maniacal grin on Willbard's sheer white face snapped shut. The eyes that glistened like polished black balls lost their luster.

"Oh," the jack-in-a-box said. "You recognized Willbard." The balloon-sized head swayed on the pencil-thin neck. "How did you do that?"

"Your ears."

Willbard patted the sides of her head with hands that could have belonged to the Pillsbury Doughboy.

"I never had ears," she said.

"There you go."

CHAPTER Thirteen

knew I was going to regret it, but looking at Willbard, who once devoured other spooks like breath mints and who now looked like the afterlife's biggest jack-in-a-box, I had to say: "You were going to scare Sophie away from the bottle. How come you're not a horrible fog? Or a big, ravenous snake?"

"Willbard was really spooky for Miss Sophie."

"And your idea of spooky is—"

"BOOOOO!" Willbard's bulbous eyes popped out farther and her jack-in-the-box head bobbed on its wispy neck. "Heh, heh, heh. Miss Sophie not recognize Willbard like this. She scream and scream. Great fun."

Suppressing the inclination to ask whether Sophie screamed before or after she passed out, I tried to sort out the nuances from the nonsense. "Exactly what did her screams sound like?"

Willbard made a reasonable replica of a hiccup. "See? Miss Sophie has scary scream." Willbard was as serious as a hiccupping clown's head gets when it's six or eight feet in diameter and balanced on a neck a millimeter or two in width.

"Willbard wants Miss Sophie to do it again."

"Why don't you try another disguise?" I struggled to find an idea with a high rating on the creep-o-meter but couldn't get beyond pumpkins and lunar landers. "See if you can come up with something more dynamic, something with energy."

"Hmm, energy."

"Yep," I said. But that got me thinking: Energy. As in a force of nature. A spectral force. An irresistible force. Something that could drop-kick an immoveable object out of the solar system.

"Give it some thought," I added. "I'll check with you later."

THE SQUID'S BEAK Inn is one of those places you can't find unless you know people who know people, and even then, those people had to be blindfolded.

I left Willbard through the roof at Margie's place, rose to a couple of thousand feet above the Richmond skyline and, locating the thickest clump of fog on the river beyond Boulevard Bridge, soon found myself settling behind the weathered gray walls and grimy gray windows of the inn.

Fred-As was in the front room. An old jukebox in the corner played a sad melody, something with saxophones hovering on the low notes, then soaring to the upper registers just when your afterlife started turning dark blue. Fred-As drifted near the machine, indifferent to the Breathers hunched over their drinks at the bar or the slack-jawed spooks clustered around the Breathers.

I had to smile. "I never saw a spook who enjoys dancing as much as you."

The little spook looked up, startled, too intent on the music to notice my arrival.

"Dancing? Was I dancing?" he asked.

"I'm just making a rough guess. Based on your feet gliding over the floor and the way you hold your arms like you're hugging a pillow."

Fred-As shrugged away that line of discussion. "Just waiting for things to calm down," he said.

I took in the nearly empty bar, the listless customers, the bartender half-asleep with an arm resting on the cash register, the shadows that seemed so pooped they piled under the tables.

"Things look pretty calm already," I said.

The little guy jabbed a finger at the door to the back room, and I became aware of a thumping and scraping behind the wall.

"Where's Red Max?" I asked.

Again the poking finger, again the door, again the sounds of things pushed across a hardwood floor.

"Think he'd mind if I dropped in for a quick question?"

"One way to find out." Fred-As waved me to enter, a gesture that flowed into a subtle twirl of his hand and an elegant bow.

I gave him a thumbs-up and headed through the door. Chaos reigned on the other side. Spectral motorcycles crowded the room, a situation made worse by the fact that the machines weren't technically on the spectral plane, encouraging the bikers to think they could cram even more two-wheelers into the space.

Members of Heck's Angels growled and grunted at each other. Astral tools spun through the air and rattled against ghostly helmets. The air was thick with the thunder of revving motors, shouting bikers and squealing brakes.

(Note to reader: The laws of acoustics are null and void in the hereafter, which is why I didn't mention the racket when I was in the front room with Fred-As. I couldn't hear it. This accounts for the rarity of hearing aids in the afterlife.)

A half dozen Breathers in headgear with rhino horns were setting up tables, unfolding chairs, and generally pushing everything around until they were stopped by doors or walls. All were shivering, for whenever a horned man crossed the room, Red Max directed a couple of astral bikers to stay in the same physical space as the rhino-man.

(Additional note to readers: Actually what Red Max told the bikers was to "squat on that idiot's intestines until he starts passing ice water and snow cones," but since some readers might find that language offensive, I'm not going to mention it.)

Red Max caught my eye. "Don't tell me. You think I'm too forgiving. Just because they're on the physical plane, they think they can barge in here whenever they want. You think I ought to stand up for my bikers. Is that what you think?"

"I was in the area," I stammered. "Wanted to thank you for your wonderful advice the other night. I went to the moon and had a nice time."

"Anything else?" Red Max had a glare next to which all other glares were smiley faces.

Unreality check: Was Red Max really interested that I wanted to pick his brain for suitably ghastly forms that Willbard could use to frighten Madame Sophie into sobriety? For that matter, would Cal consider any idea that involved scarification—however nobly intentioned—a violation of my promise to avoid pranks and snarky comments until after Halloween?

"I'll schedule another appointment with Fred-As," I said.

"You do that," Red Max said.

TO GET OUT of the back room, I was jostled by spooks in black leather while dodging Sunshiners in pointy headgear who couldn't agree on the arrangement of furniture for a meeting. Nothing can take the glow off an evening like gliding through some mortal's viscera, but, as I've mentioned before, a spook's gotta do what a spook's gotta do.

I clenched my jaw, lowered my head and plowed forward to the nearest wall. Even then, I was spinning and tripping over my own feet when I reemerged in the front room and almost stumbled into the jukebox.

The juke's lights flared, the machine jumped to the left, I caught my balance just as the jukebox turned toward me, its face of chrome and molded plastic twisted with malevolence.

"Did you just see that?" I asked Fred-As.

The little guy's eyes were closed as he glided around the dingy bar with the grace of a ballroom dancer, lost in his own thoughts, light-years from the Squid's Beak Inn or the challenges of recovering from his own mortality.

I glanced back at the jukebox. It had returned to its place against the wall and its lights now pulsed to the mournful rhythms of the saxophone. I slipped outside without disturbing Fred-As.

I WAS AS rattled as you'd expect a spook to be who'd nearly been assaulted by a jukebox. Spectral instincts kept me at an altitude where I had an unrestricted view in all directions. Each car weaving through the streets was a threat, and I could imagine one caroming off the earth and heading straight for me, the power of its headlights ripping away my ectoplasm.

In time, I noticed a familiar face peering from the edge of a tall hotel by the river. I needed a friend, so I dropped to the rooftop where Jack of Diamonds, the least flappable spook in the hereafter, dangled his spectral legs.

The horizon glowed; the river weaved nearby, and a hundred feet above the fretful waves, several boat crews worked their way inland, their voices bristling with misplaced enthusiasm, believing they'd soon be tossing their lines onto the docks of Liverpool, Rio or Singapore. One distant sail drove Hank further inland.

Was I really different from the sailors who charted their courses throughout the hereafter without a single star to guide them?

"Nice night," I told Jack.

"Yeah," he replied.

Somewhere in the distance, crickets called and were answered by the purr of the ventilation fans on the roof.

"Can I ask a question?" I said.

"Shoot."

So I told him about Fast Eddie: how he'd agreed to levitate the odd corpse so I'd have some credibility while spreading Halloween tales about the non-dead, and how Fast Eddie backed away from the deal, then how he'd turned on me, manipulating jack-o'-lanterns and artificial skeletons to attack me, and how Cal got him to stop it, although Fast Eddie hadn't, and now he'd gotten a radio to whisper threats to me and a jukebox to go for my throat. Criminey, now that I think about it, Fast Eddie probably was behind the lunar lander's attack.

"What's the question?" Jack asked after I fell silent.

"How would you handle Fast Eddie? Yell, grovel, threaten, run back to Cal?"

"What makes you think Fast Eddie is the problem? Especially seeing as how Cal has stepped in. Besides, I don't think Fast Eddie or any other Tosser is capable of shoving around jukeboxes."

Interesting points. "I can't think of another Tosser I've annoyed this week."

"Why does it have to be a Tosser? Why does it have to be anyone—spook or Breather?"

"Well, that narrows the field nicely. If no one did it, then no one's responsible. Maybe it didn't even happen."

Jack flashed me a measuring gaze. "You're forgetting the things themselves. Why can't the culprit be the radio or the jukebox or even the lunar lander?"

He was nudging a curtain I'd seen several times in the distance, and now that it was coming up again, I wasn't sure I wanted to open it. Jack must have sensed my reluctance, for he fell silent and stared into the night.

"If you listen to the traffic long enough," he said, confidentially, "you realize those cars and trucks and buses are communicating with each other. Their engines sound different if there's a tie-up ahead. They get restless and fidgety. Or if one of them passed a bad accident a few miles back. Their engines become . . . sorrowful."

This wasn't heading where I expected to go. "Have you ever picked up anything from radios or jukeboxes?"

"Just the usual—music, news, commercials."

"So, when you bring up your ideas about engines—"

"Just a thought. For what it's worth."

"I appreciate it."

I'm sure if I spent more time with Rosetta, I'd've mastered the fine art of making a graceful exit. But I hadn't, so I stayed on the roof for a while, trying to hear the messages uttered by the taxis at the hotel entrance below.

Jack of Diamonds was a spirit I admired. One night he realized that he didn't have a good reason for going from here to there—and that's any *here* or *there* you'd care to mention—so he settled on a chimney in Carytown until he could come up with an incentive for relocating. Over the years, he'd adjusted his whereabouts from one rooftop to the next, working his way eastward, but, essentially, he hadn't gone anywhere.

Sitting on that hotel roof, watching the lights from the shore gild the surface of the river, I realized the difference between Jack and me was that I needed a good reason to stay in one place.

"The weather's been good for this time of year," I said.

Jack made a clicking noise with his tongue. "Something's coming from the west. Looks like we're in for a change."

"Where?"

Jack pointed to a section of the horizon, devoid of suburbs, where the sky was black and empty. "There."

"Ah, I see it now," I said, although I didn't.

Fourteen
CHAPTER

When I slipped off the roof, I took Jack of Diamond's attitude with me. What if the radio and the jukebox weren't dependent on some spook or Sunshiner flipping their switch? Could household appliances, all by themselves, without the intervention of specter or Breather, just have a bad night? Why shouldn't a can opener develop a resentment toward someone who knocked it around? Or, having been battered on the kitchen counter all day, might a microwave oven take out its frustrations on the first person or spook who passes by?

These seemed like reasonable questions to me. After all, machinery wasn't in the same class as gourds and luminescent plastic bones, which just sat there like Larry in the funeral home. Machinery had mojo, it moved, it did things without a human—or post-mortal—hand necessarily guiding it.

After heading inland a few blocks beyond Jack's watchful gaze, I glided to the roof of another skyscraper and settled near the ventilation unit.

Now, I don't want to put all the responsibility for opening up a productive spook-to-machine dialogue on the party with the most nuts and bolts. I'll even concede to not having been sensitive to the needs of my motorized and electrified brethren in the past. But, I'd like to suggest, without starting a blame game with a bundle of fans, pipes, sensors and insulation wrapping, that I've never detected any interest on their part in meeting me halfway.

"Okay," I told the ventilation unit. "You've got my full attention. I'm here to listen."

And listen I did. To a cacophony of hums, clicks and rattles. A symphony of buzzes, whirs and whooshes. A drumroll of knocks, pops and snaps. I entered into the *machineness* of my companion, freeing my mind from the prejudices of

73

the ectoplasmic and mortal worlds so I could embrace the wisdom of electrical coils, transformers, warning lights and power switches.

"I am your sensor, ready to receive your messages," I found myself chanting. "I am your sensor, ready to—"

"Are you praying to that box?"

Gilda sat in the shadows by some pipes; her mascaraed eyes and mortuary-white cheeks and forehead were all I could see. And the purple fingernails, I could see them, too, glowing with a sort of dark blush.

"I'm trying to get in touch with the spiritual essence of that ventilator," I said. "You might want to try it some night."

"Which of the 12 steps is about talking to machines?" she asked.

All of them, would have been my usual answer. *And if I gotta explain it, you're not ready to understand.* But there's something humbling about getting the evil eye from a jukebox. Something sensitizing about meeting a Glip. I've seen what the afterlife was like without a friend, and it was enough to make me want to keep all options open. Even with Goths.

"Jack of Diamonds says machines can talk to each other. I was wondering if this ventilator could help me understand what's going on."

Gilda studied the large metal box enclosing the fans that kept air flowing into the building below. "You expect this thing to give you tips on recovery?"

"Not recovery."

"Then what?"

I winced, thought of the jukebox and said, "Things are still bothering me lately. Physical things. Objects."

"I heard that Cal made Fast Eddie cut that out," she said. "You don't think Fast Eddie would ignore Cal."

Slowly, reluctantly, I tried to expand Gilda's perspective, as Jack of Diamonds had enlarged mine. "What if you were a weed-whacker? How would the world look to you? What'd be your problems? Your dreams?"

"You're worried about the ambitions of weed-whackers?"

"And a lunar lander," I hastened to add. "I've had some dealing with a lunar lander recently, and it didn't seem very serene."

If there was anything that could add gravitas to a discussion, it was a lunar lander.

"So?"

The way Gilda said, *So*, it needed its own paragraph.

"You used to think that pumpkins and artificial skeletons were out to get you," she said. "But Fast Eddie owned up to that little hokey-pocus. And now you're worried about being pursued by industrial-sized fans. Only, they seem to be ignoring you at the moment."

"You don't understand. They've been ignoring me my whole afterlife."

"Perhaps, if I left you alone, they'd stop being so rude. I'd hate to contribute to having you shunned."

I hung my head in exasperation. "Is there anyone who isn't shunning me?"

"Sure. There's got to be a newbie somewhere who hasn't met you yet."

And on that marginally hopeful note, Gilda left. *Poof.*

I stayed on the roof, but I was only going through the motions of being open to whatever the ventilation system had to say. My ectoplasm just wasn't in it.

Meanwhile, a fine layer of fog collected on the river, barely clearing the tops of the small waves. Sunrise was on its way, and I knew if I went into my bucket in this condition, I'd have a terrible time pulling myself together at twilight.

A caring supportive moment would be a nice way to end the night. A little chaos would be even better. And I knew just the place where support and mayhem could be found in equal portions during the last hours of darkness.

BEFORE I REACHED the fine arts museum, David was eyeing my progress across the night sky. *Warily* comes to mind as a description for his stare, but on the chance you've seen David, and most folks have, if only in pictures, you'll understand what I mean when I say the best description for his stare was *David-like.*

Even without a spook bearing down on him, David was known for the intensity of his gaze: eyes fixed over his left shoulder, shaded, his smooth brow not giving away the slightest suggestion of concern. I mean, the man could have been made from marble.

Could have been. But not here.

The so-called real David, the one who hung around Florence, Italy, waiting for the last Breather on earth to agree that he was a fine-looking lad, might have more substance than Richmond's David. But local *artistes* are doing amazing things these nights with river fog.

A spook in a beret and a long white coat grabbed billowy handfuls of mist and prodded and patted and poked and packed the stuff around David's knees, trying to get the dimple on a leg just right. A few onlookers *oo-ed* and *ah-ed* at each jab and jiggle, but most were concentrating so hard I'd almost say they held their breaths. But that would be silly. Of course, they were holding their breaths. That's about the only thing spooks can do with oxygen.

Near the foot of the statue, a voice cleared itself in a way that you knew was grammatically correct. "They don't make men like that anymore," Rosetta said.

Veronica angled her head to glance around the statue's strategically placed diving goggles and said, "They never did."

"How can you say that?" Darleen asked. "Of course, they made men like that. He's right here in front of you."

"It's only a statue." Gilda caught my eye. "You can't take anything in this world too seriously."

Was that a put-down or a pat on the back? With Gilda, I'm never sure. Not even when she's explaining it for the sixth time.

I looked at David for support. He shrugged. He may be only a semitransparent entity made of river fog who will dissolve into moist air as soon as the sunlight hits him, but he knew a losing argument when it stared him in the goggles.

Next to David, another artist worked feverishly on a painting whose frame, canvas and paint were all made of fog. I glanced over his shoulder to see a scene that reminded me of Norman Rockwell channeling Stephen King.

I drifted between rows of workbenches and easels and works in progress, most with a Halloween theme. I had enough of pumpkins, goblins, skeletons, jukeboxes, ventilation systems and (*shiver*) lunar landers not to waste my afterlife looking at pale astral replicas.

At the edge of the lawn, where the fog creeping from the river was ankle-high, the afterlife's less gifted residents molded clumps of mist into something resembling eggs with stubby arms and legs.

I barely noticed a misty arm stretching toward me from the carpet of fog, farther and farther. Like a snake. Or a live electrical cable feeding a ventilation unit that'd broken loose. Or a patch of fog that absorbed all the evil in a city and now it fed on fear and in the afterlife nobody can hear you scream; or, at least, no one with a pulse, although there were the odd twofers out there, most of whom were quite odd, but wouldn't you be, too, if you spent your time around the likes of Rosetta and Gilda and Fred-As.

Where was I? Oh, yeah:

The ghostly arm crept closer, inch by inch, slow as a weary heartbeat. I hadn't died to be intimidated by a hunk of moist air. That arm of fog sprouted fingers, it reached for me. I stepped on it.

"Yikes, that smarts."

The voice was familiar, the hand less so, but the tiebreaker came when a head slid out of the fog on the lawn. I knew that face.

"What are you doing down there, Fast Eddie?" I asked.

"Having my hand stepped on."

I moved aside, then slid downward until my chin barely scraped the fog. Fast Eddie rolled over and, head resting on a hand, rose from the mist.

"How were the tectonic plates?" I asked.

"They were boring. BOOOORRRRING. They make the cemetery look like a county fair."

"I'll keep it in mind."

On a nearby table, a pair of newbies grabbed hunks of mist and formed them into crude stickmen. Fast Eddie and I watched one of the pudgy little stickmen wobble across grass toward us. With a flick of a finger, Eddie sent the little tyro tumbling, and the stickman went howling back to its creator.

Eddie waved good-bye to the foggy critter. Turning to me, his voice was calm and thoughtful. "You said something, a while back, that's been bothering me."

"Geez, I can't imagine what would stand out."

"Lunar landers."

Fast Eddie came close to knocking my socks off, a trick that hasn't happened since the funeral. "What about lunar landers?"

"I'll take the fall for my cheap tricks on you—which were, by the way, well deserved—but not for something I didn't do. And I don't know anything about lunar landers."

"But you said you did."

"That was with Cal glaring down my throat." His eyes, mouth and nose all bunched together in disgust. I'm sure he was rethinking the tectonic plates as a retirement home.

I tried to give him my own best glare.

"I used to travel with the bad boys on the spiritual plane before I found Specters Anonymous," he said. "The real heavyweight Tossers. The baddest of the bad. Spooks who'd put a brick through your attic window if you even looked at them."

"And?"

Fast Eddie smoothed the grimy collar of his wrinkled shirt, which seemed worse for the attention. "I owned up to the pumpkins and skeletons, Ralph. Why don't you own up to the aliens from Mars and their space machines?"

"It's lunar landers. And it's true."

"Yeah, yeah. Remind me to tell you the one about the spook who cried, *Candy corn*, too often."

I DRIFTED AROUND the lawn of the arts center for a while. Painters and sculptors hurried to complete their works before the sun obliterated everything. A few critics gathered around a painting to correct each other for having the wrong reasons for disliking it. David's sculptor focused on getting the toenails just so, while David grabbed fistfuls of fog and tinkered with the bits behind his goggles.

What do I have to do to get anyone to take me seriously? Show up with claw marks on my arms and legs? Trick the lunar lander into attacking me at a meeting? That'd be tough: I've only seen the lander on the moon. I struggled with my memory. Did I have trouble with radios and other electrical appliances before I went to the moon? Had pumpkins and skeletons been giving me a bad time since Cal forced Fast Eddie to apologize?

I needed to nail down a few loose ends with Fast Eddie. What did the patch of fog look like where I left the old Tosser?

"Does somebody think this is funny?" A harsh voice shattered the night. "Okay, who's behind this? Come on, people, I want names."

This voice I recognized, and I knew exactly what it meant: The show had begun.

Between the statue of David and the arts center, spooks had gathered around a wall of mist. Peering at the foggy surface, they pointed and talked with great animation or fell into shocked silence; some held their hands over their mouths while others snickered. Most shook their heads. Gwendolyn removed his head from his neck to give it a thorough shaking.

Something moved across that wall of fog, small and slithery, like a conga line of black noodles, and as I got closer, I saw things more frightening than noodles crawl from the mist. They were words. Veronica glared at a particular row of squirmy letters, her hands on her hips, and when her scowl wasn't enough to send the words back where they came from, she smacked them.

Elsewhere on the foggy wall, Gwendolyn squinted at the crawling letters and read: "Dear Mister Lovely Heart."

"That's *Lonely* Heart," I said.

"I'm not so sure," said Gilda.

From somewhere in the back of my head, in what used to pass for my memory cells, a little *bleep* started throbbing.

Veronica had positioned herself inches from the wall to block offensive language from sensitive eyes, and when a line of text expanded, she stretched her arms to cover the words.

"Something about *looking for companionship*," Darleen continued, and "*a spirit newly arrived on these lonely shores.*"

The bleep got louder, then exploded into a single white blossom that resembled the ruffles on a finely tailored shirt, and I didn't bother to conceal my grin. "You sure it isn't *lovely shores?*"

Gilda gave me a guarded glance. "I smell trouble."

"We're spooks," I said. "We don't have to worry about odors."

"We can still step into a mess and come out stinky."

"Stink is nothing but a future garden of roses," I replied.

Gilda adjusted the chains on the shoulders of her black leather jacket. "We're dead. We don't do roses. We do lilies, cypress and plastic tulips."

CHAPTER

ayers of gray appeared in the east as David's creator tried to get the heels and instep right, and the occasional photon shot across the lawn of the arts center. Fog bled into the retreating night, soon to take David and other masterpieces of Richmond's posthumous community back to wherever fog fritters away the daylight hours.

I scoured the grounds for signs of Fast Eddie to finish our discussion. He may have denied responsibility for the lunar lander, but I hadn't pinned him down for what he knew about jukeboxes and radios.

From the last large patch of fog in the far corner of the grounds, I saw Gilda watching me. I scanned the scraggly ground fog, glanced back at her, asked myself why she should seem so odd when, except for the wardrobe, she was no more peculiar than Veronica, who was swatting a wall of fog whenever fragments from Edgar Allan Poe's new blog appeared in the haze.

While I wandered over the lawn in search of Fast Eddie, Gilda was constantly shifting, sidling this way and that, always keeping herself between me and Veronica. As though she wanted to protect us from each other.

I went to her. "Doesn't Veronica know that Rosetta is the one who believes in tidying up?"

"She's not worried about neatness." She inched sideways to keep her blocking position between Veronica and me."

"Then what's going on?" I saw a line of text wriggle away as Veronica bent over, picked it up and crushed it between her astral fingers. "Poe's blog is going to dissolve into the air in a few minutes anyway."

Gilda gave me her most innocent look. Which usually required a microscope and a good pair of tweezers to differentiate from her I-couldn't-care-less-about-you-or-anything-you-say-or-do look.

"Then no one's going to object if it leaves early," she said.

"Poe will be unhappy when he learns she destroyed his priceless prose. And Rosetta. She's always touchy whenever anyone else corrects the St. Sears group for grammar and spelling."

"I guess we'll have to see about that," Gilda replied.

For a Goth, *guess we'll have to see* is an amazingly forthright declaration. An edginess ruffled Gilda's ectoplasm as she followed me back to the duplex we shared on Libby Hill. I was too exhausted by the drama to break through her veneer of indifference to her true core of apathy.

"Good night," she said when we reached the coffeepots on the dining room wall. She whooshed up the spout.

I drifted for a moment in the dark. Cuddling with my favorite beagle would be a good end to a wishy-washy night.

"Petey? Where are you, girl? Petey?"

The dog, who often stretches against the baseboard below my bucket when I return home, was absent from her post again. The last time she failed in her duties this often, she was convalescing from a disgusting snack found on a neighbor's lawn.

I scooted through the ceiling, took a right turn at the heating duct, another right at a sewage pipe and emerged in the hallway outside the room Petey shared with James William. A beagle curled at the foot of the boy's bed was what I expected to find. Instead, Petey lay over James William's legs, head erect, ears uplifted, eyes locked on the wall.

As I stood there, Petey didn't blink, more interested in a blank wall than me. Without a word, I slipped down to the first floor and retreated to my hobo coffeepot.

EVEN IN DAYLIGHT, when spooks seek the deepest shadows to despecterize into puddles of ectoplasm, I must have held onto something resembling consciousness, for I remember hearing the *clickety-clickety* of Petey's toes on the hardwood floor, reassuring but not frequent enough for the dog to be making her usual rounds to check on me. It wasn't like her to slack off.

When I finally awoke, the weight of the darkness told me the sun had been gone at least an hour. I slipped out of the pot on the wall, stretched, checked the area for suspicious radios or jukeboxes, then realized another threat lay nearby.

James William's father, visible through the archway to the living room, thumbed through a newspaper, oblivious to the television, its volume muted, the zapper balanced on an arm of his chair.

No boob tube was going to fool me. I looked down, turned to leave, then swung around to catch the television doing something sinister. But the TV was playing it cool. I pulled my lips into weird contortion, popped my eyeballs and thought unkind things about electronics. *Your mother has old circuit boards* was, I imagine, particularly insulting.

If the television was up to no good, it did a fine job of hiding it.

The standoff between the tube and me broke under the rattle of metal from the kitchen, the clink of porcelain and James William saying in an aggrieved tone, "But I'm not scared of the closet. Only babies are scared of closets. I was just asking *What if?* about the dresser."

I gave the television a warning waggle of a finger and went to the kitchen. Mother and James William were preparing the plates, glasses and silverware for their nightly ride in the dishwasher.

Mother whispered something. The boy's forehead lined with wrinkles.

"I didn't say vampires are hiding in my dresser," James William said. "I'm just saying, What if a vampire was in my dresser? Shouldn't we keep the light on in my room? Just to be safe?"

His mother kept rinsing the plates in the sink. "What would these vampires—the ones we agree aren't really in your dresser—what would they look like?"

"Dunno. I haven't seen them. I've only heard them. They go, *Ooo* and *Shhh.*"

"That sounds to me like someone left his toy train running."

In the next instant, I was back in James William's room, this time paying attention to the details. Socks, shirts and pants were strewn across the floor in drifts that weren't there during my predawn visit. The covers and sheets were twisted into contortions that would take a college football team hours to make. Toy cars and trucks peeked from under the bed.

Petey glanced at me, then, never taking her eyes off the wall by the dresser, hopped onto the floor, emboldened now by having backup.

"Grrr," Petey told the wall.

I maneuvered along the foot of the bed on the chance a Hydra-Eyed Granite Eater from the Seventh Plain of the Darluvian Escarpment was hiding behind the dresser.

Something was there, too small for a Hydra-Eyed Granite Eater, even though the species was one of the few known life-forms that achieves its maximum size at birth and shrinks as it grows older, a testament to the danger of too much roughage.

"*Grrr*," I told the shadow behind the dresser.

Petey charged the wall. I followed, rounding the corner of the dresser, prepared to do something really terrible to whatever deserved it, as Petey lunged at a red blotch on the wall, close to the dresser. With the same tactical savvy the dog showed every afternoon in protecting the front door from the mailman, she managed to stop two inches before she'd bruise her nose.

The beagle glanced over her shoulder at me. *Are you gonna stand there or are you gonna do something?* those rich chocolate eyes asked.

"It's one of those jahoozits," I explained. "A handheld vacuum cleaner."

So why's it going whoosh *when the boy's trying to sleep?*

You got me.

ONCE WE DETERMINED the vacuum cleaner had no immediate sinister plans, I left Petey to guard the bedroom while I returned to James William and his mother in the kitchen in hopes that a useful nugget of information might dribble out of their discussion, but the talk had eased into the subject of the boy's costume for Halloween, and, no doubt, I was making too much of Petey growling at the wall.

Kids are always afraid of the dark. Right? Even a kid who's trying to convince his mom that every other kid in the United States has a mother who's letting him wear a zombie costume for Halloween. Right? And why should it be unusual if a dog picks up on the kid's fears and growls at the same shadows that frighten the kid? Right?

Beam-Me-Up-Scotty, and I was gone from the house on Libby Hill and respecterizing on a residential street in Carytown. A pumpkin stared at me from the stoop of a brownstone. I stared back, glided forward a few steps, then spun around. The pumpkin's stare hadn't changed. I waved my hands. The pumpkin gave me the dumb look of a hollow shell.

Dare I dream? Had Fast Eddie truly gotten out of the business of levitating jack-o'-lanterns? Maybe some sort of ectoplasmic energy left over from Fast Eddie last night had propelled the radio and the jukebox. (Not letting myself get overly focused on the bothersome conversation with Jack of Diamonds about communicating cars.)

If you're doing the right thing, then you're alright.

That thought came from a young man who walked through me while I was trying to assess the pumpkin's intentions. It gives me the willies to share the same physical space with Sunshiners, but in this case, the Breather was actually helpful.

"Thanks, buddy," I said as the guy glanced back to cross the street.

He was somewhere in his twenties. His hair was too short and too well-maintained for my tastes; he had slacks instead of blue jeans and a freshly pressed shirt that I wouldn't be caught alive in. There was firmness in his jaw and unease in his eyes.

My kind of guy—uptight and conflicted.

While I zipped up the street, rounded a corner by a yogurt store and headed up the block to the window with its flickering neon sign, I realized I'd seen the fellow before. Wasn't he one of the young professionals who lived on Libby Hill? Or perhaps a minister who called occasionally on Father Jenkins, pastor for the church where the St. Sears group meets?

In Margie and Sophie's waiting room were two solemn coeds, a middle-aged man leafing through *Autopsy Quarterly*, which Sophie leaves on a table because she thinks it gets visitors into the right frame of mind, plus the usual assortment of spooks hoping the psychics might have some insight for the spectral crowd.

I went down the hall to Margie's office and veered into the wall to avoid a customer tucking a handkerchief into her purse. Margie was in her consulting room, counting a pile of coins on the table.

"I hate and it when they pay me with spare change," she said, not bothering to look up. "Makes me feel like a parking meter."

"Well, you can slap me with a ticket any time you want."

Margie gave me an expression she must save for dogs that poop on her front steps. So much for gallantry. She eyed me coolly. "Is there a ticket I can give a spook for having a smart mouth?"

"That's Cal's job. And he made me promise to give up my smart-alecky ways."

"I'll believe that when I see it." Head down, she kept sifting through the coins. "What's your reason for this visit? You always have a reason, you know."

"I was wondering if any of your household appliances have been acting . . . er . . . mean-spirited lately."

"Mean-spirited?"

"I meant, erratic."

"Erratic?"

"Forget I brought it up."

"No problem-o." Margie swiped the last dimes from the table with a theatrical sweep of her hand. "And that makes an even twenty-five dollars. I'm ready for the next customer."

Her eyebrows crinkled prettily. "There is a next customer, isn't there?"

"As luck would have it, there were three when I came in."

Her look was dubious. Her voice skeptical. The fingernails drumming on the table lethal.

"How many of them have a pulse?"

I held up a finger, then popped up a second, then a third.

"I'm coming, Lord, I'm coming," she exclaimed. "I have reaped the bounties of this world, and there's nothing left for me but the Pearly Gates."

With a chuckle and a spring in her steps, Margie hopped from her chair and scurried toward the hall.

I've never been accused of being pedantic—in fact, I've never been accused of knowing exactly what *pedantic* means—but I couldn't stop myself from making a few technical corrections.

"You know, they're not really pearl-colored. And I wouldn't call them *gates*. They're more like subway turnstiles."

"Then bring on the off-white turnstiles of eternity," she said.

With a twinkle in her eye, she strode toward the waiting room with no time for her or me to question whether some other destination might be a wiser choice at the moment. Like the mouth of an active volcano.

CHAPTER

The spooks loitering around the ceiling of the waiting room perked up at Margie's arrival, as did the three Breathers there.

The coeds on the sofa weren't going to be difficult for Margie. From the meaningful glances the young women exchanged, I knew that one was here for advice of a romantic nature while the other wanted her friend not to waste money on a charlatan. Margie handles this stuff every night.

Stubble-faced and baggy-eyed, the man had hair oddly clumped on one side of his head, and his shirt, although recently ironed, was a long-time refugee from a washing machine. His problem would involve money. Again, a run-of-the-psychic-mill case for Margie.

Along the ceiling, spooks quieted down, no doubt sensing that the drama was about to begin.

"Who's next?" Margie asked.

On cue, three voices started chattering at once, two expressing their divergent opinions about who should be seen first, while the third person suggested someone quit acting like a child and show some maturity.

Margie raised a hand for calm. I crossed my arms, Cal-wise, and tried not to grin too broadly.

The voices of the three waiting clients coalesced around a single topic, the meaning of *next*. Two insisted that they (the women) had passed through the threshold before the third (the man). His argument was that he would have been first if he hadn't been a gentleman who opened the door for the ladies, who weren't real ladies if they wouldn't return a favor when they had the chance.

I couldn't tell whether the coeds were offended by being called ladies or insulted because they were actually having this conversation with a derelict who hadn't used a toothbrush in weeks.

As the discussion went from animated to aggrieved, more spooks drifted in from the streets. On my side of the daisies, we're fascinated by Sunshiners arguing over the right to be the victim. Let me tell you about being a real victim. It's when someone puts a tombstone and a vase of flowers over your head.

Fast Eddie finally showed up, and the chaos shifted into a higher gear as he started taking bets on the outcome of the argument.

"Gent or ladies? Gent or ladies?" Fast Eddie drifted among the growing crowd of spooks. "Where would you put your money, if you had any money to put? The fairer sex or the callow cad?"

"My money'd be on Margie," I told him.

"That filly ain't in this race," he said, then turned back to the crowd. "Gent or ladies, folks. The finish line is in sight. They're neck and neck. Let's place your bets."

I shook my head. It was no contest. Whenever sweet reason and simple kindness are called for, Margie held all the aces. The unkempt gent showed signs of fatigue when the floor shuddered from the approach of a pair of orthopedic high heels.

"Who's this that doesn't want to call a couple working girls *ladies*?" Sophie thundered from the hallway. "Let me at him. They have just as much right to be ladies as I do."

The guy with the leaning hair took one look at Sophie and made sure his soiled collar was neatly tucked inside his grimy coat. Glancing at Margie, he asked, "Can I have an introduction?"

"We'd better leave," a coed said.

The other woman was fixated on Sophie. "I wouldn't leave now if they paid me."

Sophie gripped the edge of the doorway, overcome, although I can't say whether by apricot brandy or residual hormones, but I'm sure *Some Enchanted Evening* was playing in the background.

"Come to think of it," the man said, "I could be persuaded to give up my place at the head of this line for a little refined conversation."

Sophie tucked a wild spray of hair behind an ear. "What a coincidence. Some of my best friends are refineries."

His eyes grew larger.

Sophie lurched closer.

Margie, having gotten in touch with her inner-five-year-old, obviously wanted to stamp her feet and throw bread crumbs across the room, but was struggling to force that brat back into the shadows.

"Why don't you take this gentleman?" Margie told Sophie. "And I'll help these two women."

"I'd love to take the gentleman," Sophie purred. "To places he's never dreamed of. Not in his wildest gamination."

A bubble of oxygen must have slipped through the ocean of brandy sloshing through Sophie's veins. She arched an eyebrow and pointed it at me.

"Gamination," I agreed. "No one could put it better."

Her head lolled from side to side and her legs wobbled, but Sophie strutted across the floor to the poor gent who now had a nervous tic and a tremor in his knees.

"Let me show you how we welcomed the boys home from Manila," she cooed.

The coeds were riveted where they stood. Was it horror or fascination, or had the spirit of Fast Eddie's mobile betting parlor somehow broken through to the first dimension and infused everyone with the reckless awareness that easy money could be made if they only figured out whose pulmonary system was likely to collapse first.

Me? I inched away from Margie. I didn't know what was going to happen, but it would be memorable.

Little did I know—

—that Willbard was about to appear in the waiting room, her fearsome visage now transformed into an eight-foot blue bunny, and that she would hop onto one of Sophie's Persian sofas to sniff the dead flowers in a window vase, or

—that the door to the waiting room would fly open to admit the strange man I'd passed through on the sidewalk, the one who reminded me how simple the afterlife's dilemmas would be if I stayed focused on doing the right thing, or

—that the new arrival, seen in the tricky light of the parlor's waiting room—partly suffused through scarves tossed over Tiffany lamps, and partly blasted from LED lights that Margie had liberated from a hospital operating room—would turn out to be someone I had met before, or

—that this newcomer wasn't just anyone, but Scoop Bristow, erstwhile reporter with the *Richmond Times-Dispatch*, who had provided Margie with some free publicity when she was making her first steps toward becoming a full-time psychic.

"And I was afraid things were going too smoothly," I whispered.

Margie's scowl should have added ten years to my time in happily-ever-after, along with a year or two to my next plane of existence. She greeted Bristow and suggested they talk in her office, letting the two coeds know she'd be right back.

Willbard, who was manifesting herself as a big blue rabbit, pushed her glistening black nose almost to the surface of the world's ugliest vase on the sill of the bay window.

Sophie glanced past Margie and—*Bingo!*—realized a big rabbit was clomping over her favorite sofa. "Will someone get that creature out of here?" She pinched her nose while the fingers of the other hand twitched in Willbard's direction.

The Breathers turned in unison to the sofa which was empty for all material purposes, although those of us on the astral dimension saw an eight-foot blue rabbit nuzzling dried flowers with a nose that looked worse for wear than Sophie's.

One coed leaned into the other. "What's she talking about? If there are rats here, I'm gone. This place is beyond sleazy."

"Just one second, my little no-class hussy." Soph went from blurry to laser-focused in microseconds. "Who are you making these imprecations against?"

"*Sleazy* is the nicest thing I can say about this rats' nest," a young woman snapped.

Sophie snapped, too. She lunged for the coed. Willbard hopped from the sofa, and the women squealed as eight-feet of blue ectoplasm vaulted through their bodies. Margie, who hadn't quite managed to steer the reporter out of the waiting room, dove to keep Bristow from blundering into the giant bunny he couldn't see and ended up pushing him onto an orange plastic chair and falling on top of him.

Fast Eddie opened up a betting line on the odds for Margie and Bristow getting unsnarled within the hour. An embarrassed smile crossed the lips of my favorite twofer, but before I could even ask myself how Cal would handle this situation, the man with the cockeyed hair decided that Bristow needed help fending off a sexual assault from Margie and proceeded to tug and jerk at whatever appendage of Margie came to hand.

By all the evidence, Margie didn't appreciate a stranger pawing her as if she were a sack of potatoes. She squirmed to avoid the derelict, which brought her closer to ramming an elbow into Bristow's nose and a knee into his vital bits.

"WOULD YOU, PLEASE, KEEP IT DOWN! WE'RE TRYING TO SLEEP IN HERE!"

I froze. So did the spectral gawkers and gamblers loitering around the ceiling. If you heard that voice, you wouldn't move either, for it belonged to Letitia, a specter of feminine inclinations who, for reasons too complicated to go into right now, had taken up residence in the vase that Willbard the Blue Bunny was inspecting.

Sophie's eyes darted over the chairs and tables and bric-a-brac. Something had happened, but she didn't have a clue what it was.

Letitia's voice dialed down to its usual honey-soaked volume. "Soph, darling, shouldn't you be worried about your brandy? I know I would be. Back there in that big, dark, empty room. Alone and unguarded."

Befuddlement settled over Sophie like a damp mist. Without a word, she teetered down the hall and abandoned the derelict with the lopsided hair. Oblivious to the astral drama occurring inches away, the coeds were struck shy as Margie and Bristow writhed on the chair, sorting out which thigh went into whose hip.

So it fell to me to glide over to Margie and say, "Unless your tongue fell out during that last huddle, you might want to ask this young gentleman what he's doing here."

Margie flicked a shoulder at me. If I'd been a fly, I might've thought she wanted to get rid of me. Luckily for both of us, I'm not a fly.

"Remember he works for the newspaper," I added. "I don't think this is a social call."

That took the wind from her sails. Was Margie, my Margie, my good ol' reliable friend, who watched endless hours of *The Honeymooners* with me as I searched for clues to my real, pre-posthumous identity, disappointed because Bristow's presence might have something to do with her lapsed newspaper subscription? Surely, Margie found my wise, witty companionship enough to fill her social calendar and obliterate any desire to spend time with an unsophisticated creature still in his first life.

Bristow can't tell Margie what it was like to hide behind a boulder in the Khyber Pass when Willbard was on the loose. Or reminisce about strolling on the lawn of the Richmond fine arts center when the mist rose from the river and the afterlife's most creative spirits made paintings and sculptures from the fog.

Freed of his entanglements with Margie, Bristow arose and picked up a small decorative tea cup that had been knocked over on an end table. He put it on an eggshell-thin saucer.

"Sorry about that," Margie said, tugging her shirt into place. "I'm not used to the heels on these shoes."

If Bristow noticed she was wearing tennis shoes, he didn't admit it.

"Ask him what he wants," I told Margie.

"You think I don't know what he wants?" she hissed back.

"Pardon?" Bristow joined the discussion.

Margie's cheeks shot through a comprehensive display of shades of red before settling into a sort of flaming pink.

Then it was Bristow's turn to go crimson. Yeah, he noticed the tennis shoes and heard what she said. "You don't know what I want," he replied.

The silence that settled on the room had roots and a basement. No one, Breather or spook, could look away. And they certainly couldn't think of anything to say, seeing as how that would draw attention to themselves.

Which, of course, made this the precise instant that Edgar Allan Poe should—and in fact, did—pop up next to Bristow.

ℰSeventeen
CHAPTER

ℰ dgar Allan Poe surveyed the room with a confident smile, honoring with a glance the spooks (Willbard, Fast Eddie, the gawkers and me), the Breathers (Bristow, the two coeds and the guy with the lopsided hair) and the sole remaining twofer (Margie). Every ruffle on Edgar A-'s shirt was in place, although each hair on his head was angled as though avoiding its neighbors.

"Having had some acquaintance with affairs of the heart," Edgar A- began, "perhaps I could offer my services."

"No," Margie said.

"NO," I added.

And, "Wwwwwwiiiiiilllllllbbbbbbaaaarrrrrddd!" howled Willbard.

Bristow, of course, only heard Margie's response, which lacked the force of my voice or Willbard's, yet her frown pushed the reporter a half step closer to the door. He took a deep breath and peeked at Margie from beneath his brow.

"No?" he repeated. "A moment ago, I said you don't know why I'm here. And you just said *No* to that. Is that because you're reading my mind? Or have you tapped my telephone?"

Margie's smile was ragged and appealing. "I'm sorry. I'm having a bad night. Can we start over?"

"At the paper, we've gotten complaints from some of your customers," Bristow said, none too eagerly. "I thought—we thought—it's only fair to let you respond before we go to press."

I've been around Margie when her hormones were activated, and I've seen her come out swinging when her professionalism was questioned, but I've

92

never seen my favorite twofer when both reactions were triggered within three seconds by the same man.

Poe nodded gravely. "How little we have learned since my days in the sunshine. We still dissemble and mask our true feelings, rather than share with another the authentic—"

"Will you shut up," Margie hissed.

"I understand." Bristow resumed his slow drift to the door. "Like I said, I thought you ought to have a chance."

"Not you." Margie reached for the reporter. "I mean, you surprised me and I told myself, *Shut up*, because I was about to say something stupid."

"Take your time. Let me tell you exactly what those unhappy customers said." Bristol pulled out a thin reporter's notebook and flipped through pages covered with writing that could have been done by a myopic third-grader.

Poe glided next to Margie. "Unburden yourself, my dear. Be not proud nor courtly. Let your swain feel the warmth of your ardor."

"*Swain? Ardor? Courtly?*" I wanted to go after Edgar A- with a chain saw. "I'm beginning to understand why you were a failure with women."

Edgar A- shrugged off my barb. Critiques from the spectral *hoi polloi* weren't part of the package when he signed up for his eternal reward. "One must encourage the young to listen to their hearts."

"Can't you see, the lady is busy?" I snapped. "If you want to listen to a heart, you can listen to mine. But I'm warning you: It only makes a noise if you tap it."

While this enlightened discussion took place, a crowd of spooks descended from the ceiling to surround Bristow as he flipped through his notebook, an old-fashioned fountain pen clamped in his mouth. He didn't know what he was up against, and I'm not talking about pushback from the astral dimension. Once Margie ruled out a response that involved a left hook, she could fend off anything a mere testosterone-carrier might say.

"Yes," Margie said. "A few details would be helpful."

"No, no." I waved my hands. "You're the psychic, remember? You don't need him to tell you anything."

Margie gave me the evil eye. Bristow jerked away from that look, but Margie was quick on the recovery.

"Wait," she murmured. "Something's coming to me. Something about a girl. You were in high school together. Perhaps junior high."

I jabbed a finger at Poe's nose, said, "Behave yourself," compressed myself smaller than a flake of dust and dove into the reporter's notebook. After finding the blank pages, I worked my way to the most recent pages marred by loopy handwriting, then, working faster than a hummingbird on speed, zipped through the whorls and curlicues.

There were repeated references to *#1* and *#2*. *Marriage* was underlined four times.

When I reemerged, Bristow had found his voice. "I'm not here because of anything that happened to me."

Margie peeked through her fingers. "Are you sure? I'm definitely picking up something from high school that still bothers you."

"Well, sure. I mean, you're right. But that's not what we need to talk about now."

Time for my report. "He's interested in the two women Sophie saw the other night. They actually went to the newspaper."

"I see two troubled souls," Margie murmured and, indicating the pair of speechless coeds still in the waiting room, added, "Not these women. But two others. Who came here looking for answers and left very unhappy."

"What were they interested in?" Bristow asked.

Before I could say, *Marriage*, Margie sighed. "The affections of a man. The same man. Who has passed through the veil, who must answer for the wrongs he did to them."

Bristow lowered his notebook. When Margie was on a roll, folks on both sides of the Great Divide count themselves lucky to take in the show. Even Edgar A- seemed to enjoy the performance.

"What did you tell the women?" Bristow asked.

"My colleague, who left as you were arriving, was the one who dealt with them."

"Then I should speak to her."

"She couldn't possibly share any information about them. Our work here is strictly confidential."

"But the women told me everything. They want the newspaper to publish their story."

Margie gave a sad little smile that was one of her specialties. "But there is a third party involved, isn't there? And we can't divulge his personal information without his permission."

Big misstep. Bristow was now going to say that that shouldn't be a problem for a hotshot seer, but I'd underrated the effect of Margie's sad smile upon a young man who could still blush.

"What can you tell me?" he asked.

"Only that neither of those ladies liked what they were told. That was the real reason they left unhappy. But I deal in truth, not happiness."

Bristow flipped his notebook shut. "They also said your colleague had been drinking."

Poe gripped a lapel of his black coat with one hand, the other pointed to the northwest corner of the ceiling, and declaimed, "Quaff, oh, quaff that kind nepenthe——"

"Go *quaff* yourself," I told Poe.

Margie giggled.

"What?" Bristow asked.

AS MARGIE LED Bristow down the hall to her office, both coeds settled on a sofa, so caught up with the drama now that Margie couldn't pay them to leave, and I headed toward the back room for purely non-possessive, non-protective, dimensionally sensitive reasons.

The glass beads draped over the entrance to Sophie's room vibrated with every *snarkle* and glop of Sophie's snoring. I slid to one side of the narrow hallway to avoid the disappointed Breather with the lopsided hair who came out, leaving me unprepared when Willbard bounded from the waiting room and knocked me through the wall.

"We've got to talk, Willbard," I said.

Willbard hopped toward me again, a bouncy bundle of blue fur as big as a pickup truck, eager to get into Sophie's consulting room. I braced myself, Willbard skidded to a stop and tickled me with the ends of her floppy bunny ears.

"This is too mortifying for words," Poe said. "Have you no dignity?"

Before Willbard could answer, Poe left in a *poof*.

My turn. "You were going to scare Sophie into giving up booze."

Willbard morphed into her usual shape: a wall of fog, with lightning bolts flaring across her dark interior and mists knotted like gnarled brows.

"Willbard tried."

"You're trying too hard. Just be yourself. Be exactly what you are. No special disguises. Don't worry about doing or saying anything. Just be there, as your ol' loveable self."

Miniature lightning flashed across Willbard's storm-cloud features. "Sophie will stop drinking if Willbard is loveable?"

"She won't be able to help herself." Most of my toes and all of my fingers were crossed.

"Hmm." Willbard disappeared through the ceiling, flummoxed by the concept of anyone liking her.

I felt bad as I glided back to the waiting room, leaving Margie to work out her own problems with Bristow. *Tooth-pulling honesty* is what our 12-step program calls for, and even though I hadn't lied to Willbard, I'd bent the truth so severely it was a mere ghost of itself.

"Yo, there," Hank said as I reentered the waiting room. "You look like you missed your own funeral."

"That hearse left the cemetery a long time ago." I pointed over my shoulder. "Hank, you won't believe what Willbard thinks is scary."

Before Hank could respond, Gilda floated from a corner. "I don't know about Hank, but whatever it is, I certainly won't believe it if you're the one telling me."

I stopped at the edge of the waiting room and studied at the specters floating above the mismatched sofas and chairs. The newbies and strangers were gone. Gilda and Hank were there. So were Cal and Rosetta, Fast Eddie and Gwendolyn, plus Darleen, Jingle Jim, Mrs. Hannity, Roger and some other regulars from the St. Sears group. The two coeds were there, too, but they were preoccupied discussing Bristow, as oblivious of the spectral world as a sparrow is of trigonometry.

"If I didn't know better, I'd think this was an intersection," I said.

"See," Veronica told Cal. "I knew we weren't going to put anything past Ralph."

An intersection is a collision of spectral egos, where a group of spooks try to get the attention of an out-of-control afterlife entity. Intersections are a way of nudging someone to face the facts of the hereafter.

"I'm glad you're showing an interest in Willbard," I said. "She just left for her room upstairs. This is a good time to catch her. But I gotta warn you. I don't think Willbard will listen to anyone telling her to go to meetings."

"This isn't about Willbard," Hank said.

"Then what?" I asked. Everyone had the ol' spook-in-the-headlight stare. "Give me a hint."

Cal crossed his arms. "Candy corn."

"Lunar lander," Fast Eddie added.

"Jukebox," Gilda said.

My eyes flitted from one face to the next. No one was smiling or exchanging glances, nary a single suppressed grin broke out in the pack. These were my buddies, my friends, my soul mates. Some of them went back to my first nights in happily-ever-after.

Cal's expression was seven notches beyond stern. "I thought we had a deal, Ralph. You were going to lay off the pranks and smart remarks for a few days."

"But I have. I'm honoring my part of our bet."

Veronica stepped between me and my sponsor. You'd think she believed the big guy needed protection. "This is bigger than your game with Cal. This is about a spook who can't take his own death seriously."

"Give me credit for the fun I've brought into your afterlives."

"I'm willing to do that," Cal replied. "But let's also note the way you hide behind your pranks and snarky comments. A friendly, honest spook doesn't carry so many secrets."

Jingle Jim was so worked up, his commitment to poetry wavered and he said: "We're only as sick as our secretions."

"The phrase is about *secrets*," I shot back. "We're only as sick as our secrets."

"How would you know?" Rosetta asked.

I looked at Jingle Jim and felt sorry for him for the first time in my afterlife. I couldn't imagine opening my mouth for any reason right now, and he was ransacking his memory for a rhyme for *secretions*.

WITHOUT ANOTHER WORD, I left the waiting room. All of my friends thought I was out of line, that my stories about lunar landers and haunted radios were as wacky as my initial explanations for the candy corn. My recovery from sunshine and my transcendence to a higher plane were so unlikely to my buddies that they thought a group effort was needed to straighten me out.

Dazed and a little frightened, I got as far as the door to the street. Outside might be another spook wanting to critique my recovery. Or an empty sidewalk. I didn't know which was more terrifying. Upward to the third floor I floated, toward Willbard's domain, where floor-to-ceiling shelves bulged with legal records in cardboard boxes.

Surrounded by so much evidence of ill will, I drifted in the darkness, feeling more alone than I had been since the moment I found myself in a line of fresh decedents winding through a processing center, everyone unaware of what had happened to us or where we were or what would come next, looking in the shadows at other puzzled souls who stretched for miles.

Strangely, my mind leapt from that experience to my encounter with reporter Scoop Bristow on the sidewalk outside Margie's a short time ago. *If you're doing the right thing, then you're alright* Bristow had been thinking when I oozed through him.

And, by Roth, I have been doing the right thing. In helping Margie with

Sophie. In making Willbard feel useful. In investigating whether the vacuum in James William's room was a hazard to boy or beagle. In taking advice from Fred-As's friend, Red Max, when I needed a little boost in my recovery. And, most importantly, in meeting Cal's challenge to avoid smart-mouth comments and all manner of tricks until Halloween.

Back to Margie's waiting room I went, determined to let my alleged friends know that, sure, I might benefit from drafting a spreadsheet, but there's more to recovery than making lists of misdeeds. I was greeted by an empty ceiling, two coeds whispering conspiratorially on a sofa, and the murmur of Margie's and Bristow's voices down the hall.

"Ahem," a tiny, tinny voice came from the window. "Begging your pardon, your Magnificence. If this is a bad time, I'll come back."

The voice belonged to Sniveler, a spook entombed in the world's ugliest vase. He thought I was a divinity. The kindest thing I could do for him was not to take away his illusions.

"What is it?" I asked.

"I hope you won't smite me into dried ectoplasm if I say that I couldn't help overhearing your last conversation," Sniveler said.

"Every spook within six blocks heard that discussion." This from Whiner, the second of the specters who shared the vase with Letitia.

"Not that we blame the Great Ralph for the noise," Sniveler emphasized.

"However—" I began.

"However, it should not be heretical of us to point out—" Sniveler began.

"—heretical of *you*," Whiner amended. "I'm staying out of this."

"Okay, heretical of anyone to point out that perhaps your fellow godheads were trying to encourage you to think less about your undeserving servants, such as me. And more about your esteemed, inestimable self."

"English," I said, "Let's have this in English."

"Most perfect of deities," Sniveler began. "Whose fame reaches ninety-seven percent of the metro area, All-Knowing, All-Seeing, All-Hearing, whose gym socks never stank—"

"Get to the point."

Whiner, for once, showed some backbone. "You're losing it, Ralph. Everyone says so."

"By *losing it* you mean—"

"Your iPad has lost connectivity. Your Facebook page isn't *liked* by anyone. Your Mensa card has been revoked."

Sniveler jumped in. "Your subway doesn't reach all stations. Your deck doesn't have any aces. Your flag is stuck at half-mast. Your mother says——"

"Enough!" I stared at the cheap, garish lump of poorly shaped ceramics from which Whiner and Sniveler had been enumerating my faults, uncertain whether to smash the vase or *poof* off to the Asteroid Belt, where I understand the landscape is so barren even the most pessimistic of spectral entities stay away.

"When you say everyone thinks that, you mean——"

"The known world," Sniveler said.

"Well, it could have been worse," I added.

"And you're just the godhead who can make it worse," Whiner chimed.

Eighteen

CHAPTER

I don't remember leaving Margie's waiting room or much about the next couple of hours, although I'm sure I avoided the river and the suburbs, not willing to be reminded of the pointless cruises of the tall-masted ships over the James or to see hollowed-out pumpkins staring from windows and porches.

Whenever I have a bad night, Darleen says, *I tell myself to stop that. Just stop it this very instant. Then I can begin making a good night for myself.*

And I say: There are reasons some people died young.

Still, it's galling when my sponsor and the spooks who know me best think I've fallen so far off the track to transcendence that it'll take a team effort to get me pointed in the right direction. Their proof? Because I've made a slight exaggeration from time to time, the merest overstatement or good-natured practical joke that no one could get out of their hair for months.

Cal, especially, should know better. We had a deal. I was going to clean up my act—or, at least, keep it clean for a couple more nights—and I've always kept my word. I've earned the right for him to trust me.

Normally, when my attitude is somewhere in my socks, I know it's time for a meeting. Tonight, a meeting was the last place I wanted to be.

So I headed to Monument Avenue where there'd be plenty of company and lost myself in the spectral tour groups and local gawkers. Forty or fifty feet above the asphalt, where the residents of the afterlife were safe from the photons of streetlamps and headlights, a parade was under way.

Rank upon rank, Confederate units marched through the night sky, their uniforms ragged and patched, their steps mostly out of step, many dragging the stocks of their muzzle loaders, but all sharing the grit and solemnity.

"What's the occasion?" I asked a spook in a tux with a withered rose in his lapel.

"I believed it's the anniversary of our defeat at the Battle of Chester's Mill," he said.

A ghostly stevedore flicked a contemptuous glance at the dandy. "What are you talking about? They's celebrating being massacred at Hill House."

"Don't let the boys confuse you." A spectral matron with her hair in a bun smiled at me. "This is a commemoration of our glorious retreat from Arkham."

Wasn't it time for the rebels to stop piling up defeats and grudges? The guy in the tux and the stevedore eyed me warily, and I had the impression these spooks knew they were in the presence of a master of the snarky remark and were itching for the chance to take me on.

Letting down an audience isn't my style; for once I allowed the lady to have the last word. I thanked everyone for their explanations and, as I drifted away, realized my morale had ratcheted up a notch or two. Knowing I could've lathered on the hooey but restrained myself was sort of cool. Besides, many things about the rebel forces lifted my mood, from their plucky attitudes, handmade uniforms and quirky ways of carrying their weapons to their flowing beards, bare feet and motorcycles.

Motorcycles?

At the end of the procession, the first bikers passed above the treetops. I studied their faces and, as the leading riders pulled away, saw *Heck's Angels* stitched on the backs of their leather jackets. If any rebels questioned having motorcycles join their formation to commemorate some great rout, they had the good sense not to bring it up. The boys in gray didn't need to pick another quarrel they couldn't win.

I was about to set my astral tracks toward Shockoe Bottom for a quick visit to my favorite diner before the St. Sears group got there when a tiny hand appeared over the shoulder of Red Max. The biker chief's machine pulled beside me, and Fred-As jumped off and glided gracefully toward me.

"Just the spook I was looking for," he said.

"You missed your chance to lob a brick in my direction at Margie's." I regretted my words as soon as they bumbled out of my mouth. Fred-As hadn't joined the great let's-straighten-out-Ralph session. Why give him a bad night?

The little guy took my grumpy mood with a nod that acknowledged hearing me, while letting me know that he wasn't going to play the game of more-sour-than-thou.

"We never did get around to setting up your next appointment with Red Max," he said.

"I'm still waiting for my schedule to open up," I said, struggling against my snarky instincts.

"It's your decision." Fred-As glided back to the motorcycle with the ease of a floating dandelion puff.

"You must be quite the dancer," I said.

Fred-As froze in midglide. His smile disappeared faster than a spook specterizing in a flashlight store. "Was I dancing?"

"I can't think of another word for it. What with your feet skidding like this, and your arms waving like that."

"Dear me." Fred-As peeked at his Heck's Angels friends. Red Max was going down the line, saying a few words to some bikers, shaking his fist at others.

A big hunk of obviosity rose up and hit me between the eyes. What was a spook as gentle and mild mannered as Fred-As doing around the likes of Red Max? Or any of those posthumous hulks? Fred-As had more in common with Darleen; in fact, I could see them starting the afterlife's first quilting society.

"What does Red Max think about dancing?"

"He says it's a symptom. That once I do a proper spreadsheet, I'll realize what I'm trying to dance away from and get serious about my recovery."

"A spreadsheet, huh?" I said, wondering whether Fred-As could come up with a single bad action or thoughtless remark to enter into his inventory of misdeeds.

"He's pretty strict on that subject." Fred-As glanced toward the biker boss.

"There's a lot of that going around."

Fred-As climbed onto the seat behind Red Max and soon Heck's Angels disappeared into the night sky, leaving me with an overpowering urge to go back to Libby Hill, pour myself into the nearest coffeepot and stay there for a month.

All my friends and now my newest acquaintance on the astral plane had abandoned me to the radios and jukeboxes that wanted to come out and play. As Fred-As and his biker buddies disappeared with a thunderclap, I wanted nothing more from existence than someone who cared about my slippery hold on paranormality.

Glancing over the parade's onlookers, I didn't see a single familiar face. Faster than a gnat with indigestion, I left Monument Avenue and transported myself to the River City Diner.

THIS BEING THE time midway between dinner and the arrival of the dating set, Sunshiners were scarce at the restaurant's tables and booths, and not a single spook in recovery hovered over the sundaes and milk shakes because the best 12-step meetings were still underway.

That left the newbies.

If you worry how you're going to keep busy in eternity, Cal likes to say, *you haven't spent enough time talking to newbies.*

Several of Forever's newest residents were scavenging their way through the booths and tables, fired up by the notion that table manners didn't apply to them anymore. They were spooks, Halloween was coming, and they were supposed to be outrageous, or so they foolishly thought.

One poor spook sat by himself on the edge of the crowd. He'd gotten far enough into the spirit of things to put on an ectoplasmic mask, although his disguise was basically a blindfold with spaces for the eyes. Still, he was a newbie, struggling with the ways of the hereafter, and his mask, being of ectoplasm, was cycling into and out of existence, and when it disappeared from his face, the mask was momentarily replaced by a feathered boa, draped over his nose and cheeks.

"Mind if I take a seat?" I asked.

You'd think a trumpet just blasted in his ear. He must still be working out the details of what he could see and hear on the physical plane, and what existed only in a spectral dimension.

"Sure," he stammered. "I mean, I don't mind. Why don't you sit . . . er . . . squat . . . er . . ."

"How about I park my astrals near this chair?" I offered.

"That would be fine."

I floated into an approximately sitting position. "My name's Ralph. What's yours?"

"Jimmy."

Freckles were splashed across Jimmy's cheeks and over his nose. His eyes—when they weren't obscured by the mask that was sometimes a feathered boa—were sort of green with traces of gray and blue. Spectral manifestations in the hereafter, like spectral names, weren't necessarily related to anything in a first life, but I could easily picture Jimmy ambling across a pasture with a blade of grass in his teeth.

I gave him an encouraging smile. "I'll bet, right about now, you're wondering what you're doing here."

Jimmy smile back. "Nope. Not a lot's made sense since I woke up in this place a couple hours ago. But I don't have any problems figuring out the *why* and the *what next*."

I hadn't the moxie at the moment stuff to point out that he had many nights of recovery ahead of him before he could even start to see the rough shape of the wrongs he'd committed in the physical world that he now must fix.

"Glad to hear you've figured it out," I said, anyway.

"I must have been the worst tipper in Kenosha County," he whispered confidentially. "If you know that part of Wisconsin, you know that's saying a lot. I used to think it was cute to leave a nickel tip under my plate. And if anyone accused me of being cheap, I'd take it back and slip a dime under there."

I swallowed down the little speech I'd been putting together as he talked, the one about how it was only paranormal for the details of his previous existence to be sketchy long after a newbie has entered happily-ever-after.

Jimmy kept going with a full head of steam, as it were. "So, I figured I'd stop in the first restaurant I ran across. See what I can do that'd help the staff."

"You wanna be helpful? Try cleaning up that mess on the table in the corner."

Those last sentences came from a middle-aged waitress who stopped at our table, fixed her eyes squarely on Jimmy and planted her fists on her waist. She had the attitude of a woman who wasn't opposed to dishing out the occasional slap if that would open a pathway to understanding.

Jimmy looked up at her—this actual Breather, who was talking to him and expecting an answer—and said, "Wha, wha, wha."

The waitress dug her fists further into her waist. "Just what I expected from a spook. All lip and no action."

Jimmy looked at me, blinked and, as befits a newbie, disappeared in a confused *foop.*

Mrs. Pellywanger—for that was the name of the waitress who could stick her nose into the astral plane whenever she liked—shook her head and walked away, studying me the whole time so there'd be no misunderstanding to whom the sad shaking of her head was directed.

If Sophie exists to prove that not all twofers are helpful to spooks, then Mrs. Pelly exists to prove that not all twofers were helpful to themselves.

She had crossed paths with most of spectral Richmond when she befriended a spook who thought the afterlife would be improved if he were in charge. Then she tried to peddle herself as a mind reader during a search for

Blackbeard's hidden treasure. Margie had helped Mrs. Pelly get the waitress job to pay her bills. But I didn't give up chocolate and pecan pie so that a semicompetent twofer could make fun of my friends.

I followed her to the swinging doors of the kitchen. Surely, I could think of something appropriately barbed that didn't violate my no-sassiness pledge to Cal. The kitchen lights stung my eyes and rattled the roots of my teeth. But I'd take a few photons if that's what it cost to set Mrs. Pelly straight.

Imagine my surprise when a shiny aluminum box swaggered under the swinging doors. This toaster moved with an attitude that seemed gutsy, even though the closest it came to having guts were its heating coils. Its electrical cord flicked from side to side like a lasso in search of lunch, and its control knobs glinted as though they took my measure and found me wanting.

I backed away from the kitchen and the aluminum buckaroo. "Catch you later," I told the toaster, just to let the little fella know that I wasn't afraid of any household appliance.

The electrical cord slashed out in my direction. I yelped like a startled Pekinese and stepped through the ceiling.

$\mathcal{N}$ineteen
CHAPTER

$\mathcal{I}$ left the diner in such a hurry I was threading my way through the asteroid belt before I knew it. On any other night, I might have settled on the nearest rock to watch the earth from a safe distance. But was it really safe? How could I be sure a piece of space junk stamped *Made in USA* wouldn't zip over to pick a fight? Or the spectral residue of a life-form no one on earth will ever be advanced enough to know would stop by to swap tips on the stock market?

Besides, even from millions of miles in space, spooks still can't see stars, although we do okay with planets, meteors, comets and the odd satellite, none of which are terribly interesting after a while. It's the been-there-done-that-refused-to-buy-a-shirt attitude of a veteran traveler.

So, I went where I often go during times of trial. To the ocean. Or, more specifically, to a spot off the Virginia coast, where the lights from the cities look like cotton balls on the horizon, and the jet stream is invigorating.

No sooner had I relaxed in the stratosphere than a voice joined me: "Then upon the velvet sinking, I betook myself to linking, / Fancy unto fancy."

I spun around; my eyes tore through the darkness. For those of us impervious to wind, temperature and vertigo, 35,000 feet should be a quiet hideaway. Directly overhead was Edgar Allan Poe, twirling a silver-headed cane.

"Say what you came for, then leave," I said.

"I do apologize for this intrusion." The poet bowed. "But I just delivered my message. Shall I repeat it?"

"Give me the executive summary."

"*Executive summary*? What a novel concept. And whose execution should I summarize?"

I pointed a finger at him, disappointed at myself that it wasn't loaded. "One word. That's all I'll take from you."

"I've always regarded myself most adept at concision, yet—"

"And don't pretend you don't enjoy teasing me about the things I haven't learned yet."

Edgar A- gave a somber nod. "My, we are opening the door rather wide, aren't we?"

"One word," I repeated.

Perhaps I should give Poe credit for being one of the few spooks of my acquaintance who didn't show up at the intersection at Margie's, but I wasn't in a generous mood.

Edgar A- tapped the cane's silver head against his lips. "If I had to summarize my aforesaid insight for a busy executioner, I think that would leave us with *linking.*"

"*Linking.* Can you offer a little more information?"

"Of course, I could, old chap. But that would violate your one-word dictum."

"We can't let that happen," I said.

"It will be a struggle, yet I will do my utmost to control myself," Edgar A- replied. "Following your most . . . ah . . . interesting example of restraint."

Long after Poe swooped down to the ocean with his long black coat flung out like the wings of a bat, I bided my time on the jet stream, too preoccupied now to take advantage of the area's amenities. Though Edgar A- may have the appeal of a tub of soiled diapers, I've learned to take seriously his veiled observations and heavily draped suggestions. Not that I necessarily trust his honesty. Put it down to the old boy's vanity: a brilliant spook such as himself wouldn't stoop to lie in order to be sneaky.

Linking, linking. What would link a radio, a jukebox, a lunar lander and now a toaster? All man-made, of course, which doesn't help much. Although, looking on the bright side, it clearly disqualifies pumpkins.

EVENTUALLY, I SAW the sun creep westward over the Atlantic and knew if I loafed much longer on this spot, I'd be a former spook.

Faster than you can say *Fried Ectoplasm*, I was back at a tree-lined street where I entered the gray duplex through the roof and went directly to James William's room on the second floor. As happened yesterday, I found Petey stretched beside the sleeping boy, chin nestled between her paws and eyes focused on the dresser against the wall where a small handheld vacuum cleaner lurked in the shadows. Petey was prepared to hurl her pudgy little body at the machine at the first sign of danger.

Sitting next to Petey on the open air was Gilda, one leg crossed over the other, with both sets of toes twitching, restrained from walking to, over and through me only by grim self-control.

She was in emotional lockdown. Nothing except her toes moved. Her gaze latched onto my collarbone. Everything about her screamed that she couldn't care less about me, that only her Gothic discipline kept her from nodding off and turning into a puddle of ectoplasm where she sat.

"You didn't have to wait up for me," I said.

"You're right, I didn't." The toe of her right leg jerked from side to side. "But I was curious."

"About how badly I feel because all my friends turned against me at that intersection?"

"About what tall tale you'll come up with next. Even though you've made a bet with Cal, you can't stop yourself from making up wild stories."

"It's not a story if it's true," I mumbled.

I couldn't stop looking at the toes of her boots. How long had it been since I'd been chastised, ridiculed or scorned by an inanimate object? Somewhere in the interior regions where my small intestine used to be, a knot was forming.

"You think my boot is going to bite, don't you?" Gilda said.

"No, I'm don't."

"But you've noticed the way the bottom of that boot hangs down. Sort of like a jaw."

I squinted, studied her foot, and said, "Nah, can't say I do," when, in fact, I was sure the sole peeled away from the rest of her boot as I watched and a wide, dark, slavering mouth readjusted itself to accommodate an early morning snack that was about my size.

"Don't you want to take a closer look?" she asked.

"It's a nice boot. I can see it from here."

"Oh, I don't think so," Gilda said, playfully. And a playful Goth is a fearsome creature. "But if you don't want to take a closer look, what can I do?"

"Yeah. What can you do?"

Gilda smiled. "Well, I can always . . . take the boot . . . and give it . . . directly to . . . YOU!"

She thrust her leg at me, the one that may or may not actually have a boot with a mouth that had spittle cascading from broken teeth exposed by its dangling sole. I said, "Whoops," but in a confident and on-top-of-things way, and shot into the dining room and ricocheted for a while inside the old hobo coffeepot.

Gilda pressed close to the spout. "You're really afraid, aren't you? This isn't an act."

I pulled myself together and met her, nose-to-nose, outside the pot. "Does that mean you're willing to admit seeing unusual things, too?"

If Gilda could sigh, I'm sure she would have made a lovely sigh.

"We're dead, Ralph. We hang around cemeteries for the laughs, spend an hour each night helping other spirits to avoid the sunshine, and hope that some night, if we're very, very good, we'll disappear from here and wake up someplace that has a better quality of spooks. Other than that, I haven't noticed anything unusual lately."

"I'm glad we agree on something." I hoped Gilda noticed that my dignity was intact. And, if not intact, then freshly scrubbed and ironed.

Back in my coffeepot, I spent a couple hours sloshing around, sometimes as liquid ectoplasm, most of the time in a state of nervous excitement that reduced me to slush. Linking, linking, linking. Linking the toaster to the radio and the jukebox, but always getting stymied when I tried to fit the lunar lander into the pattern.

Setting the lunar lander aside for a minute—and even in reduced gravity, that was a sizeable hunk of metal to shove out of the way—not even I could come up with a reason for these geegaws to take an interest in me. Or anyone. What had I ever done to offend a jukebox? Besides dancing.

When I finally woke, the texture of the darkness told me the sun had been gone for hours, and I'd slept longer than usual. I heard James William and Mother rinsing dishes in the kitchen.

From habit, I glanced at the floor beneath my pot, where Petey often waited for me. Her tail waggled to welcome me to another night in the hereafter. I smiled, started to wave back, then found myself pressed against the ceiling on the other side of the room before I knew how I'd gotten there.

The figure on the floor beneath my bucket wasn't a beagle, but the handheld vacuum cleaner from James William's room, flapping an electrical cord instead of a tail.

From the kitchen came Mother's voice. "What I'm saying is that I appreciate your help cleaning the house. But when you use the small vacuum, you should put it back where it belongs when you're done."

"But I didn't touch it."

"Then who did?" Mother was calm, playful. "Your father? Petey?"

"Gilda," I whispered.

On cue, she appeared on the other side of the dining room table by the shelves with the antique coffeepots.

"You called?" From her expression, you'd think she never saw a spook loitering around a ceiling.

"Is this your trick?" I pointed at the vacuum cleaner on the floor.

"In case you haven't noticed, most spooks can count the number of tricksters who can manipulate physical objects on the thumbs of one hand."

"But is it?"

"No." A dark fire burst in her eyes, but just when I expected her to *poof* off with enough indignation to rattle the windows, she added: "When have you seen me move a grain of sand? I don't do levitation."

I pursed my lips and tapped my chin.

"What?" Gilda asked.

That got me to thinking . . . and linking . . . and ending up with a fact and a question. The fact was that Fast Eddie was the only Tosser I know well enough to be on his bad side, and I gotta believe him when he denies any involvement in my current problems with the material world. And the question was: What are the odds of a handheld vacuum cleaner deciding, all by its little electronic lonesome, to sneak up on a respectable member of the hereafter who is otherwise—at this moment anyway—minding his own business? Which is the same question that arises from Jack the Diamond's theory of car engines that pass along driving tips to each other.

If it's not Fast Eddie, and it's not self-propulsion, then it's gotta be someone else. Spook or Breather.

"You're up to something." Gilda made it an accusation.

"I'm wondering where I can get a little intelligence at this hour."

"Isn't it late for you to worry about self-improvement?" she said in her best poor-deluded-spook tone.

Don't you hate it when someone steals your best stuff before you can think of it?

FORTUNATELY, I WAS a couple blocks from a gentlespook who once had so much intelligence he needed an entire army to manage it.

I left the dining room in a hurry and hit the astral brakes a few blocks away where a figure in gray drifted near an obelisk. The memorial being to Confederate dead, a contingent of rebel spooks usually mingled around the monument, waiting to hear the bugle summon them one more time. This evening, however, the Colonel was alone.

I settled down near the officer. A moment passed, then another, then the Colonel flinched when he realized I was there.

"Sorry," I said.

I've seen the old vet in several posthumous engagements. Some specters in blue and gray thought fighting a war a hundred and fifty years ago wasn't a sufficient reason to play nicely together in the hereafter. The Colonel was the last spook I expected to go jittery.

"You see anything on your way here?" His voice was soft, his eye roving.

"Lots of buildings, parked cars, trees and"—the iron in the old soldier's glance brought me up short—"nothing of any military importance."

The Colonel smoothed his beard and mustache with stubby fingers twice the width of my own. His were the hands of a spook who, despite his courtly manners, had spent the formative years in his first life working a farm to put food on the family's table.

"What should I be looking for?" I asked.

The Colonel scanned a quarter of the horizon before answering, "Can't tell you exactly, something's in the wind. I picked it up a few nights ago. Nothing I can put my finger on, but I have patrols out now."

Or, in other words, the Colonel was on to something and he was gathering intelligence, too.

"Count me in."

"Are you any good with a weapon?" he asked.

Since he started his first life behind a horse-drawn plow, he wouldn't want to spend his second life staring at the back end of the likes of me, but I didn't earn the title of loosest cannon on two planes of existence by yielding to the obvious.

I tugged up my astral trousers. "I can do more damage with a well-aimed quip at close quarters than any spook can inflict with two bayonets and his teeth."

"I'll keep that in mind," the Colonel replied. "You never know when we'll be attacked by an unarmed enemy."

I shook my head, somberly. "Is nothing sacred?"

CHAPTER

Twenty

$\mathcal{T}$hroughout the city, in restaurants and diners, yogurt kiosks and pastry shops, delis and family kitchens, spooks were gathering for the ritual known as the meeting-before-the-meeting, a chance to catch up on the latest with friends, find out who was going later to which meeting, review the highlights of yesterday's get-together and, most importantly, see if this might be the night that the rules of interdimensional integrity would be waived to give all spooks a fighting chance to get a taste of Boston cream pie.

Me? I drifted along the banks of the river, hoping that the Colonel's patrols wouldn't discover an army of household appliances assembling in the suburbs or that none of my so-called friends who were involved in last night's intersection would take a stroll in my direction; wishing, too, that someone would come up with a logical explanation for portable vacuum cleaners wandering through a house or evidence that nothing on my current plane of existence could harm a little boy or a trusting beagle.

For the first time in months, I came upon Belle Island lying in the middle of the James. A pile of graying lumber sprawled across the sand on the downstream beach was all that remained of the old shack where I hid from the sunshine for weeks after my funeral. Nothing was left but splintered planks, jagged hunks of tar paper, and plywood that had the consistency of wet blankets. The old paint can that I used to pour my ectoplasm into before each dawn was gone.

I rose ten or fifteen feet to see if that bucket were nearby and saw instead a shadow scurry across the modernistic walkway that connected the island with downtown Richmond, a shadow that moved where no shadow should be.

I didn't die to be afraid of the dark. I slipped my hands into the pockets of my astral pants, scuffed a foot a few times through the air, then dropped faster than an agnostic's optimism as he's checking into the hereafter. Through the pile of lumber I went, then into the soggy ground, making a sharp left and tunneling through the sand parallel to the river bank, until I emerged beside a concrete pylon supporting the walkway.

"I thought we'd agreed," I began, my mouth coming online while my eyes were still figuring out exactly what I was seeing, "that this Halloween would be a *booga-booga*-free zone."

Gilda turned to me, yawning. "I was afraid the vacuum cleaner might have ambushed you before I could help fight it off."

"It's not me you should worry about. It's Petey and the boy."

"I can't see them getting sucked into that little dust bag."

She was halfway to the beach by the time I asked, "Where's *the ghostly hand of friendship?*" which stopped her in her tracks, although I'll never know whether it was because of the earnestness in my voice or the fact that I was stooping to quote from the program's literature.

"We've been over this a million times," she said.

I scratched my chin. "Let's see. Convert one million in Gothic math to standard math." I jabbed a finger in the air as though operating a pocket calculator. "Carry the eight, divide by twenty-seven, round to nearest ten-thousandths. And that totals . . . approximately . . . twice."

"Try multiplying the spooks who'll listen to you by the spooks who care," she snapped. "See if you can get a number larger than zero."

Tossing a glare over her shoulder that would send a more vulnerable specter to the nearest mortuary to look into reburial plans, she reversed course and slid toward the shoreline. I left the island. *Poof.* And respecterized—*Poof*—in the middle of the walkway to block her path back to the city.

Gilda was close enough to brush an eyelash across my cheek. Tiny jets of ectoplasm steamed from her ears. A dark fire blazed in her eyes that reminded me of a toaster flicking its power cord. And I realized it was late for me to develop self-destructive urges.

I held up my hands. "Anything you say. Anything. I'll even shut up. But you've got to believe me. If one more gadget tries to creep up on me, I don't know what I'll do."

The look I got from Gilda was exactly the expression I expected to receive when I first arrived in the hereafter, courtesy of a white-bearded geezer who should have been there to make sad, *tsking* noises as his finger swept across a thick, leather-bound book.

"Last chance," she said. "But it's going to cost you. Big time."

WORD AROUND THE cemetery was that Edgar Allan Poe had volunteered to serve as technical advisor for the fun house that the Alpha Delta Phi fraternity runs this time of year in a deserted store downtown. So, with Gilda's deal ringing in my astral ears, I zipped over to the inaptly named fun house on the street aptly numbered 5th.

Gliding through the door, I was greeted by enough cottony air to choke an Easter bunny. Since the fraternity was likely to heighten the hokum by bringing along an authentic disinterred resident of one of the local cemeteries, I went cautiously through the foggy rooms. One misstep could put me inside some poor spook's casket, and I'd be stuck with a roommate forever.

I came upon frat brothers slathering greenish-yellow paint on plywood walls. Leaning against a corner was a papier-mâché manikin with fangs approaching the dimensions of elephant tusks, which I'm sure will be quite terrifying once the gent receives a proper pair of pants.

In the middle of the next room, frat brothers laid synthetic turf over a mound of soiled mattresses, discarded paper cups, several hundred crushed beer cans, and enough plastic containers to start a fast-food restaurant. Other brothers set white crosses through holes cut in the artificial turf, their arms nailed at nightmarish angles. That's the crosses' arms, not the frat brothers' arms, although a universe with a stronger commitment to justice would give the frat boys a rougher time.

When I reached the third room, the fog was so thick I couldn't swear that the nose on my face was actually mine. Shadows moved through the mist. Not monster-sized shadows, but the bug-sized version. Creeping and squirming and whirling in the haze.

About the time I realized the wriggling shadows were letters, a murmurous babble disturbed the sepulchral air.

"*Veronica, thy beauty is to me as* . . . Nope, can't say that. Too derivative. And there's the issue of confidentiality. Although who ever heard of privacy standing in the way of art?"

I slid closer.

"*I saw thee on thy wedding day when* . . . No, no, derivative again. Confoundations! Why did I use my best material so early?"

Lines and phrases and scratched-out words careened past me in the fog.

"*Quoth the lady, Hithermore.* Now that's more like it. Let's scratch out *lady* and insert *spookette. Hithermore, hithermore.* It sort of grows on you, doesn't it?"

"Like a fungus," I answered.

After edging a few more careful inches through the gloom, I stood beside Edgar Allan Poe, an ectoplasmic quill clenched in one hand, the other pressed in creative cogitation to his brow. We were in a bubble of clear air, thanks to the vents of the fog-making machine on the floor being angled to blow mist to the rooms in front and back.

He gave me a look that would have knocked a lesser spook into the street. "Unless you've got a rhyme for *Veronica*, you can leave now."

"Harmonica."

"Hmm." Poe's wrist paused in the middle of a dismissive flick. "I believe I can work with that."

"But, first you've got to do something for me."

"And my incentive for doing that, especially considering that we've not agreed to any bargain, is——"

"I'll won't tell anyone that I've given you a tip on rhymes."

"Preposterous beyond belief," Edgar A- sniffed. "Who would ever believe that?"

"Perhaps I could say Jingle Jim is editing your stuff."

"But that would be a falsehood."

I don't usually do coy smiles, but I tried one on for size. "Not if I suggest to Jingle Jim that your work could use some help. Just a touch-up here and there."

"Name your price."

The quill mostly disappeared from Poe's fingers. Mostly, but not entirely. The vaporous trace of something else remained. A feather, a scrap of paper, perhaps a straight-edged razor?

"Ease up on spooks in your blog," I raised a hand before his outburst could detonate. "I'm not censoring you. Just ease up. Remember that dead people have feelings, too."

Edgar A- gave me a slantwise appraisal. "So those rumors are true. Cal is making you forsake your incendiary ways."

"Don't get your hopes up. It's just temporary."

"Whether temporary or permanent, the censor's chilled hand now falls on the afterlife."

"It's not a hand. It's barely a finger."

Poe shot me a look. "You're too easy."

ONE OF THE problems of mending fences is that you can't rush off in a snit afterwards. For the sake of spectral harmony, I had to look interested as Poe showed me his collection of past blogs and his system for storing his material, both incoming messages from spooks with relationship problems and his own gems of advice, in a geothermal vent. Hence, the origin of the soon-to-be-popular phrase about blogs no longer needing to be preserved on computer hard drives once they're *stored in the dirt*.

By the time I arrived at the meeting on Church Hill, enthused with the thrill of achieving a genuinely selfless good deed for all spooks nervous about Poe's blogs (and overlooking the fact that I agreed to this intervention only because Gilda would be on the lookout for knickknacks from the physical plane stalking me), the halftime break was ending and spooks drifted back inside for the final thirty minutes.

"Hank, hold up," I called.

Hank paused at the foot of the steps to the basement meeting room. Rumor has it that they didn't have *cool* in the hereafter until Hank checked in, but the closer I got, the more obvious it was that Hank was uncomfortable.

"You're the last one I expect to worry about getting a bad mark from Cal for being tardy," I said.

The pigtail on the back of his head stood a little straighter. "Cal's not the one I'm worried about."

"Well, don't worry about me. I'm fine. I just want you to know that I'm not carrying a grudge for you being at that intersection last night. I barely noticed you were there."

"Glad to hear that." Hank gave a halfhearted thumbs-up—more a thumbs-sloped gesture, actually—before slipping through the door.

"If you should see any household appliances hanging around, I'd appreciate—"

But Hank didn't hear me. I scooted after him into the meeting.

I DON'T CLAIM psychic powers, but I couldn't miss the single thought thundering in every noggin in the room: *What's he doing here?*

Rosetta leaned forward above her seat, preparing to protect grammar, deportment and table manners from the imminent danger that follows me everywhere. Cal noted my arrival with a subtle rearrangement of his crossed arms that sent shock waves through the newbies along the walls. Hank couldn't suppress a twinkle in his astral eye, which I attribute to his abiding respect for anyone who can unsettle Rosetta and Cal.

Rosetta called the meeting to order and promptly turned the program over to Roger, who was leading tonight.

Although I didn't recognize the first spook who shared, I caught myself smiling at the steady rhythms and homey undertones as he talked about his *perplexities, tremors and uncertainties*, knowing that every spook in the room had experienced the same moments of confusion and vulnerability, including myself.

Sitting next to Cal was Gilda. I gave her a surreptitious nod of my head. Mission accomplished: I'd gotten to Poe. Gilda replied with a blank stare.

Fast Eddie couldn't take his eyes off the coffeepot in the back of the room, the same pot from which I had once tricked him into levitating a few coffee beans, knowing that poltergeist activity qualifies as a *stumblie*. Cal had sent Fast Eddie for another try at the first step in his recovery, making Fast Eddie, technically, a newbie. And he dared to blame me for setting up that situation, as though anyone had ever caught me following my own advice.

In the darkest corner of the room, Veronica was rooted like a stalagmite. She gave me the kind of look next to which molten lava is a stream of ice water, unaware of my contribution—shall we say, my *harmonic* contribution—to Edgar Allan Poe's body of work, an insight I'll be happy to share with the entire afterworld after I'd outlasted my pledge to Cal to avoid all gags and snarky comments until after Halloween.

Then there was Gwendolyn, decked out in a slouch-brimmed fedora, a trench coat with the collar turned up, and the only unlit cigar stub on this side of the Great Divide. He swept his gaze over the room, and I made a mental note to thank him for protecting me from attack by the rest of the St. Sears group in Margie's waiting room. One peek at Darleen, however, and I erased that mental note. It was more likely Gwendolyn thought he was protecting everyone else from me.

Most of the regulars scrunched as low as they dared in their seats, not knowing which direction the ectoplasm was going to fly, but certain that liftoff was moments away. The newbies along the walls, being newbies, bumped into each other like balloons in front of a fan.

And I noticed, pressed against the wall on the far side of the room, a folding table with a thirty-cup coffeemaker, its beady red buttons staring holes into my ectoplasm.

Twenty-one
CHAPTER

Speechless, ignored, vilified and neglected, a prophet without honor in his homeland, a legend of the afterlife unrecognized in his own time, a crusader on a bleak and windswept moor, forlorn and storm-wracked, unappreciated by the spooks who know me best, I slumped into my gray metal chair as the room emptied after the meeting.

Gilda, from whom I'd expect at least a dollop of courtesy because of the promise of restraint I'd squeezed from Edgar A-, was the first to leave.

Specters shouted plans for the meeting-after-the-meeting or buttonholed newbies to extend the ghostly hand of recovery to decedents who still had the smell of lilies in their hair. Meanwhile, unbeknownst to the madding crowd, a large coffeepot on the table by the door turned to get a better look at me.

No way was I seeing an accident of the light, a quirk of the shadows or the phantoms inside my head. With a steady, deliberate rotation, the pot did a quarter turn until its nozzle pointed squarely between my eyes. Leaning slightly to the left, then to the right, slowly, steadily, deliberately, it wobbled toward me.

I did a *Beam-Me-Up-Scotty* that brought me in a trillionth of an instant to our favorite diner in Shockoe Bottom where there was safety in numbers, openness, and, come to think of it, a toaster in the kitchen that had once tried to lasso me with its electrical cord. I (*poof*) settled underneath an empty table.

Legs encased in support hose with purple jogging shoes soon shuffled past, and I poked my head up through the Formica.

"Mrs. Pelly, Mrs. Pelly. I need to talk to you. Down here."

Bitter experience had taught Mrs. Pellywanger, the owner of the support

118

hose, the shoes and the shuffle, that even Breathers who believe in communicating with the spiritual plane don't give big tips to waitresses who seem to talk to themselves a lot. So she tilted the tray in her hands with a resigned expression, silverware clattered to the floor and as she knelt, I drifted under the table again.

"You used to work at the state fair," I said. "You've seen people who can move things without touching them. Right?"

"I've seen acts where people look like they're moving things."

"When's the last time you saw the real deal? Someone who doesn't have hidden strings or magnets."

"That's easy." Mrs. Pelly scooped up forks and spoons, set them on her tray, then spilled the contents back on the floor to continue the discussion. "Never. They all had tricks."

An idea struggled to get comfortable in my head. "What can you tell me about the toaster in your kitchen? Has anyone on the staff been taking an interest in it?"

"You mean, besides using it to burn bread?"

"Is someone trying to communicate with it? Be its buddy. Mentor it."

Mrs. Pelly slammed the tray on the floor. Knives and forks skedaddled across the tiles. She waved a finger at me. How empty my afterlife has been lately owing to an absence of fingers flicking under my nose.

Her eyes and lips tightened, and I'm sure even her nostrils squeezed together as she said, "I've been warned about you. And now you'd better be warned about me."

I bit my lower lip.

"If you don't behave, Buster," she whispered, "I'm going to fix your wagon."

"Actually, my name's Ralph, not Buster. And I don't have a wagon to fix."

"Don't be too sure of that," she said.

In silence, she pulled herself off her knees, kicked the most visible silverware under tables and chairs and tottered to the kitchen.

I had been well and truly put in my place.

NOT LONG AFTERWARDS, I respecterized outside the brownstone in Carytown with the neon *'syck Advisor* sign in the window.

Margie sat on the outside steps, while Scoop Bristow, attired in a tweed blazer and ill-fitting black trousers, leaned toward her on the sidewalk. A strange humming filled the air. Late in the season for cicadas, I thought. Then I saw Margie's half-shy, half-hopeful smile and realized I was close to a cloud of free-ranging hormones.

"Ah, come on, Margie," I said. "There's more important things to think about."

"Then you should think about them," she said, never taking her eyes off Bristow.

"You think so?" Scoop replied. His expression was vulnerable, too young for his face. "I mean, trying to write a novel is a huge commitment."

"Are you afraid of commitments?" she asked.

Her gaze never wavered from the reporter, but when I started to say that *commitment* was a four-letter word that shouldn't be used in polite society, the fingers on Margie's right hand, which were tucked behind her left elbow, flicked two, three, four times to the side.

I said, "Okay, I understand," and her fingers stopped twitching.

I drifted upstairs, through the door, past the waiting room and down the hall. Sophie had a customer in her consulting room and, wonder of wonders, Soph stayed in her chair without a seat belt, the customer wasn't shouting, and a spook who had taken a stance on the side of the table, midway between Soph and the customer, wasn't releasing ectoplasmic steam from her ears.

"This is going to be so neat," the spook told me. She had the form of a young woman.

I nodded at the old man in the chair. "Is this your father?"

The spook giggled. "Charles is my husband. Isn't it fun to be whatever age you feel like?"

I gave her a polite smile, unwilling to spoil her night by pointing out that if that was always true she'd be chatting with a five-year-old.

Her enthusiasm was infectious. "I've been floating around the computers that run the lottery. The lottery where you pick numbers and buy a ticket at the 7-Eleven. My Charles always buys five tickets every Tuesday."

"And you know what the winning number's going to be."

"Right."

"And you'll tell Sophie the magic number."

"Right again."

"And Sophie's going to relay the number to your husband."

"Bingo!"

"And you're going to do all this in one afterlife."

"What's that? What are you saying?"

For once, my habit of figuring out what I ought to say after I've spoken didn't work to my advantage. Nor was I being compassionate for the poor spook who thought she'd found a way to give her hubby a parting gift.

As I searched for a way to help this specter prepare for a very long night, without demoralizing her so badly that she might crawl inside the bulb of the nearest streetlight and end it all, Sophie wrapped up her study of the crystal ball.

"I see games of chance. I see numbers that cannot fail you." Sophie squinted into the glistening orb while speaking to Charles. "I see a winning number. A series of winning numbers, starting with a seven. And the number one, then another one. No, that's the number eleven."

The spook hurried to Sophie's side. "No, dear. That's not actually what I said. Seven-Eleven is a store. A store."

Sophie raised a hand. Three dozen bracelets swept to her elbow in a clattering wave. "Wait, there is more. Another lucky number. It's . . . four. Seven, eleven and four."

"Store. I distinctly said *store*. Store." The spook was inches from Sophie's left ear. I expected to see apricot brandy spray out the other side of the old psychic's head.

Sophie lifted her hand, and enough bracelets to supply the metal for a tractor-trailer clinked their way down her arm. "I erred. You must forgive me. The astral frequencies are highly irregular tonight. There are two fours. Seven, eleven, and forty-four."

From there, the situation deteriorated. The spook, sensing a missed windfall for her spouse, tried to get Sophie to tell Charles not to go. And Sophie, with her gift for seizing the wrong part of every loose end, exhorted the poor man to go immediately, not to hold back, to place his faith and confidence in the advice coming to him from beyond the mortal veil.

For once, watching Sophie unravel wasn't entertaining.

I DRIFTED THROUGH the ceiling until I reached a room with legal files packed in neatly labeled boxes and stopped at a wall with boarded-up windows and a water stain on the wallpaper.

"Willbard, we need to talk."

Silence.

"I know you're in there."

More silence, although of a stubborn variety.

"Willbard, you're going to have to talk to me at some point."

That got a reaction: "Willbard doesn't think so."

Part of me wanted to transform myself into a slavering, red-eyed, saliva-dripping monster and roar at Willbard my displeasure that she hadn't been able to frighten Sophie away from the apricot brandy. A more coherent part of me recognized that I'd never beat Willbard at her own game.

"Did you show yourself to Sophie?"

"Yes."

"And you were your loveable self? Show me what you looked like?"

Willbard showed me. The red-eyed, saliva-dripping monster I thought about becoming a few moment ago would have run whining from the room if it saw the beast from the cataclysm that Willbard transformed herself into.

I took a slow gulp that went all the way to my toes. "What did Soph say to that?"

"She giggled." Willbard shrank back into wall.

Sometimes the afterlife can be so insensitive.

PERHAPS IF I'D been less preoccupied with my own fears about toasters and vacuum cleaners, I'd've given Willbard the old put-your-head-down-and-keep-climbing-upward speech. Unfortunately, hostile home gadgets had become part of my Forever, and I couldn't be critical of another spook who was terrified of giggling drunks.

I slipped out of the third-floor storage space and back down to the waiting room. Through the bay window, I saw Margie and Bristow talking outside, only now the reporter had joined Margie on the stoop and their faces had grown more solemn, their gestures less twitchy.

Less twitchy. Perhaps that should be my goal for the afterlife. I should enlist in Heck's Angels and go roaring through the second plane of existence until Gabriel blows his horn or my number comes up in the lottery run by the reincarnation bureau or my ectoplasm fades away under the assault of traffic lights, streetlamps, and the occasional rays of the sun.

"What's the matter, Godie? Having trouble getting the James River to part on cue?"

The voice from the world's ugliest vase made me imagine how a sleek panther would sound if it ever thought of something to say.

"You know, Letitia, I'm not really a god."

"That's okay, Ralph. I'm not really dead."

I glanced from the lovey-dovey session outside. "You're not? Then what are you doing in there?"

"Why don't you climb into this vase and find out."

"But your ashes were mixed with the clay that made that vase."

"Yep."

"That means your vase is a casket."

"Of sorts," Letitia qualified.

"And any spook who gets in another's casket is stuck there forever."

"And your point is?"

I closed my eyes and tried to imagine being close to Letitia as the sun shuts down operations and gravity stops pulling itself together.

"What do you say, Godie?" Letitia purred.

"I don't think that's going to happen."

The world's ugliest vase rattled, and I was—to use an unfortunate phrase—spooked. My head was halfway through the ceiling before I realized it was only Letitia registering her unfamiliarity with rejection.

Other than that, don't look to me for explanations. I'm still trying to figure out what's paranormal and what's just weird.

Twenty-two

CHAPTER

I slunk out the back of Margie's place, circled wide over the river, came back to Shockoe Bottom and found a nearly empty booth in the back of the River City Diner. The only thing that kept the booth from being entirely empty was Gwendolyn, who left his usual stool up front to join me.

"What's up?" I said, displaying my usual gift for setting spooks at ease.

"Nothing much. Hanging around, waiting for the attack of the killer can openers."

"That's toasters."

Gwendolyn shook his head, his stogie sagged with disappointment. "This isn't about gadgets, my friend. It's about you."

"Define *about*."

"Think of a bull's-eye with your face on it."

"I'm trying to forget toasters."

Gwendolyn adjusted his fedora. "What about checking out landing sites on the moon? Do you think that's a healthy way to spend your afterlife?"

My thoughts flashed back to my talk with Red Max. My littlest problem was linked to my biggest problem. And, when Red Max was talking, there seemed to be an obvious connection between sneaky appliances and my search to understand why I'd been sidelined to this loony farm in the hereafter.

"Could you rephrase that question?" I asked.

"Try this." Gwendolyn leaned closer, and I found myself wondering if his fedora was making a face at me. "What have you done lately for *the poor, still-suffering spook?*"

"I haven't added to his misery. Doesn't that count?"

"Maybe, but only as long as it brings you nearer to transcendence."

I glanced at the blender on the bar and the cash register by the door. They were edging closer. I'm sure they were. I looked at Gwendolyn. I was more likely to get sympathy from the blender and the cash register.

"I need some air."

NO SOONER HAD I left the diner and glided onto the empty sidewalk than I was surrounded by things. They were everywhere. Perhaps, not as deadly as household appliances and spacecraft, but they were still *things*. Every garbage can had a lid waiting to snap down on unwary fingers. Each automobile and truck came with a grill that could take a car-sized bite from a spook's ectoplasm. Even the fire hydrant squatting so peacefully on the corner could do something despicable once it realized I was in the area.

Down the block, a car pulled to the curb as a door opened at the neighborhood's newest nightspot for the campus-set, flooding the street with a lively melody. A young woman scurried to the car, followed by the lean, stately, astral figure of Veronica.

As a car door swung open, the young woman stepped inside. Veronica glided through the rear door, and casting a jaundiced eye at the fire hydrant on the corner, which may or may not be inching closer, I followed Veronica into the backseat.

"Go away," she snapped. "Haven't you done enough already?"

"I can do a whole lot more." I eyed her rock-like silhouette. "What are we talking about?"

Setting aside her indignation at me for the moment, she turned to the young man behind the wheel and whispered: "Wouldn't it be nice to go to the river tonight? Somewhere close to Boulevard Bridge?"

The man nodded. He pulled away from the sidewalk, made a U-turn, drove back to Main Street and turned toward downtown. The woman beside him shot the driver a glance that was a close replica of the look I'd gotten from Veronica.

"You've been drinking again," the passenger told the driver.

"I've been studying."

"You shouldn't drink when you study."

"What makes you so sure I've been drinking?"

"You're going the wrong way."

"I thought it'd be nice to take a look at the river."

"Why?"

Veronica moved her lips closer to the driver's ear. "You saw something by the bridge earlier. It reminded you of a present for her birthday. Maybe if you go back there, you'll remember that idea."

The driver winked at his passenger. "Shh, it's a secret for somebody's birthday next month. Don't let on that you know."

"I won't breathe a word," she said. "Not even to myself."

"Especially not to yourself," the driver said.

I sat back with a Cal-like crossing of my arms. *People whisperers* are always fun, although purists in Specters Anonymous are philosophically opposed to them. *First you start passing ideas to Breathers*, Mrs. Hannity has said, *before you know it, they're passing ideas to you. Then one day, they want to go to the beach and, without thinking about it, you find yourself slipping into a swimming suit.*

I glanced at Veronica.

"Don't go there," she said.

My head snapped back and whatever passed for my brain went swirling. Spooks don't read other spook's thoughts. Right?

The driver drove. His passenger tossed puzzled smiles in his direction. Veronica's chin stayed close to his shoulder, prepared to do her people-whispering thing if called upon. And I conjured up the memory of Veronica's stern visage glaring down at me in Margie's psychic parlor as every friend I had in the hereafter let me know what a disappointment I've been.

She may think that my tales about lunar landers and jukeboxes are part of an elaborate prank, but if she knew that I helped out spooks everywhere by muzzling Poe and his blog, she'd realize that I have a serious side. Somewhere.

We pulled into the small park at the base of the Boulevard Bridge, and the driver's dopey smile faded into confusion. He was miles from home with a girlfriend who kept asking where they were going, and now he didn't have a coherent idea as to what she was talking about or why he was here.

Veronica slipped through the door and I followed. A befuddled mist with no sense of direction crept from the river. Dawn had to be about an hour away.

I'd been shunned by the spooks in my favorite 12-step meeting and learned from Mrs. Pelly that looking for the cause of the mysteriously mobile household gadgets among the world of Sunshiners was —*Insensitivity Alert*—a dead end. On the other hand, I'd diverted Edgar A-'s attention from the foibles of his fellow specters. I needed another success to tip the scales in my favor and finish the night on a positive note.

"Have you ever found yourself bothered by things?" I asked Veronica.

She never took her eyes off the river. "I'm bothered by a thing right now."

"And what are you going to do?"

"I'm going to fix it. Then I'm going to find the skunk who's responsible and, faster than you can say, *Nevermore*, I'm going to fix him, too."

"I'd better be going," I said.

"No." Calculations flashed across Veronica's eyes faster than a freaked-out motherboard. "I want you to know what I've had to put up with."

"Why?"

Veronica's calculations ended with a nearly audible *ka-CHING*. She turned back to the river, and I decided, having died once and lacking any enthusiasm to find out if it were possible to repeat the experience in the hereafter, this would be a nice time to enjoy the view.

The fog grew thicker as it rose from the water and inched toward the shore. Veronica glided down the bank. Tiny, thin figures appeared in the cottony air. Stickmen, I thought, arranging themselves in rows like medieval infantry, massing for an attack. And I didn't need to see a declaration of war to understand who was their enemy.

"Be careful, Veronica. They can be treacherous."

"So can I."

She thrust a hand into the approaching wall of fog and twirled her arm. Currents swept through the mist, buffeting the stickmen—actually, letters and words and phrases that rode on the haze—pushing their neat rows into ragged ranks, growing in intensity until a tsunami pulsed through the fog and the neat rows were scrambled by blurred eddies.

Veronica was sabotaging Poe's new blog, his advice column for the lovelorn, which he was still writing despite our talk. Wasn't I clear? Had he spent so much time with his head in a sepulcher on two planes of existence that he didn't appreciate the sanctity of a promise?

Or was I being too harsh on the old wordsmith? "Shouldn't we find out what he's trying to say?"

"You're curious, are you? You really want to jump into a casket with him?"

"Perhaps in my next afterlife."

VERONICA WAS STILL slashing at Edgar Allan Poe's prose when I left. Maybe she'll have better luck than the editors who tangled with the poet during his first life.

Heading back to my bucket on Libby Hill, I realized that artistic disagreements didn't explain Veronica's anger at Edgar A-, especially not the intensity of her feelings. Poe had gotten to Veronica. The old boy had burrowed under her ectoplasm and struck the motherlode. He knew something about her. And she knew that he knew. And he didn't give a hoot.

Suddenly, the afterlife seemed . . . well . . . perkier.

Gilda was squatting beside Petey in the dining room when I arrived at our duplex. Petey's tail drummed against the floor, although Gilda didn't notice my arrival. I drifted beside her on the floor and joined in Petey's astral belly rub.

"Who do you think Veronica's boyfriend is?" I asked.

Gilda didn't look up. "What makes you think she has one?"

"She's determined to wipe out Poe's new blogs."

Gilda didn't trouble herself with a glimpse in my direction. "I thought you'd fixed him."

"So did this mortician in Baltimore."

Gilda leaned back, Petey looked up, patiently waiting for us to resume the massage.

"If Veronica has a boyfriend," Gilda continued, "I don't think she'd go to Poe for help."

I shuddered. "Can you imagine going to Edgar A- for anything?"

"You'd have to be an idiot to do that." She spoke with such finality, I knew it was time to drop the subject.

Petey's warm brown eyes flicked between our faces and I was startled to realize that Petey and Gilda had their own bond, not as strong as mine with Petey but a close relationship, nonetheless. Had Gilda been sneaking behind my back to give my favorite beagle belly rubs?

With her usual insight, Petey seemed to sense the drift of my thoughts, for she tried to nuzzle my wrist without actually touching me.

"Have you had any trouble lately with . . . stuff?" Gilda asked.

I did a quick survey of the dark room. "Yep. And now that you mention it, it's quiet here. Too quiet."

Gilda took up Petey's belly rub. "What do you think that means?"

"Why should it mean anything?" Which was a surprisingly profound notion to come rolling out of my mouth.

"Because none of us is here for the cuisine."

Twenty-three

CHAPTER

ike every good recovery sponsor, Cal preaches the value of *little-ism*, the belief that we spent so much of our first lives puffing ourselves up that it'll take an entire afterlife to deflate ourselves to the right proportions. We need to make ourselves little, hence, *little-ism*.

The implications, to use another insensitive term—and I should know, because my picture appears in the better dictionaries next to the word *insensitive*—are breathtaking.

Every spook I've ever met is brain dead, so there's no shortage of entities on my side of the Great Divide wringing every nuance out of *little-ism*. Rumors whispered by specters who venture into the noonday sun tell of galaxies of *little-ists* that can fit into the spaces between electrons.

I thought about checking out those stories as I slid into the hobo coffeepot on the wall, acutely aware that on the other side of the dining room table was another wall, and on the other side of that wall was a kitchen, and within the kitchen were cabinets and drawers and countertops crammed with all sorts of appliances, every one of which knew exactly where I was.

I had to distract myself to keep from going batty, and luckily, I didn't have to look far for a prime distraction: Veronica had a special friend. A special friend had Veronica.

Cal was the first candidate who came to mind, and wouldn't that be fun? A judgmental force meets a nonverbal object. But, given the vagaries of feelings, she'd be more likely to be enamored of someone radically different from herself. Which opened the field to nearly everyone on two planes of existence.

For as long as I could, I held onto my astral shape to keep tossing around the amazing notion of Veronica liking anyone, even though it drove me crazy to hear the buzzing and banging of photons on the other side of the pot's thin metal skin. I don't know how Breathers can hear themselves think with that racket going on.

Eventually, Petey's family shuffled into the kitchen to have their breakfasts, and I knew even the most rabid, specter-hating toaster would have to control its impulses with all those Breathers underfoot. I slipped gratefully into a puddle of ectoplasm.

MY LATE MORNING vigil entitled me to stay in my bucket until Rosetta convened the St. Sears group for its regular meeting, but I pulled myself together while the last direct rays from the sun were still packing their bags and trudging closer to California.

Although I wasn't sure what to do, I was determined not to be bullied any longer by household gadgets. If my afterlife ends at the hands . . . er . . . handles of an electronic can opener, I'll go down swinging.

Petey didn't expect me to be up this early: she was probably guarding the front door in case the mailman tried to sneak back at an unexpected hour, and Gilda was still in the art deco coffeemaker where she spent her daylight hours.

I shot through the ceiling, out the roof and got my bearings a hundred feet above the street. Cal should be a mile away by the river for his twilight inspection of the old buildings at Shockoe Slip, making certain nothing had been damaged by the daytime hustle and bustle. No spook became one of the preeminent sponsors in the afterlife by trusting in the stability of the status quo.

A silver glint flashed from the eastern edge of Libby Hill, where the ground fell away to Gillies Creek, and I was startled to see I'd been so out of touch during my daytime rest that I hadn't heard the thunderstorm that must have pounded the area. Only a first-class cloudburst could have pushed the little creek so quickly over its banks.

Another shimmer, and I pinpointed the source. Not a wavelet, nor a piece of flotsam. But a wandering ray of light reflected off the polished surface of a bayonet. I was looking down on an ocean of gray uniforms.

Officers waved their swords to rally their troops, sergeants rushed around in full-throated bellow, and privates congregated in backslapping groups to renew old acquaintances and swap stories about the officers and the sergeants.

I glided down to a lone spectral figure standing quietly to one side of the tumult.

"Good evening, Colonel," I said.

The Colonel acknowledged me with the slightest dip of his chin. The old rebel's uniform had a high, stiff collar and tired golden braids along the cuffs; his beard and mustache were meticulously trimmed; and his eyes had the gleam of an eager youth set in a face with wrinkles eroded by a century and a half of responsibility.

The old soldier never let his gaze drift from his troops.

"Looks like your boys are having trouble settling down tonight," I said.

"They didn't sign on to settle." The Colonel's voice was low and steady. "Once the dust starts to fly, they'll show what they're made of."

My eyes skimmed over the trees in the distance, the hills further beyond and the flatlands hugging the river. Anxiety snapped into full power, and this time I had something worth worrying about.

"Someone's coming? Who? Where?"

The old soldier fixed a look on me that was like a mother gazing at a fussy child. "That's the thing about enemies. They rarely send a printed invitation to battle. Sometimes, you're not even sure they're enemies."

"I don't suppose you could explain that."

"I could, but then you'd be inclined to pay even less attention."

Coming from anyone else, those words would have sent me into a tantrum. Spooks who've stood their ground when the ground was swept by hurtling steel and messy chunks of ectoplasm aren't going to flinch from any barb I toss in their direction.

So I nodded, clasped my hands behind my back and followed the Colonel's gaze to the milling, chattering mass of soldiery in the shadows of Libby Hill.

Here and there, platoons arranged themselves in rows and columns. A squadron of cavalry, one of the largest units in proper formation, moved slowly toward the northeastern flank of the assembly area, although, the hereafter not being what anyone would call horse country, the squadron lacked a certain dignity from the absence of saddles, bridles, reins, stirrups, saddle bags and, most significantly, horses.

I wasn't going to open my mouth even if a five-hundred-foot replica of Poe's raven sashayed across the field playing bagpipes.

In time, disorderly groups of specters shifted into recognizable military units arrayed, parade-style, across the floodplain. The Colonel turned to me. "We don't know who, what, where, why or how. But *when* is starting to solidify. It'll be soon. Something's in the wind."

"With everything you don't know, how can you deploy your forces?"

"I'll keep my eyes and ears open. And do the next left thing."

"*Left thing?*"

"Those with time for jabbering might call it *the next thing left to do.*"

The Colonel fixed me with a look that said he'd allow one more question and I ought to count myself lucky that on the eve of a great battle, he wasn't asking why I wasn't in uniform.

I chose my question carefully. "How do you know what's the next left thing?"

"Whatever's left that needs fixing."

AS HE DRIFTED among the gray uniforms spread across the field, the Colonel was greeted by cheers and hats waving on bayonets, and soon the men sorted themselves into regulation-sized columns and rows.

If it were anyone except the Colonel, I would have zipped into the field, planted myself directly in his path and asked whether his *something in the wind* might have an electrical cord attached to it.

But the calm authority in his gaze infused me with confidence. *Whatever's left for fixing.* I'd gone to the moon and to a posthumous analyst in hopes of finding clues to my transcendence. But had I tried to fix the things under my nose, the things that need fixing? Might that mean the next time I see a toaster swaggering through the shadows toward me, snapping its power cord like a whip, I should volunteer to help it find an electrical outlet?

Whatever needs fixing. The phrase rattled around in the portion of my head that used to hold a brain. Passing over Shockoe Bottom, I found myself drawn to the Poe museum. (*Note to reader: Spooks don't have a sixth sense. In post-mortality, we pick up the seventh, eighth and ninth senses, which are further from intuition and closer to hearing. Our hunches are more reliable than a psychic vibration, although they're adversely affected by crowds and thunderstorms.*)

I came down on a street corner opposite the small, low building appropriated for Poe's reputation and joined a lean figure draped head-to-toe in a dark ectoplasmic cloak and a hood that nearly covered his/her/its face.

Think of death waiting on the sidewalk for a taxi. Then take away the sickle, turn up the thrum of sinisterosity and you'll get a feel for how that gaunt figure must work a room.

"Have you come for Mr. Poe?" I asked, struggling to contain my hopefulness.

"I'm not sure he's inside? Do you know?"

The voice was familiar. Clipped and unhurried, with sharp edges on the consonants and vowels that snapped.

I peered under the cowl. "Veronica? Is that you in there?"

"Shh. You're going to give me away."

"How can you possibly say that?" I asked, meaning: *How does a spook who is a genuine people whisperer, able to communicate across different planes of existence, think that a Trappist monk standing on a corner in a major American city won't arouse suspicions?*

But, of course, that was it. Not the bit about the street corner or the Trappist monk. But the part about the people whisperer.

"I happen to know someone who knows Poe real well," I said, thinking quickly. "They go way back."

Veronica pushed the hood off her head. Whatever Poe was writing about her on the fog must be pretty juicy. I could scrape anxiety from her face with a butter knife.

"How far back do they go?" she asked.

"This was when he was struggling to get a grip on limericks."

Veronica's eyes went glassy. If she were still a Breather, we'd be looking for an ambulance and a jump start, but she said, "I don't see what that has to do with me."

Give a spook a rumor, and she has a rumor. But give a spook a twofer, then that spook can manufacture her own rumors. Throw in a fishing rod, and the twofer will have something to do with her hands while I'm working this out.

AFTER ASSURING VERONICA that I chatted practically every day with this friend of Poe—and omitting the bothersome detail that the person I had in mind was totally oblivious to most of our conversations—I led Veronica to a street in Carytown where *'syck Advisor* blinked in neon letters from a window, and dangling underneath were pieces of paper taped to the glass that added:

Also:

> *Romance Advisor*
> *Financial Advisor*
> *Interior Designer*
> *Gardener*
> *Babysitter*
> *Dog Walker*

Veronica's eyes hit the words *Romance Advisor*, and she exploded out of her monk's robe.

"I'm not going to sit still while another charlatan tries to tell me how to straighten my afterlife," she hissed. "Especially not from Breathers who make a life's work of hopping from one disaster to another."

"Gracious me, nothing of the sort. If you want to unmask a fraud, then you have to go to——"

I don't believe Veronica realized I gagged before reaching the end of that sentence. She was too involved with giving me a glower that would have burned a hole in my retina if I hadn't had the foresight to leave it at the funeral parlor.

"Let me make an introduction," I said, recoveringly. "If this woman can't offer a clue or two about dealing with Edgar Allan Poe, then you can pack up your broom and go back home."

"Pack up my what?"

"Stack up your *room* when you get back home."

I saw Veronica's squirrelly little thoughts wonder why I thought she should clean up anything. Or why she would go back to the hotel suite she called home so early in the evening.

I, on the other spectral hand, focused on the bigger picture. The next left thing.

Twenty-four

CHAPTER

ope, Rosetta once said, *is a thing with ectoplasm.*

During many crises in the hereafter, my thoughts have loitered around those words. Maybe if I'm dead long enough, I'll figure out exactly what they mean, but for the time being, I squeezed some comfort out of knowing that *hope* and *ectoplasm* could fit into the same sentence. And that I couldn't be accused of playing a single prank or uttering a single snarky comment since I decanted from my coffeepot this evening.

Still, I couldn't shake this thing about household appliances. Or understanding what was so familiar—yet so foreign—about Fred-As. Or figuring out what I'm supposed to accomplish in the hereafter.

But I had finally discovered a workable *next left thing.* And it wasn't helping Veronica sort through her problem with Edgar Allan Poe, although, if that should happen, it'd be the first train wreck that fell into the category of *easy fixes.*

No, the pending accomplishment was using Veronica's skills as a people whisperer to nudge Madame Sophie into doing something about her problem with apricot brandy, thus upgrading my friend Margie from a chronic state of desperation into mere panic. And if Veronica could pry useful information from Madame Sophie that provides leverage with Edgar A-, everyone goes home happy.

All it took was the right astral touch, which now looked achievable, despite the fact that Sophie wanted to keep drinking and Veronica was only interested in having Edgar Allan Poe quit scandalizing her in his blog.

I glanced at Veronica as we drifted outside the brownstone where Sophie and Margie had their business. Veronica watched me as though I were a puppy who thought her leg was a fire hydrant.

She said, "Remind me exactly why I want to take my personal problems to a couple of flimflam artists."

"I've heard that Madame Sophie has some influence upon Mr. Poe," I said, which was true, in a highly technical sense, for I distinctly heard those words as they rolled out of my mouth seconds ago.

I led Veronica up the outside wall of the building and directly into Sophie's psychic consultations parlor. Persian rugs layered the floor, purple curtains as thick as mattresses lined the walls, and in the center of the room a crystal ball rested on handmade antimacassars, glowing with a brilliance that was creepy to anyone who didn't notice the electrical cord snaking under the linens.

Electrical cord. I shivered.

"She's not here," Veronica observed. "I'm going back to the museum and deal with that reptile myself."

"Don't do that." I maneuvered myself between Veronica and a trash can overflowing with empty brandy bottles. "She's got to be here."

Veronica and I slipped through the string of beads that hung from the door frame. An eerie humming drifted down the hall from the waiting room, a tune that might have been a nursery rhyme if nursery rhymes included snorts and cackles and giggles that could only come from heavily caffeinated elves.

Madame Sophie was stretched on a couch, her eyes half-closed, a hand rocking back and forth in the air to keep time with the tune she was humming. Surrounding her on the floor and the sofa arms and even the back of the ottoman were a half dozen toddlers. Some held pieces of lint over Sophie's mouth and released them to see whose flew the farthest. The younger ones had stripped flowerpots and vases of their foliage, which they tore into petals and twigs to place along Sophie's legs and hips.

"How quaint. The Munchkins are practicing for a wake." Veronica studied the bottle locked in Sophie's motionless fist. "And the relationship between this boozer and my problem is—"

"Oh, dear, Madame Sophie must still be fighting that cold," I empathized.

"Madame Sophie's only fight is to free the material world of its last drop of booze."

I crossed my fingers behind my back, took an earnest look at Veronica, then crossed some toes, too. "What a pity. She has such a close relationship with our esteemed poet. I'm sure if she put in a good word for you, he'd give up his blog and return to poetry."

Snarkle. A cloud of alcoholic fumes burst from Sophie's lips. Toddlers fell on their diapered bottoms, gurgling and snickering. The two closest to Sophie's head rubbed the stench from their noses.

I took a valiant effort at what I remembered a sigh felt like. "She would have been so good for you. If she could only stay away from the bottle for a day or two."

Veronica gazed down on Sophie. Perhaps I was being too subtle.

"Look, I've got a great idea," I said. "Why don't I have a chat with Edgar A- myself? Sure, he didn't listen the last time we spoke, and we've had our disagreements over the years. But what friendship doesn't have its rocky moments?"

Veronica straightened to look down on me from a greater height. "Don't put yourself out."

"No, really. As I think about it, the idea really grows on me."

"Don't."

She packed so much iron and ice into that single syllable that Madame Sophie shivered and most of the toddlers whimpered and slunk away with trembling lips. Slowly, Veronica slid through the carpet until her lips were inches from Sophie's ear.

"What is going on here?"

Bursting into the room from the hall, Margie took in the scenario at a glance—Sophie passed out on the sofa; the toddlers, who were clients for her new babysitting service, in a wailing, pitiful, confused state; me, trying to look as though I'd just arrived at the scene of the accident; and Veronica, who was unaffected by the uproar.

"What's she doing?" Margie asked me.

"Helping."

"—is poison," Veronica whispered into Sophie's ear. "It makes you sick. You don't like it. You'll drink from the toilet before you touch any liquor."

"Whatever." Margie scooped up two toddlers distressed by the voices they heard in places where they couldn't see anyone talking.

"Repeat after me," Veronica whispered to Sophie. "Liquor makes me sicker."

Sophie mumbled. "Lick . . . Ugh!"

"Liquor makes me sicker."

Margie smiled. At least Veronica was trying. "Liquor makes me sicker."

What the Roth. "Liquor makes me sicker," I said, joining the choir.

"Who's sick?"

This last from reporter Scoop Bristow, who appeared in the hall leading from Margie's living quarters with a small bowl in one hand and an eggbeater in the other.

All he needed was an apron to become the picture of domesticity— walking, talking, joking, mugging, breathing homeyness. Resplendent in the remnants of a tan, his breath swelling his manly chest with each inhalation.

I could almost feel sorry for the poor creature. Who knows when he will leave the vale of tears and enter into the joys of . . . of . . . not worrying about earwax or belly button fluff?

Bristow squatted beside a toddler who pressed a blanket to her cheeks. The baby gazed over the room with huge eyes, no doubt trying to pinpoint the astral presences that she could almost see, an ability infants are born with and retain, in varying degrees, into childhood.

"Auntie Sophie isn't feeling well," Bristow told the toddler. "Maybe she'll feel better with some food. Do you want to help Uncle Scoop make an omelet?"

Bristow held out the eggbeater to the child. The toddler looked squarely at me, scared I might take the gadget away, not knowing that the only kitchen appliances I had issues with were the electrical ones.

"You're so good with children," Margie said.

"Aw," I answered.

"Thanks," Bristow answered, too.

I squinted at Margie. Funny thing about planes of existence. They're pretty straightforward and unambiguous. Except when they're hopelessly muddled.

Speaking of muddled, Veronica whispered into Sophie's ear a few more times, straightened up and glided toward me, passing close enough to make Margie flinch, although Veronica acted as though acknowledging any Sunshiner was beneath her. She was the clear winner of tonight's I-notice-you-less-than-you-notice-me award.

"I've done all I can do here," she said.

Bristow crawled on his knees from one toddler to the next until a little boy in a sailor's cap was willing to try a few flicks of the eggbeater. Soon every kid in the room gathered around Bristow and his fascinating bowl of yellow gunk, eager for a chance to spank it with the funny paddle.

Margie wore a smile I last saw on a painting of Madonna, the original Madonna, the one with a Nazarene zip code.

"Aren't you a little old for this?" I asked her.

She fired back, "Aren't you a little dead to care?"

"Huh?" Bristow asked over his shoulder.

Margie shot me a look. "I said, I'm too dead tonight to care about food."

"Nice recovery," I told her.

Bristow gently pried the beater from one set of pudgy fingers and handed it to another.

"Speaking of recovery," Veronica said, "We're late for our meeting."

"Off you go," Margie whispered.

"Yes, off I go," I bandied back.

I was halfway through the wall when I heard Margie say, "Thanks for trying," and Veronica replied, "I'll be back."

Ain't it sweet when spooks are appreciated? What do I have to do to make that happen to me?

CHAPTER Twenty-five

When Veronica and I made our entrance at our regular meeting, Hank and Gwendolyn were still chatting on the church steps that led to the basement room of the St. Sears group. With one glimpse, my friends slid discretely through the wall, too cool to raise in any minds the suggestion that they were avoiding us. Veronica was too self-centered to notice anything that wasn't attached to her own ectoplasm, and I was perfectly content to be misunderstood so long as an on-off switch wasn't involved.

"Did you mean what you said back there?" I asked Veronica. "The part about going back to see Sophie?"

"I fail to see the point of spreading falsehoods about my own intentions."

Veronica's voice was crisp. In fact, if she were crisper, I'd expect to see her ectoplasmic essence drift to the floor in flakes.

"Edgar A- must know something pretty spicy about you," I said, "to make you put up with Sophie."

Veronica spun around. She slipped through the concrete steps until I was looking levelly at her. Which didn't feel differently from having her glare down at me from a pedestal.

"Gilda was right," she said. "You don't have a clue what *Yes* means."

I stared back. If I said that, Yes, I knew what *Yes* meant, wasn't that a double-positive, and shouldn't it have the same effect as a double-negative, which meant I didn't know much of anything, especially why my head was starting to hurt?

"Right," Veronica said and proceeded through the door.

Fast Eddie was right behind her. "You're losing it, kid."

"What, exactly, am I losing?" I asked.

But Fast Eddie merely shook his head and followed Veronica inside, and when I looked around for moral support, most of the spooks still in the vicinity were newbies who looped around the church to slip into the basement without getting close to me. I felt as out of place as a ghost at an exorcism.

A pair of rebel soldiers straggled down the stairs, either desperate for a meeting or playing hooky from the Colonel's deployment. Not many vets showed up at our meetings, and why should they? When you've got an entire army behind you, you don't need civilians to back you up.

"Do I look like some kind of pariah to you?" I asked them.

"Eh? What makes you think you look like a piranha?" one said. "You ain't got fins."

"He said *pariah*, not *piranha*," his friend replied.

"What's the difference?"

"Nothing worth mentioning," I said and followed them inside.

WHEN ROSETTA CALLED the meeting to order, the gray metal chairs in the center of the room were already taken by the regulars: Cal, Gilda, Hank, Gwendolyn, Fast Eddie, Mrs. Hannity, Roger and Jingle Jim to name a few. Cal recrossed his arms in greeting; I twitched my nose in reply and slid above an empty chair next to the Confederates where I could keep an eye on the table with the radio and the coffeepot.

"I asked one of our newest members to lead our discussion tonight about our *perplexities, tremors and fantasies*," Rosetta said, footnoting her talk with excerpts from the approved literature. "I'm sure he's been delayed while *extending the ghostly hand* of comfort to one of our spectral brethren——"

"——or sistren," Hank and I chimed.

"Quite." Even decades after her last meal, Rosetta still had a look that showed she remembered the taste of spoiled milk. "So, perhaps someone else would care to——"

Spectral clothing rustled and astral voices murmured. I looked up from studying the floor and expected to see the radio swagger toward me with a wicked grin. Instead, Fred-As and his sponsor/analyst/biker boss Red Max entered the room.

With a may-I-present flourish, Rosetta said, "Ah, here's our leader for this evening's discussion."

Fred-As and Red Max took places on either side of the table holding the haunted radio and the ectoplasm-eating coffeepot.

I nudged one of the rebel vets. "Now, you'll see what I've been talking about. The radio there. Just keep your eyes on it. Watch what it does. And they said I was crazy. Ain't that something?"

No response from my Confederate confederates. I turned in time to see the toes of their scuffed boots melt into the ceiling.

"My name is Red Max," the biker chief said. "I've been dead so long I'm not afraid of sunshine any more. It's afraid of me. The last time I laid eyes on a photon, it excused itself for existing, turned into a gas and puffed away."

Rosetta dug up her curdled-milk expression. Cal crossed his arms, and I knew that any stone wall that got in his way was going to regret it. Hank and Fast Eddie, on the other hand, drifted on the edges of their chairs, certain that the ectoplasm was going to fly and confident of having the best seats in the house. Gilda's eyes grew larger, sensing, no doubt, that Red Max was like a Goth, only louder.

"I know the custom at these meetings is to talk about whatever we want to talk about," Red Max said. "Tonight, I want to do something different."

If the afterlife had pins, we could have heard one drop.

Red Max swept the room with a glance that reminded me of the Colonel's. Like the rebel commander, he wasn't talking to a group; he was delivering a personal message to every spook in the room, letting us know that expectations were being set, and it'd be in everyone's interest to pay attention. The Colonel had a way of making me want to please him, while in contrast, Red Max was letting us know that whatever anyone else wanted wasn't the point.

"What I want to hear," he said, "is whatever you *don't* want to talk about."

Mrs. Hannity whispered to Rosetta. "Is this going to be a Zen meeting? One of those New Age thingees? If nobody wants to talk, what are we supposed to do with our ears?"

Red Max glanced at Fred-As, and the little fellow nearly snapped off a salute.

"What don't I want to talk about? My, that's a large topic," Fred-As stammered. "There's so much unpleasantness I remember from my first life. And even more that I see in the lives of the Breathers that I run into these nights. Having to pick one thing that I don't want to talk about, that's a pretty tall order."

"Then let me help you," Red Max said. "It begins with the letter *S*."

If a single spook in the room thought the afterlife was supposed to be tranquil, those notions skidded into a sharp U-turn with a glance at Fred-As's face. The little fellow was as close to physical pain as anyone gets without a body.

Fred-As began slowly, as befits someone stepping into a snake pit. "I was in a store last week. I saw people in uniforms running. They were pushing this metal bed. It had wheels. I knew someone was hurt. And, maybe if they were hurt really bad, I'd be able to be the first spook to welcome a newbie to the afterlife. I've never done that before."

I glanced at Veronica and recalled our first meeting. It had been at the spectral state fair, the one held when the Breather's state fair closed down for the night, and although she was then in her first week on the dark side of the Great Divide, she was giving some spooks the benefit of her ideas about making the afterlife a destination of choice for post-mortal travelers. I worked with her until sunup—and for several nights after that—to teach her how the afterlife worked. Those were special nights, and my recollection of them might be called tender if the phrase *lethally uncomfortable* didn't come to mind first.

My thorny relationship with Veronica wasn't on anyone's agenda for the evening. Fred-As glanced at Red Max, who stared back with the calm of a thunderhead that hadn't decided yet to assert itself.

"These men in white were running in the store, and they pushed that metal bed on wheels as fast as they could." Fred-As took a deep breath, but, since his lungs have retired from heavy labor, his lips pursed together like a guppy's. "Someone told them the person they were trying to help was on another floor. So they pushed their metal bed onto this . . . this . . ."

"Thingee?" Mrs. Hannity volunteered.

"This thingee. It was like a floor, but it wriggled up to the next level. It was like . . ."

Rosetta leaned forward and tried a guppy-mouth squinch to help Fred-As find the word that kept squirming away. "Yes. It was like—"

"Wriggly and flowing," Fred-As offered. "Up and up it went, like a stream climbing a mountain. And Breathers were standing on it, except for those that were walking up it."

"How did the stream get in that building? And what for?" Mrs. Hannity asked. "Have they done away with toilets?"

"No. It was metal. And it was too crinkly to do a proper job of flowing upward. It sort of marched to the next floor."

Fred-As shot a look at Red Max, who said, "And what's the word for that crinkly, flowing, metal thing?"

"Escalator," Rosetta offered.

"It begins with an *S*," Red Max countered.

"'Scalator," Fred-As counteroffered.

"You mean, *ssss*—" Gilda said.

The groan that came from Fred-As was the most pitiful thing I've heard outside of a funeral home. He screwed his eyes shut and gritted his teeth, while his ectoplasm pulsed with a queerish radiance that came, not from light nor even from darkness, but from flickering transparency.

He looked at me across the room and, as his spectral being faded into the puzzled air, said, "Don't you just hate it when this happens?"

Twenty-Six

CHAPTER

The rebel spook closest to me slid his finger to the trigger of his ectoplasmic rifle as Fred-As disappeared like smoke from a burnt-out candle. Panicked, the reb's eyes flashed over the specters in the meeting room, uncertain which way to charge but convinced by a century and a half of military training that even the problems of the afterlife could be helped by fixing bayonets and having a good run.

I nudged him. "You boys don't get to many meetings, I'll bet."

He exchanged glances with his buddy. Was this was a trick question? Slowly, carefully, he replied: "Can't say that we have."

"Happens all the time," I answered, nodding to the chair where Fred-As had faded away, not quite lying, because it could happen all the time, although I'm personally unaware of it ever happening before.

Spooks using the *Beam-Me-Up-Scotty* mode of astral transportation leave in a *poof*, and spooks who've fixed the problems that sidetracked them into this part of the hereafter are gone in a *bing*. But specters who leave in a drawn-out dribble of ectoplasm were new to my experience, and based on the anguish on Fred-As's face, I decided to revise my list of *10 Things to Avoid When You're Dead*.

The rebel soldiers relaxed, although they kept their hands close to their triggers. Red Max took Fred-As's departure in stride.

"Who wouldn't like to share next?" he asked. "What don't you want to talk about?"

A half dozen hands shot into the air. Fast Eddie didn't wait to be recognized but started talking about how he didn't want to talk about the Harvard Classics. Anyone who'd attended more than three meetings of the

St. Sears group knew that the last thing Fast Eddie did in his first life was reach for the top shelf of a very tall bookcase. I've heard more times than I care to remember how Fast Eddie died happy that he didn't have to read Plato's *Republic* because it had just been stamped on his brain.

Cal crossed his arms at me. I gave him my best syrupy smile and went back to scrutinizing the radio on the other side of the room while a succession of newbies gave vent to the traumas, injustices and slights they're otherwise too noble to mention.

Even some regulars got antsy to talk about the things they don't want to talk about. At halftime, Rosetta went through her usual midmeeting routine, asking if any newbies wanted to introduce themselves or if any spooks were celebrating the anniversaries of their expiration dates or if anyone had an announcement. An argument broke out between a spook who was determined to keep talking about something he didn't want to talk about, and his neighbor who didn't want to hear what the other guy didn't want to say.

I had to get some air.

Hank and Gwendolyn followed me through the door to our usual spot at the top of the stairs outside. I had a few choice words that I didn't want to tell them about friends who weren't supportive when I had an intersection I didn't need, but as soon as I hit the night air, I knew something was amiss, and I didn't need a flashing neon sign to give me the particulars. The wall of a three-story house across the street delivered that warning. I blinked, but it was still there: a flickering, silvery glow—eerie in a non-spectral-friendly way—flashing on the side of a house.

"Why does that look familiar?" I whispered.

"Let me guess," Hank said. "Might it be because you pass that house every night?"

"I'm talking about the light, not the house," I said.

The glow was as gray as fog, only brighter, and it wavered as though a strong wind was blowing the photons around.

"My investigative experience says it looks familiar because you've seen it before," Gwendolyn offered.

But where had I seen fog that set off such a glow?

"Actually, it's toasters," Fred-As said, respecterizing on the church lawn. "I noticed them on the ride here. Looks like every toaster in Richmond has gathered in the back lawns on that block."

"That's a relief," I said. "For a moment, I thought something strange was happening."

"You want strange?" Fred-As replied. "That would be the hair curlers that are rallying in the two blocks. If you listen carefully, you can hear them clicking and rattling."

"Everything is starting to fall into place," I said.

But did it really? I wanted to ask Fred-As to account for the faint, foul smell I detected whenever the breeze blew from behind the church, but I didn't dare. No one had mentioned the zombies' plans for the evening.

"Let's talk about this." I waved for Fred-As to join us at the bottom of the stairs. "Why don't you come down the . . ."

"NO!" Fred-As threw up his hands and inched away. "Don't say the *S* word."

"Which *S* word would that be?" Gwendolyn offered, helpfully. "Sturgeon? Samovar? Stallion? Perhaps satellite?"

I elbowed Gwendolyn. "Ease up. Can't you see he's scared?"

"I can see right through him," Gwendolyn offered.

"Anybody can," Hank added.

Fred-As was doing another slow fade away, and the outline of the waxy leaves on the magnolia by the curb were clearly visible through his chest.

"Wait." I tried to keep him in focus. "Would this *S* word have something to do with this concrete thing on the ground, the concrete thing between the railings that helps Breathers walk up and down?"

A hopeful, pained smile came to Fred-As. Slowly, he nodded.

Inside, Rosetta called the meeting to order and Red Max asked for volunteers to talk about anything they didn't want to discuss. I, on the other hand, was faced with not mentioning something when I wanted to have a full conversation about it.

I picked my words carefully. "I can think of two *S* words that might do the job. One rhymes with *pep*. The other with *chairs*. Which one is it?"

Fred-As shrugged. "Funny, but I don't remember."

"That's a real hardyhar answer," Gwendolyn said as his cigar bobbed in agreement.

"You want to hear something really odd?" Fred-As glided forward and sat down on an *S*-word block of concrete. "I'm not even sure I'm afraid of it. It's more like . . . it reminds me of something that's going to happen to me. Or that's not going to happen, even though I want it very much."

I dusted off my hands. "Things are really starting to fall into place. Does everyone get the picture?"

"No," Fred-As, Hank and Gwendolyn said in chorus.

TO MY FRIENDS, I may appear carefree, debonair, unaffected by the petty nuisances of the afterlife, always in control, except for those features of the second plane of existence that I don't have a clue about.

But I didn't even try to put on a brave face now. It was no coincidence that the city's entire population of toasters and electric curling irons had decided to hold a mass meeting a few blocks from the church basement that I've visited for a meeting almost every night of my afterlife.

I wouldn't be surprised if the radio or the coffeemaker in the meeting room were responsible. They didn't fool me for a moment, sitting there all innocent-looking and not saying a word.

I told Hank and Gwendolyn to let Cal know that the spooks inside should prepare for some kind of unpleasantness when the meeting broke up. I'd keep watch outside.

"You'd better go with them," I told Fred-As.

"I don't want to see Red Max right now," Fred-As said.

"You can't avoid your sponsor forever."

Fred-As gave me a look for which Gilda held the patent. "Isn't Cal your sponsor?"

So we changed plans and I slipped inside with Fred-As, leaving Hank and Gwendolyn outside to let us know if the household appliances did anything suspicious.

I motioned to Cal to join me in the church overhead, but Cal shook his head. So I drifted next to his chair and whispered that if I couldn't talk to my sponsor, I'd have to share my concerns with the entire group. His eyes went wide. He followed me through the ceiling and into a side aisle of the church.

The main lights were off; votive candles flickered along the altar railing. Angular shadows and tired, gray air littered the cavernous room. Breathers were gone at this hour, although a couple dozen spooks were spread across the pews, mostly dazed newbies checking out each hymnal and prayer book in the hopes of finding an up-to-date edition of *Ralph's Death for Dummies* or perhaps a good flowchart that shows the process for being dead.

"You look like you've just seen your own casket," Cal said.

"It's not that bad," I replied. "I think it might be yours."

"Would you care to explain that?"

"I'm not sure I can work up the energy right now. Something else is on my mind."

So I told Cal about the toasters and curling irons that were massing around the church for an attack. He crossed his arms. So I added my experiences with the lunar lander.

"I thought you'd sworn off tall tales until after Halloween," he said.

"I have."

The corners of his astral mouth took a downward wrinkle. "How much of this story do you expect me to believe?"

"The bit about the toasters and curling irons. Hank, Gwendolyn and Fred-As saw them, too. Outside, just a few minutes ago."

"And what makes you think these gadgets are violent?" he asked.

"The lunar lander took a serious swing at me."

"And where was this lunar lander?" he asked.

"On the moon. Duh."

NOW, I'VE ARGUED with Cal, called him names to his face (when I didn't know he was there), flashed exasperated expressions from time to time, and even rolled my eyes once or twice, but I'd never *duh-ed* Cal before, and I was pretty sure I wasn't going to do it again.

Ectoplasm boiled from his nostrils. I couldn't take my eyes from his forearms, which he squeezed with vise-like thoroughness until he could get a grip around my neck.

I just deleted *duh* from my vocabulary.

"Yeah," Cal said through clenched teeth. "Gotta see my sponsor." And he disappeared in a *poof*.

"Well, I got to talk to my sponsor, too," I told the spot where Cal had been.

That empty spot in the aisle practically hummed with ectoplasmic energy. I'd never seen Cal so upset, and the fact that I caused it was so far-reaching in its implications that I couldn't get beyond thinking, *Wow*, before slipping back to the time-sensitive problem of the moment:

How do I tell a meeting full of specters that they were about to be assaulted by every toaster and curling iron in central Virginia, when they weren't willing to believe any warning that came from me? And don't get me started on what the electric can openers, microwaves and blenders might be up to.

I looked forlornly over the specters scattered across the church, hoping none of them were here when Heck's Angels chased everyone outside. A spook drifted up the central aisle toward me. Determination was in her stride. She was having a very bad time in Forever, and she'd decided to share her unhappiness with every entity within shouting distance. Starting with me. And it didn't matter that we'd never laid eyes on each other before. She wouldn't be deterred if I were hiding behind a bank of grow lights in a florist's window.

"I've got few questions," she said when she reached hailing distance.

"Lucky for you, I've got the answer." I raised a finger, pointed at the distant roof and said, "Grow lights."

Twenty-seven

CHAPTER

$\mathcal{I}$t was simple. No one at the St. Sears meeting had to believe me. All they had to do was get out of the basement as quickly as possible and in as many directions as they could manage. And if yelling *Fire* is a time-tested method for clearing a crowded theater in the material world, the post-life corollary would be yelling *Grow lights* in a roomful of spooks.

So back to the 12-step meeting in the basement I went.

Red Max was in the process of remembering a story that he didn't want to talk about that involved a bag of sugar, a motorcycle left outside a beer joint in his first life and a Breather who had made uncharitable remarks about Red Max's mother.

I cleared my throat, raised my hand and observed: "GROW LIGHTS!"

A spasm of relief flashed across Red Max's face as his reflexes took him through the floor. Rosetta, Mrs. Hannity and some of the other pillars of the meeting jumped as quickly as the newbies through walls and ceilings. Hank, Gwendolyn and Fast Eddie didn't care for once about hanging around to catch the fireworks. Only Gilda and Veronica stayed in their places.

"Did you have something resembling a coherent thought before you opened your mouth?" Veronica huffed.

"He wanted to empty the room quickly," Gilda answered. "I'm sure he wants to help. For some reason."

Veronica looked down her nose and across the room at me, which even a spectral entity has trouble doing. "What's the point? He scared the afterlife out of a few dozen spooks. But it's okay because he meant well. That's supposed to put my mind at ease?"

"Don't take my word for it——" I started.

"I haven't," Veronica finished.

"Take a look outside," I said in a bid to finish my own thoughts.

With the slow majesty of a queen going to visit the court jester, Veronica slid through the brick wall. I blocked Gilda before she could leave.

"Thanks for standing up for me," I said.

"I was sitting down."

"Whatever."

Gilda wore enough white makeup to camouflage a Confederate battalion, still I knew something I said had touched her. She dipped her chin and shoulders in an ambiguous yet significant angle as she brushed past me; the chains on her black leather jacket had lost their old, self-confident luster.

Veronica, Gilda and I leveled off near the treetops. The night was quiet. Most lights in the nearby homes had winked off hours ago. For once the hum of traffic on the interstate highway didn't reach us.

"Now I can see why you felt a need to end our meeting so abruptly," Veronica said.

"You can?" I peeped through the trees at the house where the reflected glow from hundreds of toasters had lit up the night and checked the houses in the next block where an army of electric curling irons had been assembling.

Nothing.

A jack-o'-lantern squatted on the porch of a brownstone down the street, its candle extinguished for the night, while on the next block a lone plastic skeleton hung from a tree, looking as fierce as drying laundry. Hank and Gwendolyn were gone. Had they run away, gotten bored and drifted off, or were they at this very moment surrounded by snarling toasters and snapping curling irons, being interrogated for what they could reveal about the Colonel's defenses and the afterlives of my fellow spooks?

Veronica took in the asphalt, grass, sidewalks and stoops with a regal gaze. "From what I see, you're not matching last year's debacle."

There it was again: the shadow of Halloweens past.

"Can I explain about last year?" I said.

"I doubt it," Veronica twitched her nose. "I have a patient to see." And she disappeared with an indignant *poof.*

When I turned to Gilda, she swept a toe through the leaves.

"Will you let me tell you what happened when I talked to Poe about his blog?" I asked her.

"Is that what you want to talk about?"

"'Natch."

The starch came back to Gilda's expression. "Then don't let me get in the way of a wonderful conversation between you and yourself." And she was gone in a *poof* that was twice as indignant as Veronica's.

I HUNG AROUND the street, hoping that Gwendolyn and Hank would show up, on guard for toasters and curling irons that might be lurking around the next corner, telling myself that they'd be sorry, those other fair-weather spooks of mine, once they found out the meeting really was going to be attacked and I saved them all, although no one bothered to hang around to save me.

Barely a whisper came from the breeze in the leaves. A gauzy glow rose over the downtown streets. From the river, the scents of rotting timbers and drying moss were strong.

"Ah, the fairer sex." Edgar Allan Poe specterized in the lower branches of a nearby tree. "Can't die with 'em, can't die without 'em."

"Isn't there some abandoned house where you're welcome? Where the rats will greet you with open . . . hmm . . . claws?"

"Rats are always glad to see me," the master answered. "But sadly, they're able to manage their relationships without my professional advice."

"What makes you a professional?" I retorted.

"Do not underestimate me, my quasi-ethereal friend. I was quite the rake in my day."

"I heard you were more like a backhoe."

Edgar A- adjusted the cuffs of his flouncy white shirt. "At least, when I had an admirer, I wasn't so terrified that I pretended not to see her."

Gongs went off, only they were drowned by a sea of buzzers, which, in turn, were buried under pounding of the bells. Ah, the bells, bells, bells.

"Are you suggesting that . . . I mean, Veronica's old enough to be my . . . Why should she . . . That is to say, I don't believe you."

"It would be indiscreet of me to betray a confidence," Poe said.

"However—"

"There's only one proven cure for the broken heart."

"Which is?"

"Burial."

Poe, who's been experimenting with triple rhymes lately, disappeared with a hearty, *roof, poof, woof.*

I LOOPED AROUND the church, looking for armies of toasters and radios or my buddies Hank and Gwendolyn, expanding my search with each circuit until I covered all of Church Hill, then Libby Hill, then dipped into the flatlands along Gillies Creek, looking for the Colonel and his troops.

The old soldier had sensed an enemy was closing in on the city and mustered his forces to beat back an attack. Might the appliances skulking outside our meeting be scouts for an approaching horde? Perhaps with ovens and refrigerators in their ranks. Or a lunar lander or twelve.

And why couldn't I shake the idea that Edgar A- might be somehow involved? And Veronica?

The vaguest thought about Veronica was enough to give me a bad case of the post-mortal willies. Sharing eternity with that whirlwind of righteousness was as close as I wanted to get. Or that she wanted. Right?

Or was it possible I'd lost what passes in the hereafter for sanity? That I'd become a raving, delusional, apoplectic bundle of neuroses, driven over the hill and through the psychotic woods with Veronica in full pursuit, her arms outstretched for a hug?

It was time for an unreality check, and if the Colonel wasn't here to give me the unvarnished truth, I'd have to stoop to ask my sponsor.

But Cal wasn't around his favorite blocks on Shockoe Slip, which bought me more time to sort through the implications of really infuriating my sponsor, and when I went a few streets away and twenty-some stories upward, I couldn't find Jack of Diamonds perched on the edge of his now-favorite hotel.

Was somebody throwing a funeral and not inviting me?

OPTIONS WERE CLOSING rapidly, so I set my astral feet towards Carytown and didn't stop until I reached the brownstone with the *'syck Advisor* sign in the bay window.

For those who include daylight hours in their reckoning of time, we were less than twenty-four hours from Halloween, and I didn't relish the idea of waking up on the appointed day to find (A) the Colonel was right and we were overwhelmed by an enemy force, (B) the curling irons and radios were in league with the lunar lander, or (C) this side of the Great Divide had its own version of the funny farm and I'd become a resident.

Fog rolling in from the river was thick enough to reduce visibility to a city block, but it wasn't its usual fuzzy self. It was different, less cushiony, more squirrelly and restless. As though bugs were darting through the mist, hither and yon. I flapped my hands at the foggy air.

When a dark shape wriggled toward my nose, I followed it closely, dodging and squinting, angling my head this way and that, and soon determined it was worse than a bug. It was a sentence. Half the hereafter seemed to be sending text messages on the fog to the other half.

You only die once, so dare to dream!!!

--E.A. Poe

Howling and flapping, I bolted to the door of Margie's building, past the shadows on the unlit porch, then through the door. Then back out through the door and onto the stoop. Margie stood in the darkness outside the door with Scoop Bristow, who patted his hands against his shoulders.

"It's getting chilly," he said, as I came out of his back. "Maybe we ought to call it a night."

Margie fixed me with a look that was enough to convince the most savage toaster to sit up straight and quit misbehaving. "It's not chilly. A ghost must have run through you. It dare not happen again. It simply wouldn't dare."

"A ghost?" Bristow chuckled. "I haven't heard that one before. But it makes more sense than shivering if someone steps on your grave."

Margie laughed, too, but there was fire in her eyes. "Yes, it does make more sense. I hope any ghosts in the area get that message, loud and clear."

"I got it, I got it," I mumbled. "Geez, you don't have to shout."

I slunk back inside.

FITZSIMONS' THIRTY-SEVENTH Observation on the Characteristics of Ectoplasm holds that, since each plane of existence has its own distinct residents (e.g., humans or spooks), any lasting interdimensional mingling of entities will have to occur on a plane of existence not native to either mingler.

Fitzsimons lived during the early Victorian era and his use of *mingling* in this context was considered so provocative his work was placed on the restricted list in the library where it was lost after being pushed further into the back shelves by naughty books that had better pictures.

I didn't need Fitzsimons to point out that I was a spook and Margie was a human, albeit a twofer with rare abilities to communicate with the spirit world. Our relationship was based upon her ownership of the 1950s sitcom *The Honeymooners* in DVD format and my need to explore those episodes for clues to the problems I caused in my first life that need fixing in my second life.

That was all. Really. I'm dead, not stupid. What kind of a deceased idiot would form an attachment to a Breather? Besides, I don't know where I'd find enough cinnamon to see if there's any truth to those old stories about the psychic properties of certain spices. And, believe me, I've tried.

Fitzsimons was the last thing on my mind as I drifted toward Margie's waiting room. Not that I'm checking up on her. I mean, if I were doing that, wouldn't I turn around and leave once I saw her outside with Bristow? Yes, that would show there's clearly more going on than meets the crystal ball, whereas, having me go into her place obviously shows I'm not affected by whatever was going on, on the stoop, in the shadows, which I don't care to dwell on.

I barely heard the whooping and laughter that filled the hallway until I turned the corner to the waiting room Margie shared with Madame Sophie and saw a line of spooks.

Harold, a specter with the bedraggled expression of a bloodhound who'd been threatened with a bath, was the only spook in line I recognized.

"What's going on?" I asked.

"Madame Sophie just opened her eyes. I mean, really opened them. And she's seeing things."

"What things?"

"Us."

$\mathcal{T}wenty$-$eight$

CHAPTER

f the Über-Spirit ever decided that He/She/It needed a vacation, I'm sure the spook at the top of the list to be a temporary replacement would be Veronica. I'm sure she thinks so, too. She has a commitment to doing *the next left thing*—and doing it properly—that makes the rest of us look like we'd been shunted off to the hereafter for slackers and ne'er-do-wells.

Still, I was surprised by the way she coupled her skills as a people whisperer to the natural desire of spooks for a good show in order to sober up Madame Sophie long enough to pick through the old hag's brain for ammunition about Edgar A-.

"Not a word from you about grow lights, searchlights, or lighted matches," Veronica said without looking in my direction.

"Not a syllable from me," I said. "Not even a vowel."

I could've slapped my own face silly. Was I flirting with this banshee? I might've had an autopsy, but that didn't excuse me from being mindless.

Sophie was sprawled across a tasseled ottoman in the waiting room. Her head rested on an embroidered pillow, and a hand dangling over the edge of the sofa gripped a bottle of apricot brandy. Veronica had glided through the sofa until her mouth was next to Sophie's ear.

"Liquor makes you sicker," Veronica whispered. "Liquor makes you sicker."

Sophie swung her head from side to side like a petulant child. "But a little nip? A wee little mouthful? Just to clear my head. What's wrong with that?"

She dragged the bottle from the floor, rolled onto her side and puckered her lips. Her eyes focused on the mouth of the bottle. I could almost believe she'd never seen an uncorked container before or maybe she didn't recognize what a bottle looked like that wasn't clamped to her face.

"That's a bad idea, Sophie," Veronica said calmly. "A very bad idea."

"Nothing's bad about a friend. And this is my closest, bestest buddy."

The bottle was three or four inches away. As her mouth stretched to align itself to the exact contours of the oncoming bottle, a demon popped from the brandy. Its eyes were the red of a lava chute, its skin had green scales speckled with black mold, its miniature lips parted to reveal more teeth and saliva than a mouth that size should be able to handle.

"Eek," Sophie eeked. The bottle dropped to the floor, though Sophie's fingers kept their grip.

As the brandy skidded across the Persian rug, a spook emerged from the glass container, giggling and waving to the specters around the room, and another spook shrank himself smaller than a cork and slid into the bottle.

"They have a contest," Veronica said, never looking from Sophie. "They're seeing who can transform himself into the ugliest, most disgusting, most hideous sight imaginable."

"What does the winner get?"

"My high opinion of him."

"That explains the crowd."

Sophie's head lolled on the pillow. I saw fear ebb from her like a retreating wave: a cunning glimmer lit her eyes although her hands and feet trembled. The spook who'd moved into the brandy now had the head of an insect on a body of yellow-green slime.

"Tut, tut, tut." Veronica's finger wagged in time with each *tut*. "Wait for it."

"Sure," the spectral slime-insect said as it oozed back inside the bottle.

I wondered if this might be a good moment to let Veronica know that Sophie doesn't really have any insight into Edgar A-, that I'm not sure she's ever met him, given her spotty connection to the astral plane and Poe's reluctance to spend his afterlife around Breathers who were unlikely to burnish his reputation.

Sophie smacked her lips. "Kinda dry in here, don't you think? Maybe I've still got a little something to lip the pucker."

Pulling the bottle from the floor, Sophie grinned in amazement. "Look what's in my hand. A bottle. The very thing I was looking for. It's a sign, I tell you, a sign."

She adjusted her mouth into a bottle-sized opening, slid to the edge of the cushion, and tilted the brandy ever so slightly. Veronica said, "Now," and a slimy insectile spook emerged from the bottle, flexing its mandibles.

Sophie squealed. The bottle thumped to the floor, but again her fingers kept their death grip on the neck.

"This isn't worth it," I told Veronica. "You're never going to get her sober."

"She hasn't had a drop since yesterday."

"How can you be sure?"

"As that good spook told you, she sees every spook in this room—"

"—and probably a bunch who aren't here."

Veronica straightened. "The point is—she sees them. She's not hiding in a cloud of booze. Her head is beginning to clear. Soon she'll become a contributor to my. . . ah . . . *her own* well-being."

Next in line for terrifying Sophie into sobriety was Willbard, the polymorphous spook who last tried to scare Sophie by changing into a blue rabbit.

Veronica gave Willbard a look that could peel paint. "Fear. I want fear. Nothing from the petting zoo. Understood?"

"Willlllbbbbbbaaaaarrrrdddd," Willbard said.

"Good."

Willbard, currently manifesting herself as a thunderhead, shrank to the size of a sewing needle and zipped into the brandy bottle.

When Sophie's eyes cleared, she wiped the back of her hand across her mouth and said, "Thirsty."

Sophie yanked the bottle from the floor. Veronica said, "Action." Sophie's lips puckered and closed in on the mouth of the bottle. Willbard sprang from the brandy. Sophie screamed. Veronica howled. Sophie lost her grip on everything, and the bottle fell to the carpet and kept rolling.

I watched each revolution of the brandy, unable to sort out what I'd seen and what it meant until the bottle bumped against the base of a Tiffany floor lamp. Mini-Willbard drooped over the lip of the brandy, dazed, and as the spook shook off the cobwebs, I realized what the commotion was about.

Willbard had made herself into an image of Veronica. A pint-sized—or was it quart-sized?—duplicate of Veronica, complete with shoulder-length brown hair too cowed for frizzies, a mouth that hadn't smiled since her diaper days, and an aura that let everyone know, at a purely noncognitive level, that disapproval carried consequences.

"Hhhhhhhrrrrrrrraaaaaa," Veronica explained.

Willbard sprang from the mouth of the bottle and straightened to her full height. If the Über-Spirit had become manifest in Margie's waiting room at that very moment, the creator of the universe would probably have mumbled, "S'cuse me, folks," and snuck into a more manageable cosmos.

"That's it," Veronica said. "That's the very last straw. I'm going to deal with this my way." She glared at me and aimed the tip of her finger between my eyes to add, "And you keep your trap shut."

"I was about to suggest that very thing."

YOU HAVE TO go around the cemetery a few times in the paranormal plane before you get the hang of the way things work. Normal doesn't exist in the paranormal world, except for those bits of normal that become paranormal without calling attention to themselves.

Spooks go through Breathers like a spring breeze flits through candle smoke, although there's no record of candle smoke complaining of a draft the way a resident of the physical plane reacts to a bit of ectoplasm gliding through their spleens.

Spooks don't go through spooks at all. And if we're able to touch each other, the gate is open for two other questions. First, shouldn't specters be capable of tearing each other to pieces, or at least, of registering disagreements by the conjunction of fist and nose? *(Note to readers: I forgot what the second thing was. Don't worry, it'll come back to me.)*

Anyway, Hank, Gwendolyn and I have spent many a night debating what would happen if one of us snaps and starts going after his spectral friends. Would the aforesaid spectral fist actually land on the previously mentioned nose? Would the Über-Spirit personally intervene to referee the fight? Or would all the participants be transported to some bleak galaxy, surrounded by life insurance salesmen, telemarketers and teenagers with earbuds cemented to their heads?

Fortunately, Veronica was going to do the research for us.

She left the waiting room with an indignant *poof*, and I, having a sudden intuition about the spook whom Cal would blame for this latest froufrou, *poofed* after her.

First stop was the Poe museum. I reprised the old *Grow light!* routine to polite applause. Everyone seemed to think I was part of the show. When Veronica asked the leader of a spectral tour group winding through the tiny rooms if they'd seen Mr. Poe, I lost all hope of controlling the situation.

Conversations popped up all over the narrow hallways and soon Veronica admitted that she'd actually met the poet. Soon, she had more spooks than she could point her nose at clustered around her, peppering her with questions about what the great specter was really like. A French tour group got a whiff of the discussion, and reason, common sense and Gallic good manners got lost in translation. Veronica was besieged by spooks jabbering in wonderful French.

Veronica left the museum at a Breather's pace, leading a line of tourist spooks through the fog, half of whom thought Veronica had agreed to introduce them to Edgar A-, while the other half thought she *was* Monsieur Poe. All those references to burial sheets in his stories, I heard one of the guides sniff, were clear evidence of the great man's fondness for dresses.

The parade went a half dozen blocks to the River City Diner. Veronica skimmed the empty tables and the deserted booths, looking for a meeting-after-the-meeting that was still meeting, where someone could answer some questions about Poe's whereabouts. The Paris contingent clustered in the kitchen around the carving knives and cleavers. From the gestures that didn't need translation, I knew they were trying to determine which blade was the inspiration for the swinging weapon in "The Pit and the Pendulum."

By the time we left the diner, Veronica's entourage had doubled. I picked out Hank in the crowd.

"Where've you been?"

"Trying to track the toasters." His pigtail pressed against the back of his neck, and I knew it was ready for action. "Word's going around that Veronica's spoiling for a fight."

"Misunderstandings keep snowballing," I said.

He eyed me skeptically. "Funny how that keeps happening. When you're in the neighborhood."

"I have nothing to do with this."

We watched Veronica dip beneath a highway overpass favored by spooks who'd always wanted waterfront property. With the fog concealing most of the spectral horde, the voices drifting through the haze were appropriately eerie.

A figure bulldozed through the fog; the outline of a fedora and an upturned trench-coat collar identified Gwendolyn better than a name tag. Letters and sentences and a few paragraphs swirled around him in the murk.

"I didn't do it," I said.

"That's how I figure it." Gwendolyn straightened, but his cigar drooped in puzzlement. "Someone's writing here about a *love-worn* spook. Do you think that's really possible for our kind?"

"Don't you mean *lovelorn*?"

"Nope, there was a definite *W* there. I could see the squiggles moving around."

Hank pursed his astral lips. "We've been hanging out with the wrong crowd."

"I'm more concerned with hanging on," I said. "Something's going to happen here. And whatever it is, it's going to be unpleasant and I'm going to be blamed for it."

"*Comment dit-on en anglais?*" asked a spook, beret sagging over an eyebrow, a tiny piece of text squirming between his pinched fingers.

The letters were *P-o-e*.

"*Poop*," I said. "We pronounce it, *poop*."

Twenty-nine

C H A P T E R

If a spook can't be found at his favorite museum or cherished diner, there are only a few places left, with the highest priority going to cemeteries close to the river. For Poe to post his text on the fog, he needs to be near the source.

Veronica must have reached the same conclusion. She started in the eastern edge of the city and worked her way west along the James, past Richmond National Cemetery, Evergreen, Oakwood, Riverview, and Mt. Calvary. As she left each burial ground, the number of her followers kept growing until, by the time her glide path put her on a course to Hollywood Cemetery, the caravan included regiments of Confederate infantry, spectral tour groups from the West Coast and representatives from most of the city's Specters Anonymous meetings.

We were several hundred feet above Hollywood Cemetery when I pulled out of formation and hovered in the mist. Something wasn't right. I couldn't give it a name, but I could picture its face. It was snout-nosed, mostly orange with silver highlights, and it had an extension cord as vicious as an anaconda. My eyes tore through the fog for signs of curling irons. Or radios, electric knives, motorized can openers or vacuum cleaners.

A single spook stared at me from a headstone in a section of the cemetery that hadn't had a new arrival in decades. His hand was cupped over his eyes to block the glow reflected by the fog.

I drifted down.

Jedediah was the first friend I made in the afterlife. His waist-length beard and ragged, knee-length coat were faded by the moonlight of tens of thousands of nights spent guarding his grave, but the long, lonely vigil had done nothing to take the sparkle from his alert eyes nor the wisp of a knowing smile.

"Good evening, Jedediah," I said.

"If I'd known my grave was going to be on a racetrack, I'd've set it elsewhere."

"That's the sensible thing to do," I said. Of course, Jedediah didn't have a voice in his own burial, which was one of the many unacknowledged injustices faced by the nation's spooks.

"I'd likely go off with the rest of them and put it over there." Jedediah tossed his hand in a gesture that took in the northern hemisphere. "Closer to the reviewing stand."

Jedediah was a tomb-squatter, a spook who'd found the actual resting place for his bones. Crawling into his casket (which he couldn't do unless a Breather or an earthquake opened it) was the only thing that interested him.

I braced my knees and cleared my head. In a nano-sized portion of a nanosecond, I would be settling down on the grass by the edge of the river next to Veronica.

"My best to Mr. Poe," Jedediah added.

In mid-despecterization I reversed course so quickly that the place where my stomach used to be sagged.

"Poe?"

Jedediah's smile had aw-shucks written all over it. "Why, the legendary writer and pioneer with this new-fangled *blag*—"

"No, that's—" I rolled the word around in my mind. "Forget it. *Blag* says it all."

"—Mr. Poe is dedicating the new clubhouse across the river for Heck's Angels."

My view of the far shore was obscured by Veronica and her crowd of spectral gawkers while she interrogated newbies who must've thought she and the hundreds of spooks surrounding her were the welcoming committee for the afterlife.

Glancing at Jedediah, I said, "Let's see if I can bring reason to the table."

"'Bout time someone straightened out the likes of me," Jedediah agreed.

Before he could offer another nugget of homespun wisdom, I was respecterizing on the other side of the James River. Heck's Angels had formed an honor guard in two parallel lines leading to a green aluminum shack, the sort of place where lawnmowers and garden tools were stored.

Had happily-ever-after really come down to this—a haunted toolshed? And how would Cal manage to blame me for the spiritual dimension sinking so low?

Still, a respectable crowd of spooks had come to hear Poe orate over the new home for the hereafter's rowdy bikers, but Red Max was unaware of the larger horde of spooks gathering across the river or, more significantly, the tall, lean, infuriated brunette in their lead.

The safest way to avoid responsibility for a pending accident was to reschedule the mishap.

"Why don't you send everyone home?" I told Red Max. "Thank them for coming, wish them a safe and raucous Halloween, and clear out yourself."

Red Max glowered at me. "I can't end things before they've properly started." His glare became more glaring.

What's the *next left thing?* I asked myself, flounderingly, while to Red Max I said: "The goal of every successful event is to have your audience leave smiling. Look at 'em: They're smiling now. Why don't you cut to the bottom line? Eliminate all the junk that second-rate minds call an agenda. Quit while you're ahead. Nothing but nice memories all around."

Red Max's interest was piqued. "I don't see that many smiles, and the ones that are out there are pretty feeble."

"Perhaps we should have some music. Anyone have a guitar? A tin whistle?"

The big fellow spun on me with surprising speed. "Do you need to be reminded where you are?"

"We can sing," I improvised. "Name a few songs that everyone knows?"

"*This Little Piggy Went to Market* and *Rock of Ages* would be my guesses," Red Max said.

By now, Veronica had noticed the gathering of Heck's Angels on my side of the river. She'd taken on a flowing cloak and let her hair stream out behind her, a trick of considerable skill when you remember the wind is restricted to the physical plane of existence, mainly to aggravate Breathers and spare birds from having to do much walking.

I nearly stumbled over Fred-As. "What do you want?"

"I could dance."

"Whatever," I mumbled, while I asked Red Max, "Where's Poe?"

"Behind the shed. Finishing his dedication poem."

"See if you can stall Veronica."

Red Max smirked. "That little thing will be putty in my hands."

"Just remember that bricks were once putty."

I FOUND EDGAR Allan Poe near a gully behind the shed where the fog rising from the river collected and congealed into a fine writing surface.

"*Ten Tips for Getting the Attention of that Special Someone*," I read. "Do you really think public address systems belong on that list?"

"We waste precious time worrying about subtlety in affairs of the heart." Poe didn't look up from his work.

"Cargo nets?" I added, still reading.

"Ditto."

From the other side of the shed came the rumble of hundreds of spectral voices competing with the roar of dozens of astral motorcycles, and above the pandemonium, two voices, one feminine and commanding, the other masculine and growling, spoke at, over and around each other.

My money was on the female of the spectrals.

I faced Poe. "Look, you've got ten great ideas there. Why don't you hit the *send* button or whatever you do to get your blags moving? Then we can check out this new diner by the campus. I hear they make amazing milk shakes with herbs and chocolate syrup."

"Capital idea." Poe honored me with the suggestion of a smile. "Let me fulfill a brief speaking engagement, then I'll be right with you."

He jabbed an index finger into the fog; the lines of text divided and subdivided and kept on splitting until they resembled a swarm of bees circling a hive before shooting across the river in the fog. Thumbs fixed into the pockets of his vest, Edgar A- sauntered toward the shed.

"I understand you've written a poem for this grand opening," I said, meekly.

"My muse, perhaps not too strangely, has been silent on the matter at hand. Fortunately, I have the perfect dedicatory piece in my literary trousseau." He clenched a lapel and uplifted a single finger. "*O, Times! O, Manners! It is my opinion / That you are changing sadly your dominion.*"

"That'll be perfect," I mumbled.

At least Poe was in a festive mood when he rounded the side of the shed to face his impending dismemberment. I was almost . . . almost . . . willing to take his place. And then I turned the corner myself, saw Fred-As—decked out like a 1930s Hollywood star in a top hat, tails, a silver-tipped cane and glossy shoes that floated on the breeze—high-stepping between the ranks of Heck's Angels, tap-dancing elegantly to a tune only he could hear. And I realized that I should put my ectoplasm where my mouth was.

As a specter, I can transform myself into anything I want. Several nights ago, Willbard had chosen to become a giant blue rabbit. What's more appropriate for the Halloween season than wearing a disguise. If a youngster can become a ghost, then a ghost can become—

Edgar Allan Poe!

A dark light flashed across my eyes. My knees quivered, and a strange dizziness overcame me, making me feel giddy, a sensation I can only describe as *breathfulness*. I looked down at the simple black trousers I was now wearing, the knee-length coat, the ruffled shirt. I felt a thin mustache twitch into place along my upper lip, the hairs on my head darken and uncoil.

Poe glanced at me and lifted a hand to straighten his simple string tie as I, matching his movements, twitch for twitch, lifted my hand to adjust my own.

When a spook decides to look like someone else—specter, Sunshiner or nine-headed slime creature from Alpha Centauri—there isn't a molecule's difference between the original and the spectral version.

Veronica didn't miss a beat. "Good. I was worried what I'd do after I straightened you out. Now I can straighten out the other one of you, too."

"Other one?" I parried. "Other one? But you have underestimated us, my friend. Or should I say, undercounted us."

Red Max, who'd been cringing next to Veronica, was the next spook to decide on a rapid transformation that, in future nights, we'd describe as *doing a Poe*.

Once Red Max sported a simple, black and white ensemble, soulful eyes and a mustache that could have been a mouse asleep on his upper lip, his fellow bikers dropped the motorcycles they weren't actually holding and did a Poe, too. And remember: When spooks put on costumes, we go beyond clothes. We also adopt the face, build, gestures, movements and atoms of the creature we're representing.

Veronica held on to her dignity and her usual manifestation. A few spooks customized their Poe outfits: Gwendolyn kept his cigar stub, for example, and Fred-As couldn't countenance having a mustache. The rebels were the next to follow the trend, eager to get rid of their rifles and packs, although I noticed a significant number who weren't willing to eliminate all personal preferences when they assumed their disguises, appearing as identical, cloned replicas of the master poet, albeit without shoes.

"Why are you doing this to me?" Veronica beseeched the starless heavens. "I was only trying to help."

She lunged toward the original Poe and the Poe-like me. By this time, the spooks who'd followed her across the river had entered into the spirit of the occasion, and a tidal wave of Poes swirled around Veronica, sweeping her up in eddies of pirouetting Poes and waltzing Poes and hoedowning Poes.

A wayward spectral elbow sent one Poe crashing into me. "S'cuse me," he said.

"Nothing to it."

"Sorry, too, about earlier. At the funeral home. I laid there like a stiff when you wanted a little fun with your buddies."

"Larry? Is that you?"

More jostling and bumping, and Poe-Larry spun away into the flood of prancing Poes, and if my ectoplasm depended on it, I couldn't pick out the Poe who'd just spoken to me from any one of the hundreds of Poes twirling around the shed, and soon it didn't matter.

The tune for *Stairway to Paradise* was taken up by the birds nesting in the trees by the river bank, and when I tried to trace the source of the music, I saw Fred-As above me in the night sky, sliding and hopping as though he were dancing his way up a gigantic spectral staircase.

I sighed and nudged the Poe closest to me and said, "Look at that. He's a regular Fred Astair."

And, of course, that was the point about Fred-As.

He twirled on a toe of his glossy black shoes, and his satin tails flared out behind him and his silver-headed cane was tucked debonairly under an arm as he transcended with a *bing*.

CHAPTER Thirty

There's a phenomenon in Specters Anonymous called a *mortality hangover*, which occurs the night after an excess of emotions or memories make the most dutiful, recovery-oriented spook feel as though he woke up in a clothes dryer.

Every spook stumbling into the meeting-before-the-meeting fourteen hours after the Great Clubhouse and Toolshed Dedication was a good example of what a mortality hangover looked like.

I headed for the first Breather in the River City Diner with a mug of coffee in front of him. It was Halloween, and I couldn't care less. Being close to a warm stream of caffeine was the only thing that mattered. I closed my eyes and let energized air rattle around the space between my ears.

"Thanks for inviting Veronica to dance last night."

I pried open an eyelid. Gilda was on the other side of the table. Her black leather jacket was dulled and the metal chains on her shoulder drooped.

"It's too early for me to respond creatively to sarcasm," I mumbled.

Gilda started to rise. "Well, excuse me for being dead."

"Wait a minute." I snared the cuff of her jacket. "You don't know how to be snarky."

She gave me a look that would have taken another spook several minutes to reproduce, what with all the innuendoes, subtexts and footnotes shoehorned into the glance. In the end, she summarized her position with the flick of a shoulder and said, "I felt sorry for Veronica. She and Cal were the only ones out there last night who weren't doing a Poe. I knew you had to be the Poe who asked Veronica to dance."

"A gold star for detective work," I said. Truly impressive. And this from a spook who didn't like Veronica.

"You made a good dead poet yourself," I added. "What was it like to be in someone else's . . . er . . . combat boots?"

"Weird," she said.

After buffing her purple nail polish and checking the piercings on a spectral ear, she leaned into the chute of steam rising from the coffee mug. The Breather sharing our table flinched as Gilda's ectoplasmic neck slid through him. His head popped up, startled, not sure what had just happened.

If Sunshiners only knew how rarely they were alone, it'd do wonders for their personal habits and posture.

Rosetta entered the diner, followed by Mrs. Hannity, Darleen, Veronica and a few newbies I recognized from the regular meeting. With a toodle-oo wave to us, Rosetta led her group to the tables in back.

"Gotta go," Gilda said. "My sponsor calls."

With Cal respecterizing inside the front door, I said, "Yeah, mine's here, too."

My eyes met Gilda's, and I believe we wore the same half smile. Relaxed, trusting, aware, accepting. We'd passed some threshold and reached—if not an understanding, then—a compromise, and from here, our nights would be better, with less tension and drama and more uncomplicated communication.

Of course, it's also possible I might sense things were going too smoothly and couldn't cope with this goodwill and earnest specterhood.

"Before the dancing started last night, Veronica said something about *trying to help*." I spoke with the confidence of a Sunshiner about to pat the nice little shark swimming beside his boat. "Do you think she might have been talking to Edgar A- about someone else's problems?"

"I surely wouldn't know. And I don't care to know." Gilda waggled a finger under my nose. It'd been hours since I'd been waggled at. "And I think it'd be a good idea for everyone's transcendence if no one tried to know anyone else's business."

"Does that mean you think Veronica wasn't really telling Poe about herself?"

"What part of shut-up-and-mind-your-own-business-and-don't-bother-me don't you understand?"

I gave her my sweetest smile. "Could you repeat the question?"

Rosetta was only twenty feet away, but Gilda did a formal *poof* and reappeared *(repoof)* next to her sponsor.

170

Cal arrived at my table as she left. "What was that about?"

"Do you really want to know?"

Cal mulled my question for as long as he'd need to weigh the pros and cons of stepping in front of a searchlight. "Does it look like I ask questions when I'm not interested in the answers?" And for good measure he added, "Duh?"

"Can we forget I ever said that?"

He sniffed the cloud of caffeine above the coffee mug. "Except for a careless *duh*, which I'm willing to overlook, it seems to me that you won our little wager. No snarkiness or pranksterism, despite having every spook in town thinking you were putting them on. It must've been painful."

"I almost lost what's left of my mind. But other than that, it was okay."

Cal's smile was hopeful. "You won the wager, and it's time for me to pay up. So what's it to be? What's my Halloween costume for tonight?"

I arched an eyebrow, was about to tell him to forget about it, but common sense settled back on my rattled nerves like a pachyderm taking the stool next to me.

"Let me think about it."

"Okay. While you're working on that, why don't you tell me what you've been up to?"

"You're not going to accuse me of telling tall tales or pulling tricks, are you?"

"Our bet is over except for my penalty."

So, I filled him in on the latest. About the background, foreground and sideground of the war I had with common household appliances, which none of my other spectral friends seemed very concerned about and which I couldn't, to this very night, explain.

"You're not pointing a finger at Fast Eddie, are you?" Cal asked.

"Nah. He's been a real prince among spooks."

I swiftly transitioned into telling him about going to Red Max for advice when a better sponsee would have reached out to his top-notch sponsor for guidance, and how that led me to the moon where I listened to this peculiar creature I couldn't understand and was chased by a demonic lunar lander— another apology inserted here for *duh-ing* Cal—an encounter that everyone still thinks I made up but which I know actually happened. Then, how I tried to help Margie by getting Veronica to use her people-whisperer powers to send Madame Sophie into a detox program.

And about Veronica going to Edgar Allen Poe for romantic advice, which Poe wrote about in his blog, which was distributed by the fog to every specter in central Virginia, and which I later realized might have been a case of Veronica pretending someone else's problems were her own.

At about this point, I paused, not that, being a specter, I was becoming breathless. It was more a practical matter of not overheating whatever I use for a brain.

Cal uncrossed his arms, rested his hands on the table and, not accustomed to the position, twitched his fingers like a dying spider. Then he asked, "Was it a Glip or a Glurp?"

"Pardon?"

"That little fellow you couldn't understand on the moon. Which was it? A Glip or a Glurp?"

"Has something changed since our last talk? You're sounding like the loose cannon in this relationship."

With a somber nod, Cal explained the Glips and the Glurps.

They were two related, but mostly hostile, groups of entities who inhabited the moon, back when the moon wasn't entirely uninhabitable. Don't waste your time wondering how they survived with gobs of solar radiation but no oxygen or water. They just did, okay?

They were mortal enemies, these Glips and Glurps, and over the eons they slaughtered each other until only a handful were left in each camp. The Glips were about as nice as nonterrestrial, non-carbon-based entities could be. And the Glurps were every bit as unpleasant. But toward the end, both groups were sorry about what they'd done to each other and, despite not having a formal 12-step program, understood the importance of making a good spreadsheet of their dirty deeds and unkind thoughts and discussing it with someone else. Or, as the lunar population extinguished and only their spectral residue was left, with any astral entity who might wander into the neighborhood.

"So that's what was happening up there when that little fellow couldn't stop jabbering?" I said. "You think one of them was discussing his spreadsheet with me?"

"No doubt about it."

"That's a lot to swallow, even for me."

Cal traced an exclamation point above the table with a finger. "The proof is in what happened next. You were besieged by gadgets—toasters and radios and vacuum cleaners, all sorts of things made for an electrical current."

I winced. Cal had finally lost it. "That doesn't prove anything."

"Think it through. The Glips and the Glurps are on the moon. What do they know about us? Practically nothing. Then we started sending them all kinds of junk, stuff made of metals and circuit boards and electrical wires. They probably thought the higher life-forms on this planet are the toasters and electric can openers."

I felt a headache coming on. "And the connection between my conversation with these creatures and the attack of the killer appliances is——"

"If it's a Glip—the nice ones—it was trying to return the favor by listening to your spreadsheet. It sent you a toaster because it thought you'd be more comfortable talking to one of them."

"How did it manage to do that?"

"You'll have to bring that up with the next Glip you meet."

"And if it was a Glurp?"

"Then it wanted to be sure you never told anyone its secrets. So it decided to readjust your expiration date by arranging for members of this planet's master race—which is what a hair curler might look like to them—to silence you."

"What a relief. I thought I was losing my mind."

"Yeah, it all ties neatly together." Cal rocked on his astral heels. A lesser spook would have smiled, but Cal realized what his mouth was about to do and stopped it.

"What about Fred-As?" I hastened to add, while my sponsor was in the mood to chat. "Was he really Fred Astair? And what was it about hearing that last name—Astair—that triggered his transcendence?"

"We never know what effect our words have on someone else. I'll bet his sponsor Red Max was afraid that hearing that name too soon would keep Fred-As from focusing on his transcendence. Sort of like a tomb-squatter losing interest in recovery once he finds his actual grave."

"But I mentioned his name. And it ended up being precisely what he needed to hear in order to transcend."

Cal gave up all resistance and permitted himself a wistful smile. "Yeah, funny how that works sometimes."

In the back of the diner, Gilda and Veronica had squared away at opposite ends of a table. Rosetta, Mrs. Hannity, Darleen and the others in the middle seemed to do most of the talking. Whenever Gilda shrank into her black leather jacket, a spook would haul her back out. And when Veronica's nose seemed to lengthen, Pinocchio-fashion, the better to look down at Gilda, Darleen gave it a shove and took some of the air out of Veronica's hauteur.

"What's going on over there?" I asked.

"Nothing you need to be concerned about."

"Far be it from me to stick my nose where it isn't wanted," I said, while this strange echo in the back of my mind added, *If, however, my nose should be invited to stick itself somewhere, I can't really speak for where it'll end up.*

Cal seemed eager to change the subject. "Might I offer a suggestion for my costume?" he asked, as his hair took on a wild, untangled look, purple circles appeared under his spectral eyes, his skin went paler than a self-respecting spook would tolerate, and his clothes morphed into a black-over-black motif.

He was doing a Poe.

I'll never know if Cal was seriously proposing to spend twenty-four hours in Edgar A-'s ectoplasm because Margie chose that moment to plop on the chair next to me.

For once, my favorite twofer didn't seem to notice me. Or anything else. Her complexion was pale, her eyes fixed and glittery, and she clasped her hands on the table as though not wanting to be accountable if they got out of her sight.

"You look like you lost your best friend," I said.

"*Best annoyance* is more like it." Margie studied my face, then Cal's, then her own hands before adding: "I had to call an ambulance for Sophie."

Cal reached for her shoulder, then stopped when he realized he was dealing with a card-carrying member of the physical dimension. His transformation into Poe halted, the ruffles on his shirt still blurry. "How serious is it?"

Margie opened her hands. It was up to the Über-Spirit.

"There goes the neighborhood," I said.

Faster than you can say, *Nevermore*, Cal fixed on me the glower of a sponsor who'd just heard a snarky comment. He crossed his arms over his broad astral chest as every trace of Edgar Allan Poe disappeared from his ectoplasm.

– The End –

SPOOK NOIR

By Phil Budahn

~ *SAMPLE CHAPTER* ~

CHAPTER One

There are a million stories in the city and I know them all. Especially, the ones that make your lower lip go *thump-a-thump-a-dee-thump* as you drag it down the stairs.

This is one of those stories. About Richmond, I mean. Not about some palooka dusting his shoelaces with his chin, although I'll get to Johnny Spivey in a minute.

The night I'm talking about was a few weeks after Halloween, and my friends and I were sticking to the shadows. You've heard about drunks staying close to home on the holidays to avoid the novice drinkers? Imagine what someone in my condition thinks when he sees the first jack-o'-lantern of the season.

Amateur hour.

My boss Big G, not having a sentimental disposition, gave me an assignment on the edge of the Fan District. My buddy Hank tagged along.

"What's the job?" Hank asked.

"Observe and report."

Hank nodded, and the tiny pigtail at the back of his *café au lait* neck twitched in agreement. I've seen the freest spirits hereabouts go weak in the knees when that pigtail shimmies.

Settling under a magnolia on the lawn of what Big G identified as the residence in question, I started to explain the technical palaver to Hank until I realized he'd start dithering about what the question was and who asked it.

Across the street, a day-glow plastic skeleton dangled from a spindly tree, waving howdy-do, while all the pumpkins in evidence quietly decomposed into the floorboards of porches. Down the block, a figure in black that could've been the Ghost of Halloweens Past lurked behind a wrought iron fence. A cat tiptoeing on the top of the fence eyed the joker hiding in the shadows and made the fur on its back stand at full attention before departing with a good-bye hiss.

The ambience put me in mind of Sophie, a good ol' gal of my acquaintance who was probably elbowing her way at this very minute into the best seats of the Choir Eternal. Wherever she was, I hope they enjoy tornadoes.

Hank shifted my focus with a grunt. On the porch in front of us, a guy was jiggling his key in the lock. As the Breather turned to come down the steps I knew that, yep, that was Johnny Spivey.

Spivey had dark hair parted down the middle and swept back along the sides where a couple strands tended to wander around his ears as if speculating where they're supposed to go. His eyebrows were frozen in an upward arc, and his lips rippled gently, like he was trying to finish a conversation with himself before he got distracted and forgot what he wanted to say.

"I'm on him," Hank whispered before I could spell out a few crucial details for him. Such as the fact that this was my caper and he was my sidekick. Tagging along was the only thing I expected him to do. Yet there he was, shooting out from the shadows and coming up behind Spivey.

Hank was antsy to sign up with Big G's Triple-A detective agency, but Big G wouldn't give Hank the nod without my okay. Me, I was still working the angles. It'd be nice to have my buddy around for those long stakeouts. On the other hand, as I was just reminded, patience wasn't in the top tray of Hank's tool kit.

Trust is a place, Cal says. *You don't get there until you get there.*

I had trusted Hank not to screw up my assignment, but now he was close enough to Johnny Spivey to use the hair whipping around the guy's ears as dental floss. Perhaps I should have told Hank that neither of us should hitch a ride in Spivey's back pocket. That's the kind of helpful nugget he needs to hear.

I trailed them out of the shadows, keeping it slow and stealthy, and by the time Spivey hit the sidewalk, I reached around Hank's shoulders, cupped a hand over his mouth and brought him quietly to a halt while Spivey kept going, unaware of the tussle in his wake. When I eased my grip, Hank spun on me. Lightning glinted from his eyes, his fingers rolled into fists. The dark scarecrow that'd been down the block was now a couple of lawns closer to get a better view of the upcoming fracas.

Before the situation went from bad to stupid, a new variable ambled into the equation. Spivey murmured, "Aw, nuts," and reversing course, headed back to the house, walking right through me.

Some of the regulars in my support group insist that we should be beyond irritation, but none of them was standing in my shoes at the moment every pointy edge in Spivey's rib cage sliced through me. His lungs sloshed their way into my gut. Then came the heart, thundering like an overcaffeinated drummer. Finally, the spine. Don't get me started about the spine. That witches' potpourri of neurochemicals and electrical impulses, slick sheathing, icky tendrils and vertebrae with the consistency of old clam shells.

A more delicate spirit would've fallen to his knees but I managed to steady myself with my hands on my legs, bending over, wishing I could bring up my last dinner, although it came out of the microwave years ago. My neck twisted to one side to make sure Johnny Spivey didn't change his mind—or direction—again.

Hank was so surprised he forgot to be pissed at me for jerking him around. "You didn't actually think Spivey was one of us?"

"Nah, I can spot a Breather a mile away," I wheezed, so relieved at being out of Spivey's intestines that I lost any grudge against Hank.

"Glad to hear everything's under control."

EVER SINCE I woke up with the memory of a funeral that I hadn't so much *attended* as I was *wheeled into*, I've spent part of each night in the 12-step recovery program of Specters Anonymous. Following the wisdom of *The Teeny Book*, I go to nightly meetings, try to fix whatever I fouled up during my days on the physical plane and help maintain Cal's illusion that he was running my afterlife, anything that'll keep me on cordial terms with the neighbors until I find out what comes after the hereafter.

Life goes on, says Cal, my recovery sponsor, *but we're not part of that parade.*

He wasn't keen about me signing up with Big G's Triple-A detective agency. Anything not directly related to kicking the sunshine habit is time wasted digging my grave deeper, Cal says, though he cut me some slack once I made the case that acquiring a few skills of an investigative nature might help me pinpoint the first-life problem that sidetracked me into this off-ramp on the second plane of existence. Still, letting an assignment from Big G make me miss a meeting was pushing my luck.

"No telling how long Spivey's going to be inside," I said as our suspect reentered the house. I gave the nutcase in the Grim Reaper costume down the block a cold glance to make sure he wasn't creeping up on us. "I don't want to be late."

"Shouldn't we stay with Spivey?" Hank asked.

"You go ahead," I said. "I'll let Cal know you're busy. That you found something more important than recovering from sunshine."

A mind reader wasn't needed to sense that Hank's enthusiasm for the stakeout was rushing away like water down an unclogged toilet.

Quicker than a mosquito's sneeze, a spectral technique known as *Beam-Me-Up-Scotty* brought us to a street on the hilly, eastern edge of the city. Rosetta was waiting by the stairs to the church basement where the St. Sears group meets.

"Did you pass Strathhorn on your way here?" Rosetta asked.

I gave Hank a glance. Hank gave it back.

"Don't know anyone named Strathhorn," I said.

Rosetta scanned the dimly lit sidewalks and empty streets. "He promised to lead tonight's meeting."

Rosetta was our group's chairspook, a position she achieved by virtue of being the only spook with the foresight to bring comfortable shoes and a wrinkle-free tweed suit into the hereafter. She was also our resident grammarian, able to spot a wobbly preposition long before it could dangle.

"Don't worry," I said. "Hank can lead the meeting tonight."

My buddy's glare was prickly, but he knew a price must be paid for getting too eager with Spivey. He even seemed relieved that payback wouldn't be worse.

"Sure," Hank wisely said. "I'm here for you, Rosetta."

Rosetta gulped. Was it Hank's testosterone-saturated pigtail that gave our leader a moment of discombobulation? Or was it her sudden recollection that Hank liked to refer to the residents of the spiritual dimension as *roadkill*, *carcasses* and *daisy food*?

"Perhaps we should wait a little longer," she said. "Some of our friends inside have come a considerable distance to hear Strathhorn."

"We certainly don't want to disappoint any of our brethren," Hank said.

"Or sistren," I added.

IF YOU OVERLOOK a certain transparency among the participants, a Specters Anonymous meeting isn't that different from 12-step gatherings in the so-called real world. Often they take place in church basements with tile floors and walls painted off-yellow, off-green and off-everything else. Gray metal chairs circled the room for the regulars, while seats along the walls are favored by newbies who'd rather have another funeral than be noticed.

Like any collection of the recently deceased, the newbies are in constant motion, forgetting they didn't technically sit on chairs or stand on floors or lean on walls or bump their heads against ceilings.

Cal had his usual place at a chair facing the door. He greeted me by crossing his arms and giving me a glance that started at my belly button and didn't last long enough to reach my spectral collarbone. Any meeting with newbies was a good meeting for Cal and a better one for me, since Cal will have plenty of other spooks to talk to.

Not paying attention to where I was going, I settled at a chair that had me rubbing shoulders with Gilda the Goth. Nodding at the newbies, I said, "What's the lowdown on the tourists, Doll?"

"Speak English, Ralph. And don't call me *Doll*."

If I'd've had a fedora, this would have been the perfect moment to slick down the brim. Give it that certain angle that separates the champs from the chumps, the winners from the whiners, the leaders from the losers, the spooks from . . .

Gilda eyed me closely. "Your mind's stuck again, isn't it?"

. . . the girls from the squirrels, the masters from the disasters, the scorers from the borers, the victors from the . . .

She put her mouth next to my left ear and blew hard, which came out *blat*, her being a specter without a working respiratory system, and I expected a spray of ectoplasm to shoot from my ear on the other side. Still, my thoughts broke free from an ever-tightening vortex.

"Thanks. I needed that, Doll," I said.

That earned my first wagging finger of the evening. "I warned you about *Doll*."

"No offense, kid."

"That, too."

As a member of a spectral investigative force, my usual MO is to take a .38 round in the face before backing down, but I'm not sure those rules apply around Goths. What makes anyone think he can influence a spook who accessorizes with snowy-white makeup, purple fingernails, black leather and chains? I mean, we're dead. What's with this *nouveau mortuary* fashion?

Gilda studied the newbies; something about this bobbing, weaving, shuddering and shimmering assembly of ectoplasm was different. Put it down to their sincere expressions and intense, hushed conversations. If I'd kept more neural connections entering post-mortality, I might be wondering now if they were waiting for a concert to begin. Say, something by Beethoven, where every instrument does its best to move your ears to the back of your head.

A collective "ah" rose from the newbies; I traced their stares to the door.

Eyes the color of spoiled butter glowed at me from a spook of the old school standing in the doorway. It was the joker who'd made a fine imspookination of a lawn ornament near Spivey's.

He was covered in a dark dusty robe that hid everything from the top of his head to the bottoms of his feet. Or maybe he'd found a way to layer himself in old spider webs. Strangely, the guy gave off the scent of lilacs and freshly watered ferns.

"Just in time," Rosetta said with unshakable propriety. "I am delighted to introduce tonight's speaker. Please welcome Strathhorn."

She patted the seat of a vacant chair, and Strathhorn glided toward her. Spooks don't cast shadows, but Strathhorn managed to dim the glow seeping through the windows as thunder rolled through the night.

"MY NAME IS STRATHHORN, AND I AM A PHANTOM OF NO SIGNIFICANCE." His voice was deep and hollow, as chilly as an abandoned mausoleum. "FROM THE LEGIONS OF DARKNESS, I BRING YOU A MESSAGE."

The newbies leaned forward. Concern rippled across Rosetta's features. Hank and Fast Eddie grinned: they knew they'd arrived on the right track moments before the train wreck.

Strathhorn's eyes pulsed like a fevered dream. "I WANT TO TALK ABOUT"— He paused, and the silence was so intense you could hear a pin starting to drop long before it hit the floor—"ABOUT STAYING CHEERFUL IN THE AFTERLIFE."

- End of Sample Chapter -

ACKNOWLEDGEMENTS

The author gratefully acknowledges the support of his writer's group buddies: Rebecca Ruark, Carol Rutherford and Barbara Weitbrecht.

Thanks to Bailey Hunter for her wonderful cover design and internal design.

Special thanks to my wife, Lee T. Budahn, for her support, humor and eagle's eye.

For the latest about the St. Sears group, check out our website at SpectersAnonymous.Com.

Other books in the Specters Anonymous series are available on Kindle and from Amazon.Com.

Made in the USA
Middletown, DE
10 September 2023

38072914R00106